Other books in The Horseshoer Mystery Series:
The Clincher
Dead Blow

Other books by Lisa Preston:
The Ultimate Guide to Horse Feed, Supplements, and Nutrition
(Skyhorse, 2016)
Alternative Treatments for Animals (Skyhorse, 2020)

FORGING FIRE

FORGING FIRE

A HORSESHOER MYSTERY

Lisa Preston

ARCADE
CRIMEWISE

An Arcade / CrimeWise Book

Chapter 1

THE KIDNEY-BUSTING DRIVE DOWN THE GRAVEL road to the Buckeye is extra rough in a diesel with stiff suspension like Ol' Blue's, but rolling closer to the ranch always makes me smile. My teeth air-dried by the time I eased the truck under the gate header. Charley got up from his snooze, shook his furry, yellow self, and did a chortle-woof in appreciation of our destination.

"No herding today," I told him.

My dog didn't look best convinced. The second I opened the truck door, which bears the decal DALE'S HORSESHOEING along with the house phone number, Charley bailed out with hope in his heart, staring at the faraway rangeland like anyone with a working soul does, before he got busy with his sniffing.

"No good, no good." Manuel, the guy who works seasonally for the Nunn Finer Hay Company, was muttering under the hood of the pickup between the main barn and the all-quiet ranch house.

"Hey, Manny." I don't know if he heard my greeting as he continued to commune with the innards of his engine, but I reckoned Skip and Harley, the geldings I planned to shoe, were in the corral at the run-in shed on the other side of the house. Soon as I found the horses, I'd move Ol' Blue so I wouldn't have to haul my anvil too far.

"Miss?"

"Miss"-ing me—instead of calling me by name—is one of Manuel's things, but I try to have the kind of faith my dog does and gave him another chance.

"Rainy," I reminded him.

"Miss, you know a phone number for the Mister?"

I always enjoy when anyone makes the mistake of asking Hollis something about ranch plans and Hollis directs them to Donna, who's Hollis's new wife and the real owner of the Buckeye ranch.

"Mister Hollis, he gave me money to take the bull to the sale down in California, but today my truck, it has problems, and I cannot do it."

"Oh." I sort of got it now. Not due in 'til after this weekend, Donna and Hollis. Ranch folk don't often get to get away. "They're kind of out of town."

"Yes, but you have a way to talk to them?"

"They're not cell phone people." No way, no how was he going to reach the honeymooners. Their wedding was last November. With spring around the corner, the old newlyweds were more than ready to ride off into the sunrise. They'd gone so deep in the back-country with four horses, they'd probably slipped back in time a full century.

Manuel spun his eyeballs a lap like I was the one a little deaf or half-stupid. "The bull is supposed to be at the big sale tomorrow."

"Oh!" Now I got it extra good. Donna's killer bull was supposed to go to the Black Bluff bull sale, down California way, and Manuel was supposed to haul the blasted beast there. Suggesting Manuel to Donna and Hollis as a ranch hand had been my doing. They'd needed help, didn't need to be breaking their backs as hard as they did. Donna has given me all the pull to shoe her horses when and how I thought best. Plus, her stock are so well-handled, they stand like a dream, no fussing or yanking away while I work on their feet. I even shoe the ranch geldings in the pasture sometimes. Real well-behaved, old-style Quarter Horses. With most clients,

I require a person be there to handle the horse, but I trust Donna and her stock, and she trusts me. I just about love Donna. She's become like another mother to me, and her horses behave so well that I shoe them when my schedule's open.

Fact is, the horses I'd planned to end my afternoon shoeing, they could wait a couple days just fine. Twisting my ponytail around my thumb made the idea come quicker. I've always wanted to go to the Black Bluff bull sale, even though Hollis has said a time or two, kind of weird-like, that I ought not visit there. Now fate was handing me a great excuse to go. I'd be helping out Hollis and Donna by getting a bad-news bull off the Buckeye ranch. It'd get me to the best-of-the-West sale I'd long wanted to see—horses, cattle, and herding dogs worth big bucks would compete and change hands at the Black Bluff sale. Tonight, my Guy was going up to Seattle to buy special food at a big market for our wedding, which was slated for Wednesday.

Rare is the night and day I'm alone, but right now I could make the free time to do Manuel's hauling job. All kind of good could come from me hitching Ol' Blue to Hollis's stout stock trailer, loading that bull, and hitting the road.

If I left right away, I could be back before Guy had a chance to miss me.

My boot heel ground the dirt as I turned for the barn to call home off the landline. I let the phone ring 'til the message machine came on, hung up, thought hard, then called the restaurant. This road trip idea of mine was coming together. I'd put the diesel charges on my debit card, sort it out later with Donna and Hollis. Tomorrow was Saturday. I had no clients scheduled until Monday afternoon. The last day of the bull sale was tomorrow, and I could maybe send Charley on cattle at the sale, which everybody knows is cooler than ice. I mean, herding at the Black Bluff bull sale, for mercy's sake? Everyone in the world wants to work their herding dog there someday, it's the cream of—

"Cascade Kitchen," a gal's voice said, sounding rushed over the clink of coffee cups and plates and whatnot.

"Guy still there? This is Rainy." This last bit of information would make sure she didn't just put me on hold. My husband-come-next-week always takes my calls.

"No, he left like a half hour ago. He thought he wouldn't go 'til five or six, but he made it out of here earlier even though he thought he'd have to get the dinner rush moving before he could go, but he didn't."

Yeah, that was Sissy on the phone, that server-and-dishwasher Guy hired. She talks in funny circles, always. I thanked her and called our house again, this time leaving Guy a message that I was going to take an all-of-a-sudden road trip to get that bad bull Dragoon to Black Bluff since Manny couldn't do it. I promised to call him later and be back tomorrow night. The big thing on the list—getting my horses taken care of while Guy and I were both out of town for a night and a day—would need more than a phone message left on an answering machine, but my best friend was probably working right then. I left a message on Melinda's cell. I'd call her again later, go ahead and hit the road now.

It was that simple. Manuel and I got the stock trailer hitched up to Ol' Blue, checked the lights and brakes—the left signal flickered, but mostly worked—then opened the trailer and backed it to the pen gate. That big Brahma gives me the heebie-jeebies. We didn't need to risk getting into the pen with him. We swung the gate open to the inside then hollered and waved around the outside until Dragoon decided the hay in the trailer looked like a better deal than a bare pen being circled by a couple of shouting idiots.

So what kind of an omen is it that as I pulled off the ranch road onto the two-lane highway that would take me to the interstate, a marked deputy's car with a man and woman in the front seat was coming in the opposite direction? I flashed my lights, then eased Ol' Blue and the stock trailer onto the highway's shoulder. The cop car activated the spiffy, rotating up-top lights, did a one-eighty, and came up behind me. The male cop stayed in the patrol car as the uniformed woman left the driver's seat.

Charley thumped his stubby tail as she sauntered up.

"Hey," I said, when probationary Deputy Melinda Kellan stuck her nose in my window just a hair. Ever since she went to police school, Mel's got all these weird habits, like the way she stood just back of my truck's door post and leaned to talk to me.

"Hey, yourself." She nodded at me, then gave Charley a proper howdy. "You being good as gold, pretty boy?"

It's like Melinda thinks she's the funniest thing ever, every time she says that about Charley being gold. True, his long coat is all shades of yellow—not super-common in Aussies—but he's no beauty queen, he's a worker. As though to prove he's come from some school of tough knocks, his ear tips are missing, though the long fringe pretty well covers the flaw. Charley's a fine example, considering he's a stray I picked up along the interstate on my way to Oregon.

When they got done nuzzling each other, both glanced at me. Charley's eyes said I was really the only girl for him. Melinda asked, "What's up?"

"Wondering if you could maybe swing by tonight and tomorrow to feed the horses and Spooky, too, if the spirit moves you. Guy's gone 'til tomorrow afternoon-ish and now I'm going to take Donna's bull down to a sale. I'll probably make it back late tomorrow night."

She swung her head the quarter turn it took to squint at the swaying stock trailer Ol' Blue was towing, and wrinkled her nose.

Bulls have a more than manly scent, it's true. Dragoon smells like the bad news he is. Manuel and I had put plenty of hay in there and a water bucket tied up that I could fill without having to open the escape door. Not one to turn your back on, Dragoon. I planned to rest the bull's legs by stopping on the three-hundred-plus-mile drive, but I wouldn't let Dragoon out of the trailer until I backed up to a waiting pipe corral at the Black Bluff sale grounds.

Melinda stood with her arms folded across her chest, then shifted to rest one elbow on her pistol, the other wrist across a couple of extra magazines in her gun belt.

"You know," she said, "the only reason I ran from that son of a—"

"Bull," I put in, doing my part to keep her from cussing all the damn—oops—all the daggummed time. "Son of a bull, Dragoon is."

She glared at the trailer. "I didn't have a gun on me at the time. Now, I could drop him at a hundred yards with a twelve-gauge slug. Or six of them, if that's what it takes."

Carries a grudge, my friend Melinda does.

"At this sale you're going to," she asked, "will there be mules?"

"Not officially. It's a stock dog thing and beef cattle thing, mostly. Replacement females. And some real nice geldings will be sold. But I'll keep my eyes and ears open for your mule."

She nodded. "You said you'd find him."

One thing that's a little annoying about this buddy of mine is the way she remembers everything. There's that, and the block on her shoulder she packs around.

Melinda glared at me good and hard, up one side and down the other. "Do I still have to wear a dress next Wednesday?"

"Well, yeah. Since I do."

"But you're the one—"

I waved her off. Best she not get started and dig too deep. "I'll find your mule."

"You'd better."

Melinda is sometimes a bit of a jawbone.

Guy says we could be sisters.

***

I made good time crossing the state line not too many hours after dark. It's a border I hadn't touched since I found my way into Oregon looking to get back my childhood horse, Red, nigh two years ago. Touching the northern edge of California then had been lucky, as it's how I acquired—and named, come to it—good old Charley.

He'd watched me as I relieved myself at an unofficial interstate pull-off, wary and tired, though he wasn't in too bad of shape, just alone. I'd known his feeling purely. He'd needed someone. Back then, I wanted to need no one.

"Sorry, Charley." That's what I'd said, crushing the half hope glimmering in his gold-ringed brown eyes. But then, as I'd opened my truck door, something in my soul made me pause, changed my mind. I'd waved the stray into Ol' Blue's cab.

Within a few miles, Charley and I had started calling each other by our first names. What and all with him having no collar, I took that "sorry, Charley" and made it something we could both live with.

Charley wasn't sorry as a dog, and he never seemed sorry to have joined me. He's loyal and a good judge of character. He had Guy figured for a keeper way before me. And his herding's solid, fun, and a time-saver. When a killer loosed Dragoon on Melinda and me last fall, Charley was a genuine lifesaver.

***

At a spot along the dark interstate with an extra-wide shoulder, I pulled Ol' Blue over for a snooze and wrapped myself in the familiar scent and creak of my worn leather jacket. I prefer this kind of rest stop to something full of truckers and tourists and weirdos and what-not. It swerves on the nerves something fearsome, a lack of space. Here, the interstate is bordered by real ranch land. Charley stared across the freeway, up the steep hill that angled down to the north-bound lanes. Stock dogs always want to work, but my good old boy finally settled, curled against my ribs, and we kept each other warm.

Being on the road, on my own, was a good rinse for my brain. I'm trying not to get too clutched up in the throat about what's going to happen next week. Until the last year of my life, I'd fig-ured I was best off with a good dog as my hot water bottle and general nighttime warmer.

This Friday night alone, my first in forever, was the reason I was able to jump in and get this blasted bull gone for Donna and Hollis. Guy had taken as much time off as he could for the coming celebration and would be back tomorrow night, cooking up a storm. My coming wedding would be followed by a lazy, married weekend, which would make two Saturdays in a row with no horseshoeing scheduled or even contemplated.

***

Dragoon woke me in the dark, rocking the truck with his motion in the trailer, but at first, I didn't remember where I was or why. My brain's transmission was stuck two years back, when I'd driven north in search of my horse Red. The warm breath on my neck made my hand reach to feel Charley's fur, remember I had a dog, had already found Red and established myself as a horseshoer up in Cowdry, and had fallen in love, for real.

"Look how far we came in two years," I told Charley as I redid my ponytail.

He wiggled and stared at Ol' Blue's condensation-coated windows. Four a.m.

We went out in the dark to do what comes natural. Dragoon was fine, as was his hay and water. I called Charley back from too much nosing at the hill across the northbound lanes, and we got gone.

Interstate 5 is blessedly calmer after midnight. The easy driving gave me thinking time. I need plenty of pause to chew on things, and I don't often get it. Miles zinged past.

The famous Black Bluff bull sale had a canvas banner across the main entrance. The red-haired cowpoke with a gray-flecked mustache at the main check-in gate looked right across Ol' Blue's cab, eyeing my dog instead of me. I like that real well in a person. Given where we were, the attention wasn't unusual. This yearly sale is not just about the bulls and other cattle on the offer. No, the running of the working dogs, one right after the other, moving rough stock with reason, is the other big draw of the Black Bluff sale.

I leaned toward the man to be heard over Ol' Blue's diesel engine. "Got a bull here from the Buckeye Ranch up in Cowdry, Butte County, Oreg—"

"Bring it over there." He waved and jabbed his pointer finger toward the heaviest pipe corrals at the back of the sale grounds. He was already making a phone call as I pulled away.

Trucks and trailers of all sorts lined the acres of open fields beyond the many pens surrounding the huge main arena, but I couldn't gawk, had to pay attention to backing in where I was directed. The way it is, is the bull's my responsibility 'til it's out of the trailer, then the salespeople have the charge of moving him and handling the auction. But if Dragoon didn't sell, it'd be my job to get him home again. After I backed the stock trailer to a stout corral, the receiving stockman complimented my driving and asked if I minded unhitching the trailer, so he could get Dragoon out when he had a couple more hands at the ready.

"Makes sense," I agreed.

Clear of the trailer, I parked, let Charley out for air and a pee, then hupped him back into Ol' Blue's cab and opened the rear slider window for ventilation.

A good stock dog has to watch his person, has to have access.

One or two fellows checked out Charley and me. Eager to show my dog's skill, I strolled over and asked the most relevant question of the day to a fellow leaving the check-in booth. "When're dogs working?"

"You got something to exhibit, little lady?" His lopsided grin gave way to a leer. Flirt Boy seemed to have an idea that he was all kinds of charming, which didn't exactly sugar my grits.

"Maybe so." I spoke gruff enough that he'd rethink whether I was meaning my words, like him, in extra ways. I'm average-plus height or more and made out of trim muscles, nothing little about me.

"Then you're up." He jerked a thumb over his left shoulder to the main arena and pressed a button on his radio to tell someone to release six steers to let a demo run before the official program started.

That's more like it. Ready to run my dog in this thunderdome, I whistled. Flying yellow fur bailed out Ol' Blue's driver's window, and we slipped into the ginormous arena, first of the day.

The Kelpie that was officially entered downed at the gate with a word from his handler in that way we call honoring. The dog wanted to work but was going to honor Charley and me.

At the far end of the arena, a gate clanged, admitting a half dozen rowdy cattle. They snorted, stamped, and scattered. Near me, two green metal fence panels were set up with a ten-foot gap between them. Charley would have to drive the cattle between the panels.

"Away to me," I told Charley.

Distinctive in his work, my Charley is. Plenty of eye, confident, with a knack of knowing when to use which kind of manipulation to make cattle stop or move where needed. Younger dogs have faster out runs, sure, but Charley possesses the wisdom of experience. He ran to the end of the arena and gave the milling steers the benefit of his glare. They pretty well gathered up and began to move down the long line of the fence. Charley would have to force the loose steers toward me through the panels, then around again and out a gate at the far end.

One crusty half-breed steer decided he liked the original end of the arena better. He whipped around and charged my dog.

Feinting, Charley whirled and told the steer to get back, told it he wasn't giving up ground. In two seconds of stubborn, Charley further explained that he was fine with either one of them dying over the issue of whether that steer should move along peaceably and join the others.

It went like that. These rough cattle didn't cotton to being herded at all, but Charley wasn't intimidated.

Without a wave of my hand, I verbally directed Charley to bring the stock through the panels. Charley bossed them right and proper, until he could deliver them again to the end of the arena where we re-penned the lot.

The nods we got, well, we'd earned 'em.

"That'll do, Charley," I told my old fellow.

Both our hearts were brimming with pride and love. We thought we were pretty much the coolest thing on the planet. I'd run my dog, my Charley, at the Black Bluff bull sale's first run of the day. Bucket-list life item, check.

It's a herding-dog thing. Maybe everyone wouldn't understand.

A microphone clicked on with a squeal. They were ready to get started with the day's official program. An announcer asked my name, my dog's name, and where we were from. He repeated it all over the loudspeaker to clapping and cheering from the hundred or so early spectators, and he welcomed everybody to the last day of this year's Black Bluff bull sale.

They released more burly cattle, rough enough, barely dog-broke. The first official man up gave me a considered, congratulatory nod, then sent his Kelpie, who spent a lot of air yipping. The tough little dog would need that energy for the extra out-runs he'd have to do when his stock scattered. And now Charley had to honor the Kelpie, ignore the fresh steers he wanted to work.

A big fellow across the way looked above the crowd to eye me and mine. Seemed like too much attention. Another feller—this one smaller and dark-skinned with straight black hair and no hat—eyed the one eyeing me and then stared at me way too long. He edged my way and paused, then faded back, 'til I lost him in the milling crowd.

Then I saw him again. I'm not all that given to the heebie-jee-bies, but that dark-haired wiry man moved toward us in a way that made me not want to turn my back.

It's always a sign when I start to think ill of others that some-one around here needs a nap. And I was hungry, having not so much as a stale half-box of Milk Duds to munch on since I'd left the Buckeye. I'd done my road trip in hard hours. If I caught a few more winks, I could maybe unofficially run Charley again during one of the program breaks, take a gawk around, then hit the road. I just needed a small corner of the world, some open space at the end of the sale property. I fired up Ol' Blue and cranked the wheel hard, rumbling slowly through the less traveled parts of the ground to gain a patch.

Shady, without such long grass that the bugs would have me for breakfast, and quiet, way back from the hollers and truck sounds and stock smells of the mighty sale, this was a spot where a gal could catch herself ten or twenty winks before she turned her sweet self around and rolled north again.

I slid out of Ol' Blue then turned to ask Charley for an opinion on where we should rest, the grass or the cab.

Crack! Something smacked the back of my skull.

Chapter 2

FAINT SOUNDS FILTERED IN AS I fell face-first on the grass. There was a clanging sound and a diesel engine fired up. Footsteps rushed around.

Someone helped me up. Then, under the comforting rumble of a loud engine and the rocking of a truck's stiff suspension, I took that nap I'd been wanting.

***

Panic whispered at the back of my brain. A pair of legs in dark jeans loomed at my side. Wishing for better circumstances, I squeezed my eyeballs shut.

Opened them to a man squatting in front of a white car.

"Are you all right?" the man said.

I registered the gist that someone was asking a question, but before my brain cells could assemble a response, the quiz kept coming, about one question every five seconds.

"Can you see me?"

"Can you talk?"

"Do you need an ambulance?"

I wished I wasn't on a game show on a road shoulder with the worst headache ever recorded in human history. I posed one bonus question to the dark, blurry head leaning over my body. "Did you hit me?"

Blurry Head shook, like an ocean roller from my perspective, but I was on the far side of woozy.

"You need help." The accented voice reminded me a bit of Manuel's, but it echoed from a distant tunnel. Seemed to belong to the dark blue legs with the floaty head on top.

I closed my eyes again. Better, less ooh-I'm-gonna-barf, which was the way I'd felt when the truck stopped moving and I'd stumbled onto the road shoulder of dead grass. Yeah, I'd been glad when we'd stopped moving.

What truck? I sucked in a breath, ready to throw up like Guy's cat if that's what it took, 'cause what was I doing here, and where was here, and who was the man leaning over me?

I looked around and had no earthly idea of where I was, though I knew I had been at the Black Bluff bull sale all the way down in California. Yeah, I'd finally made it to the big sale and managed to unofficially run my dog on cattle in the Black Bluff arena. But I wasn't at the sale now. An expanse of brown, slightly hilly, undeveloped land pocked with manzanita and a few oak trees lay beyond the little two-lane road at my heels. The only vehicle in sight was an odd white car behind the man kneeling beside me. The car was a Jeep Compass, which is what happens when a small car—like the tiny thing Guy has—gets carnal knowledge of an adult Jeep. It's got southern-bad breeding written all over it. Under-powered, undersized, and white is an ugly car color, too.

I gave the just-sometimes blurry fellow a wave intended to convey all my questions.

He tilted his head. "Sabino Arriaga."

That was his favorite sentence, I guess, because he said it a couple more times. And the way he said it seemed like I was supposed to know a whole lot of people named Arriaga, and he was merely helping me understand which one he was. Then he turned to study my face in a way that made me wince.

"I'm Sabino Arriaga."

"I'm not," I said, my voice croaking. I groped around, realized I was on my butt in the dirt.

"You know the ranch?" He pointed a fence that stretched both ways from a white metal gate. Rolling hills of scrub and occasional oak trees swallowed up the wire fence lines separating the land from the road. I assumed the border continued beyond those hills.

I shook my swimming head. "I'm not from here. I live in Oregon. Who are you?"

"My name is Arriaga. That is my family name."

"And?" I prompted.

"And I am the one who is helping you."

"You're helping me?" I was about to spew that the usual form of help involved wading in when the fight began or fetching the police or taking the victim to a hospital or—

"A man helped you out of a truck and then drove away. I was too far away to see him well." He pulled a little pair of binoculars out from under his shirt, scanned the countryside across the road.

"You were watching through binoculars?" The morning glare made me squint, accelerating the headache. I wanted my sunglasses, which should be tucked in Ol' Blue's visor.

"I am searching for my uncle. He used to work on that ranch but he disappeared."

After some time, I realized I hadn't responded and started thinking about what might be a good response, which made me try to remember what he'd said.

Then both of my working brain cells grab on to the idea that I'd been robbed—Ol' Blue was stolen when Charley was in the truck. I'd lost Charley. Charley, my good sweet old found dog who'd slept within arm's length of me every night for two years. Charley was with me the night I refound my horse, Red, the night I met Guy. Charley loves Guy as much as I do. Charley's been to hundreds of

Oregon shoeing jobs with me. All my clients know him. Charley holds my heart.

Charley and I had even run cattle together at the Black Bluff bull sale in California. Oh, yeah, I was in California, not Oregon. I'd gotten rid of Dragoon, Donna's killer bull. Why was my mind stuck in replay mode? Focus.

My Charley was gone, 'cause someone had taken my truck with Charley in it.

Now I remembered the clanging sound when I got hit. That would have been Charley jumping from Ol' Blue's cab through the slider window into the bed, banging over all my tools and gear. He never jumps into the bed from the cab. I felt sick. Plus, losing Ol' Blue means not just the truck but also my tools. My newer, better tools, my anvil and stand, the propane bottle, my bar stock and shoe inventory, my old backup tools. My clean shirts and fly spray and lead ropes. In the cab I'd had my day planner, the one Guy gave me and wrote all my clients into, my cell, a bottle of lotion, and a canteen of drinking water. Ol' Blue's my livelihood. It's my truck, and I'm the one who organized everything and mounted my crappy forge into the bed on a swing-out arm.

Me losing Ol' Blue, well, that's like other folks who love their jobs losing the building they work in plus all the stuff in it after having had to buy that workplace plus the forge and anvil and shoes and all the tools it contains.

It's everything.

I swung my right arm to the butt of my skull and winced so hard tears dribbled out my eyeball corners. My knees drew up to my chest of their own accord.

"Charley! Come to me, boy. Charley—"

The man looked over his shoulder and hissed at me, drawing one finger across his throat. "Quiet."

There was absolutely no reason to be quiet. No one was around, and we were in an unknown remote corner of California.

I inhaled a lungful and bellowed from my sitting position. "Charley! Come, Charley!"

The man put a finger on his lips to shush me. I yelled until my headache made me stop. He winced and rubbed two fingers on his forehead, but at least he didn't give me any more orders. Instead, he asked, "Should I look at your head?"

"It's right where I left it." I didn't want to shake my noggin to tell him no, 'cause moving my skull around felt like a really bad plan. No one should move my head again, ever.

"My uncle, Vicente Arriaga. Do you know—"

I cut both hands across my body to shut him up. After I'd thought and thought of how to respond, I offered, "Both my folks were only children. I got no aunts or uncles."

He pulled a photograph from his back pocket and faced it to me.

With less than a glimpse, I raised one hand and squinted. I wanted to get to my feet but wasn't sure if I'd fall over trying. "Stop. Just stop it. Where am I? How did I get here? Where's my truck?"

There was something about him that reeked of suspicion, the way he measured his words and watched me too much. The way he'd been handy enough to see my attacker—or claim to, anyways—but not so handy he could actually do a daggummed thing about it.

He waved at a white metal gate in the fencing across the road. "A man dropped you off and then drove that way, onto the ranch."

I placed my eyelids under orders to open all the way and stay there to study the shoulder of the ranch's nearest low hill dotted with occasional oaks. That's pretty much all the eyeball was offered. Beyond the fence line, another dirt road like the one we were on cut a curving brown line through the earth, making the only relief to what appeared to be faint green rangeland. It looked from afar like land that could support thousands of cattle, but I knew better. It was land like under my knees, nearly desert from overuse, the grass thin and weak as the soil.

It looked like I felt.

Fire season's long past where I live, but it could strike any time in this part of California.

I stood, feet planted wide, straightening my knees and back slowly, keeping some flex in them. The hill on my left dipped and straightened. A pounding recommenced in the back of my head like someone was beating down a door.

My mood was ready to beat down a door. "If my truck went that way, then that's the way I'm going."

He shook his head. "They say I will be arrested if I go onto the ranch again."

"Who says?"

"The people with the ranch." He waved his hand toward dusty hills that might be hiding Ol' Blue.

"You know who took my truck?"

We stared at each other and I started getting a whole 'nother raging case of the creeps.

Then he said, "I know your truck went through the gate, but I cannot go there."

I finished this for him, just to prove my headache was a little better and I'd been paying attention. "Because *they* say you'll be arrested if you go there."

He nodded but looked like a man with a glimmer of an idea. Speaking slowly, he pointed to his car and muttered, "But they don't know this car. Maybe I could give you a ride."

Getting into a strange car with a strange man is usually a dumb idea for anyone, but especially for a young woman who's been attacked and now doesn't know where she is except she's on an abandoned dirt road, un-assed of her own truck, and in too bad a mood to watch her language.

No two ways about it, getting in that car was a bad idea.

I got in.

It gave me a minute while he went around to the driver's side.

Why I reached for the glove box and turned the knob, I have no earthly idea, but I did. And the rental contract looked at me and I looked at it and then at this what's-his-face fellow, who looked away.

"Look, um . . ."

"Sab. Sabino Arriaga."

Yep, the rental contract was issued to Sabino Arriaga, from Hertz.

He blinked openmouthed at the open glove box and looked at me, a question in his eyes. "I was going to give you a ride, remember?"

I'd managed to get into a car. I could manage walking. Mama and Daddy didn't raise a brilliant girl, but I was smart enough to pass on this offer of a ride. I opened the passenger door and pushed myself back out and to my feet, staggering my sick self in the direction of the ranch gate. He didn't come after me, didn't call out. I kept going. That's what I do.

Standard No Trespassing signs hung on the wire fence at regular intervals. I passed three of them before reaching the white metal pole gate. In the middle of the gate hung a sign.

TRESPASSERS WILL BE SHOT. SURVIVORS WILL BE SHOT AGAIN.

Chapter 3

I SLIPPED THROUGH THE RANCH GATE, past more No Trespassing signs, and walked up the ranch's snaking two-track road. It rose up to meet me, which is not a good thing, because the exertion in the slight climb made my stomach turn and my head pound. Bile seeped into my mouth. I called for Charley, called and cried, called and got mad, tamped down the threatening puke-fest.

Beyond the little hill, on the side of the ranch road in the distance, sat Ol' Blue.

Minutes was all it would take to reach my truck. From the little rise I'd climbed, I spied that white rental car on the public road beyond the ranch. I'd lose sight of that fellow—and forget his name, whatever it was—by the time I descended to Ol' Blue. I was aware enough to see a four-wheeler paralleling me on a hill to the north, deeper into the ranch. He motored along barely above idle, slow enough that he didn't raise dust.

Then the four-wheeler cut switchbacks down the hill toward the two-track that was taking me to Ol' Blue. I saw the rider plain—a man in a cowboy hat, western shirt, and faded jeans. Saw that he'd reach Ol' Blue before me.

The four-wheeler's dust cloud boiled at my truck. The man

stopped hard, dismounted, walked around Ol' Blue with his hands cupped around his eyes as he peered in the cab and the topper windows. He tried the passenger door but didn't open it. I couldn't see if he also tried the door on the driver's side.

Then he remounted the four-wheeler and gunned it straight at me.

Here's a tip for men who want to bully a woman having a real bad morning: don't. In this game of chicken, I'd be damned—oops, but not really—if I stepped out of the way of this man and his big loud machine.

He swerved and cut the engine. My ears popped, adjusting to the sudden quiet. I walked on like he didn't exist, seventy-five yards from Ol' Blue and happy to be closer to my truck than the stranger was, though he could certainly power up again and beat me to it.

He called out. "Morning, miss. This is private property. I've got to have you turn around and leave the ranch now."

I walked on. Fifty yards to go.

The roar of the four-wheeler coming back to life killed what should have been peacefulness in remote country.

I walked. The four-wheeler pulled up beside me and matched my pace.

"That your truck?"

I nodded painfully, and so we reached Ol' Blue, where he cut his engine again.

He unclipped a little radio from his belt and held it to his perfect teeth, flashing a smile worthy of a toothpaste ad. "Yeah, I've made contact. A girl, by herself. Turning around now. No problem."

A squelch sounded, then a Spanish-accented male voice came back over the radio. "Okay, got it, thank you."

Ol' Blue was dead quiet. Nothing. No rustle, no furry yellow head with little cocked ears. The truck windows were still half open, the way I always leave them when Charley's in there, so he has ventilation and can get out if the cab gets too warm.

"Charley? Come on, boy." I turned my body to look and call in all directions.

Then I peered into Ol' Blue's locked cab. My ignition key was missing, which meant my house key and the key for the truck topper were also gone. I called for my dog again, tried to ignore my headache, and touched my truck's hood ornament, a little replica of an anvil Guy glued on especially for me.

Ol' Blue's hood wasn't too toasty, given the heat we were basting in, and California being what it is. The sun even works in the winter here. Diesels stay warm a while. Had it been an hour since I was at the back of the Black Bluff bull sale grounds? Way more? Less?

Like I was just learning to tell time, I studied my watch—ten a.m.—and wondered if that fellow who'd claimed to be helping me could have messed with my watch when I was woozy.

"Ma'am," Four-Wheeler said, jerking a thumb in the direction I'd come from, "you have to go now. I'm going to escort you to the closest gate, which is that way. Okay, ma'am?"

Ma'am. He was probably a good thirty years old, five years older than me. He folded his arms across his chest. His dog wasn't missing, and he hadn't had been hit on the head, and had his truck stolen, too. Yeah, his day had shaped up just fine. Me, not so much.

I opened Ol' Blue's topper with dread. "Charley?"

I didn't really expect him to be there, since I hadn't heard a rustle inside the bed, but I couldn't help checking for a silenced dog in the bed of my truck. There was no still body there. Well, that was good news. I studied the bad news, too.

It could have been worse, but it was pretty bad and feeling way worse. My whole shoeing box, the one I set beside the horse every time I'm working, was there and so was my stall jack, but the gate-mouth bag that held my new track nippers—the top-notch model that set me back nearly two hundred dollars—was wide open. I'd definitely left it zipped shut. It held all my backup tools and they were there but the new nippers? Gone. The nail cutters, the crease nail pullers, and two good rasps were missing from their slots in the wood toolbox, the one I set on the ground and rack my working tools on while shoeing. My forge was still on its swing-out arm—the one piece of gear I was least attached to, maybe the sorriest piece of gear I owned. I really need a better forge. I'd have to crawl into the truck to know if my pocket anvil was still there, but I'd seen enough for now.

I whistled for my dog and felt a stabbing pain in my skull. "Charley? Come to me now, buddy. Come on, boy. Charley!"

The four-wheeler cowboy racked a boot heel against his handle-bars. "You lose something, ma'am?"

What started as a favor to get the bull off a friend's ranch and get me to the famous Black Bluff bull sale had played out in the worst way. I was a long day's drive from home, missing some of my working tools, on a dusty ranch road in the middle of nowhere. I didn't know how to get myself home from here. I'd been hit and dumped. Worst thing was, my dog was gone. So, yeah, I'd lost something.

Closing my eyes again, I remembered the sound of Ol' Blue being driven away as I'd met the grass with my face, as my brain took a lap inside my skull from the whack. The sounds. I remembered hearing Charley in the bed of the truck. He about never goes through the rear slider window and climbs around my tools in the back. But I remembered the clinking sound, his rushing body, the mad scramble that I'd somehow known in a flash was Charley. Had he been trying to get to me? Trying to defend me?

There was no sound now but the light breathing of the man on the four-wheeler. I didn't know him and didn't trust him, plain and simple.

Guy, I wish you were here.

I peered into the cab through the driver's window. My cell phone was still in Ol' Blue's open ashtray. Sunglasses hung from the visor.

"You have to go now, ma'am. I mean it." He sat up straighter on his stupid four-wheeler.

I turned on my feet, but there was no sign of Charley in any direction. "I'm looking for my dog. I kind of woke up over there. I don't know who moved my truck. But my dog's gone." I pointed beyond the ranch, though we couldn't see the public land from this little hollow.

"Well, you should have kept him on a leash, and you shouldn't have been on this land in the first place. There's, like, a hundred signs all around the property edge that tell you—" He looked at me, then away, fidgeting on the four-wheeler. "Aw, don't cry. Look, it's okay, it's just that—"

"I'm not crying!" I wiped the tears away and again turned in place, searching as far as I could see in every direction. "I want my dog. And someone hit me and dumped me out on that road and I just want my dog back. Charley? Charley, come on, boy. Come to me."

"What do you mean, you got dumped out on the road? You all right?"

Jeez, I'm not a crier, I swear, but the shuddering breath I sucked in was near enough to bawling. "Charley? Charley!"

I tried to think it through. Someone had taken my truck, drove it here, stole stuff from it, and abandoned it. So he didn't want my truck, it was just a sleazy way to set himself up with some shoeing tools. He must have had another vehicle waiting here, where he'd driven Ol' Blue. Robbery in broad daylight. Even in my muddled state, I thought it seemed like a lot of trouble for a few tools.

Whoever hit me took quite a chance that he wouldn't be seen smacking me at the far reaches of the bull sales ground, then taking my truck. He also took a chance that Charley, who'd apparently tried to get himself clear of the thief, wouldn't bite.

Well, Charley wouldn't. He might stare or growl to warn people off. Generally, that's all it takes. Most people aren't more trouble than that. Charley and I both understand such a situation. I have no quarrel with him not taking his forty-five-pound self to a life-and-death battle over a big chunk of metal. He'll back off any animal that I've sent him to gather, he'll guard any gate I leave unattended when we're moving livestock. He collects Guy's geese, puts them in the shed for us, brings the ducks off the Buckeye pond when Hollis wants to fish. He's Charley, he's my friend, he's great.

How in the world could I leave this place with him lost? How could I drive back to Oregon without him?

Maybe the sound of Ol' Blue starting up would bring him in. I remembered, then, that my keys were gone from the ignition.

"Charley? Charley!" I cupped my hands and yelled at the hills north and south, down the dusty road, east and west. I held my breath and listened, wiped my face, and called him some more. I climbed on top of Ol' Blue's hood, then cab, and hollered some more, making myself dizzy, hoping my voice would carry farther and I could see farther, far enough to see Charley come loping back to me.

"Ma'am, please come on down from there." The man swept his hat off and ran a hand through his clumped, dark wavy hair.

"Mister, I want my dog back," I said, teetering on top of my truck's cab as I called for Charley.

"I'm Gabe."

He just got scared, I told myself. Charley skedaddled when the scumbag stopped the truck and started stealing from it. I could picture it in the back of my eyeballs, my little dog scooting from the clangy, crowded truck bed—a place where he never rides anyways. I could picture the nervous eye he'd have given to the unknown man who'd struck me down. Sure, I could understand my dog clearing out. Protecting Ol' Blue isn't Charley's job. He's my buddy. Yeah, he works, moves stock for me, but I have that dog because I met him at a time in my life when I truly needed—and flat didn't have—a friend in the world. And he was willing to take the job.

He's sterling. I so love my Charley dog.

And he loves me, I just know it. I could understand him running off. From his perspective, he'd about been kidnapped. No one ever drives my truck but me. Even Guy doesn't drive it—though that's a story for another day—so anyone but me behind the wheel would look pretty far from cricket to my good old dog.

Guy.

I wanted to call my Intended, tell him what had happened. I went to my butt on Ol' Blue's cab, slid down the windshield, then fell off the hood, landing in a heap on the dirt like I'd been run over by my own truck.

The man jumped off his four-wheeler and moved to help me up. I hauled myself up by grabbing my truck's grille, lacing my fingers into the hard metal edges. It hurt.

Four-Wheeler's expression seemed to grow darker when I staggered to Ol' Blue's left hind tire and threw myself to the ground. He didn't move while I lay on my back and wiggle-crawled, reaching up above my truck's springs to undo the baling wire that holds my spare key up there. I'd have to pick a new hiding spot for the key. The cowboy was eyeballing me so hard when I wiggled back out from underneath my truck.

"Oh," he said. "Locked out. You're all right now?"

I gave one half-nod, made it back to the driver's door, then threw myself into Ol' Blue's cab. The air in there hung hot and stale. I turned the key halfway and waited for the glow plugs to tell me to start the truck.

That's when I lost it and wept alone in the cab, unable to fire up because I couldn't leave Charley. The quiet of the truck was the most disturbing thing, far and away worse than missing tools. I switched the key off in the ignition. I wasn't going anywhere. I shoved the truck door open.

"Charley?" Wrapping my mind around the fact that my Charley dog was really gone was going to make my skull explode. Had he run from the truck? Jumped out when the thief started to unload my tools?

The cowboy-hatted rider of the four-wheeler watched me, looking around this way and that while I checked my little cell phone. Nothing. I held the phone up high but got no bars of service.

On the other side of Ol' Blue, the reception offered one flickering bar. I'd have to get the truck started, find my way back to a cell connection, maybe to the Black Bluff bull sale grounds, and call the police. The missing shoeing tools, I'd live without. They weren't missing me, but I knew Charley was. He's irreplaceable, the one thing I couldn't go to my insurance company for fixing.

A scared dog can cover some miles, avoiding people. I didn't want to drive farther away from him. I waved my stupid little cell phone in the air.

"I can't get a signal."

"No, that's why we use the radios on this part of the ranch. There's one big hill with pretty good service, but that's the only reliable connection. I can radio to have a call made for you if you need someone to come pick you up."

"I'm not from around here. I don't know what road I was on or how I got here. I'm all turned around, and I just want my dog."

How could I leave this spot where Charley had disappeared? Dropping to my knees, I puked spit and bad air. Waves of nausea kept coming. Sweat beaded off my nose. Palms in the dirt, I retched again, realizing as I wiped my mouth that I was probably streaking dirt all over my face.

"Charley? Come on, buddy. It's over. That'll do. Come back to me now. Charley!"

A terrible scream rent the air over the ranch's next hill, then was cut off by two gunshots.

Chapter 4

F OUR-WHEELER WATCHED ME AND EXHALED. "OKAY, how about this," he said. "How about I take you to the house. You can use the landline, and there's easy access to get you on the main road from there. We'll get you sorted out. Okay?"

So, we were going to act like those screams and gunshots didn't just happen? I swallowed. "I want my dog back."

"You can't stay here. We've got a party fanned out over those low hills. They'll be at it all day unless they score early."

"Party?"

"Hunting party."

It was February. "What's in season?"

"Pigs."

I didn't like the idea of Charley being lost in the ranch's oak woodlands while some city-folks-who-think-they're-hunters types took potshots. Not that my gold Aussie looks like a wild pig, but there's people who take what they call *sound shots*, meaning they fire at sounds in the woods.

"There's an active hunt going on, and you have to be escorted."

"A pig hunt?"

"Yes, ma'am. You're standing in one of the top pig-hunting areas in the entire state of California."

"Dandy." I scanned so hard against the horizon for my Charley, my vision blurred.

"Look, are you okay? Can you follow my four-wheeler back to the house? You have to stay with me. Don't stop. We'll find your dog later."

"I don't want him out here when there's people shooting."

"You against hunting? Eating meat?" His jaw stiffened. "People have to be careful when they shoot. They have to be sure of the target and what's behind it."

I shook my head, stopped, grabbed my skull with both palms, sickened by the swimmy vision. "I just want to find my dog."

He fired up his four-wheeler and looked at me over his shoulder. "You stick close, okay? Get in your truck, follow me, and I'll take you to the house."

My stomach flipped, and my mouth tasted terrible. There's toothpaste and a travel brush in my glove box, but I didn't feel coordinated enough to clean up and drive. I was ready to retch any second anyways. I didn't like driving away from the place Charley might associate with the truck, assuming he'd been in Ol' Blue when it was abandoned.

***

The horse was a powerful Appaloosa mare, black with a white hip blanket and a decent mane and tail for an Appy. Picked up a lope on cue and covered the sand arena in jig time. The rider had a lot of long blonde hair with more wave and big curls than she could have come by without a fair bit of styling time this morning. The western shirt and jeans fit tight over her Barbie body. One of the beautiful people and probably knew it. She wore red leather chinks with fringe that must have been over a half-foot long. Every one of those long thin strips of leather lifted in the air and swirled in slow motion up her thighs and around her knees when she reined the horse in.

The four-wheeler angled toward the arena gate and shut off within thirty feet of the white wood rails. We probably hadn't driven a mile, but the two-track ranch road was so windy and I was so woozy the route was disorienting. Climbing out of Ol' Blue, I stumbled on a stone and leaned on the front fender. The hard, rocky ground would have been murder to put those posts in, which is why most arenas in this part of Northern California are portable panels, just setting on top of the dirt.

"She's doing great, Gabe."

"Yes, ma'am, I thought you'd be pleased."

"Picks up either lead with a whisper from my leg." She swung off the horse and draped the reins over the top rail where her stylish leather and denim jacket hung. One of those women who's probably old enough to be my mama—mine was barely legal when she had me—but takes attentive care of herself.

"Yes, ma'am."

She hooked one perfect boot heel on the bottom rail. "And what's going on here?"

Gabe pointed at me. "This girl was on the property near the perimeter."

"We have a hunt."

"That's why I stopped her. She's kind of out of it. Says she got turned around and needs to use the phone, needs help to get back to town."

"Like, needs someone to go with her?" The woman looked at me. "You want someone to go with you? I'll send Gabe. I can spare him for an hour or so. Actually, that would work out wonderfully."

He started to raise a hand and shake his head, but the woman was already turning away and didn't see his protest.

She called over her shoulder, "Gabe, you go with her. Give us a call afterward and Oscar or I will come get you."

She pulled a Bible-sized brown package from her jacket on the fence and flounced toward Ol' Blue. I'd left the driver's door open, I noticed now. Maybe Gabe and I both couldn't believe it when she put her goodie on Ol' Blue's bench seat. "Drop this at the shop for me while you're in town, okay?"

Gabe set his hat just right and spoke a little loud. "You said Eliana was going to do that."

"Well, she's not around or busy or something. I think she's making dinner."

He took a step toward the four-wheeler like they all had better things to do. "Stuckey's not answering the radio. Oscar's been asking me to check on him."

Swiveling on my feet, oddly woozy, I looked around and took in the two houses and a barn behind me. I felt like I was wearing out my welcome, though I'd no real notion how long I'd driven to get here and only sort-of noticed the buildings while tailgating the four-wheeler. Tunnel vision isn't like me except when it comes to studying horses' feet. I blinked at my surroundings. The farther house was fancy-big, new, with an arched flagstone entrance on the close end, a triple garage on the other. The other house was nearer us, a good sixty yards from the fancy place, right close to the long wooden barn. Probably the original farmstead house. A beat-up green Ford Bronco with out-of-state plates sat near the farmhouse. I watched the houses blur in and out of focus. My right hand went to the back of my skull. It had felt good to get out of Ol' Blue, I realized, because the big goose egg under my ponytail was tender and had been rubbing on the truck's headrest.

"Honey," the woman addressed me, the wobbly statue between the four-wheeler and the arena, "are you okay?"

"My dog's missing. I want my dog back." My knees went of their own accord, and I swooned like some girl in need of a fainting couch.

"Gabe, grab her!"

She berated him for letting me drive, and he defended himself, saying he didn't realize I was that bad.

"I'm not bad," I protested.

Things grayed out, maybe just for seconds. Powerful hands on my upper arms kept me on my feet then started walking me out of the sun toward the shade of the older, closer house. Hadn't realized the fellow was so strong. He sat me down in a glider on the porch, and I planted my heels on the wood planks because I could tell the rocking motion was going to make me seasick. This north side of the whitewashed house's clapboard rested in the shade and practically exhaled coolness. I realized I'd been out way too long in the sun. Who knows how long I'd been lying on the roadside before I'd come to? Back home, it's a sight cooler than most of California, and this seemed to be turning remarkably hot for early spring.

"Do you need to lie down?" The woman's voice came from some tunnel I couldn't see. "She needs a cold drink. Is Stuckey back from escorting that group? Or is he checking the flock?" Her voice doubled in decibels. "Oscar!"

"Oscar's doing the group," Gabe put in.

"Oh, right. Oscar's turn. My bad. Eliana! I think she's up at the house."

The footsteps on wood I heard were Gabe's, crossing into the farmhouse, running the tap, returning with a large plastic tumbler of water that she took from him and forced on me.

"Flock?" I asked before and after big gulps of water. These people had sheep. My Charley would be called to sheep like an ant can't resist a picnic. "You got sheep on this place?"

The woman laughed like tinkling bells, ridiculously pretty. "Oh, that woke her up."

"Wait," I asked, "do you have a guardian dog?"

Like herds, flocks have to be protected from predators. These days, more and more, ranchers use livestock guardian dogs. Every European and Near East country has a great white breed, the Pyrenees from the French-Spanish borderland, the Komondor and Kuvasc from Hungary, the Maremma from Italy, the Polish Tatra, the Anatolians and Karabash from Turkey. They're all giant, fierce, flop-eared dogs that live with a flock and protect it from wolves.

And here in California, a guardian dog would kill a strange herder as quick as they'd take down a coyote. My Charley might be swooping toward this ranch's flock while I sat in the shade sipping water. I started to push myself up. The glider was a lousy push-off surface, and I fell back on my butt.

"What's your name, honey?" the woman said. "Mine's Ivy, and I think you still need to sit down."

My escort from the four-wheeler and general man-handler, Gabe, asked, "You mean a livestock guardian dog?"

I nodded. Made my head swim. Didn't like nodding.

Gabe said, "She's worried we have a big dog that'll take hers out."

"Oh, I see. No, we had a shepherd—"

"We've used the collars," Gabe said. "Lots of different things."

Ivy nodded. "But I think we're going to go with that guardian dog idea and get a couple of those big boys. We used to have a real shepherd. A man."

"Mmm . . . shepherd's name . . ." I croaked.

Ivy narrowed her gaze at me. "Um, Vicente. Vicente Arriaga. Why?"

"He moved on," Gabe said.

Arriaga. I rubbed my head as hard as my headache allowed. "Mine's Charley. He's an Australian Shepherd."

"Oh!" Ivy waved and smiled. "You were talking about the dog. Oh, honey, I know Aussies. I used to have one of the top working stud dogs in the country."

I tried to raise my voice enough to make a difference above their nattering. "I need to call . . ." But then, who did I need to call? I wasn't home in Butte County, and, even if I had been, Guy was up in Seattle today. I wiped my eyes. "Please radio whoever's out there hunting to be careful of my dog."

"Look, nobody in the hunt is going to shoot your dog thinking it's a pig," Gabe told me, then spoke like an aside to Ivy, though I was right there. "She said someone dumped her out on the boundary road."

"Oh. Oh! You were assaulted? Are you okay? Do you think you need to see a doctor? I could get you a doctor." She paused after I declined, asked if I was sure, and made me nod before she continued. "So, you need to talk to the police? I didn't realize. Okay. Okay, let's see, where did it happen?"

"I was at the Black Bluff bull sale."

Ivy turned to Gabe. "Isn't that . . ."

He was looking at her horse, still standing in the sun, reins looped over the fence. The mare cocked one beautiful hip, looking like she'd wait all day and then some.

Ivy said, "You need to go back to the sale grounds to report it to the police."

"Can't I call from here?"

She shook her head. "There's a whole jurisdictional thing. It has to do with whether you're in the city limits, which we're not, or the county or what. Like, this ranch is in two different counties. So, you should go back to the sale grounds to make your police report."

"Getting my dog back is my priority. He ran off or something when I got hit and they took my truck. I want my dog back."

"Oh, you poor thing. Being worried about your dog is something I completely understand. I'm still not over mine and he's been gone—" She waved and shook her head, long hair flying around her face. "Sorry, off topic. You know, dogs usually turn up."

I nodded with as little motion as could convey the idea of yes, somehow unable to form the syllable.

She turned to Gabe. "Where exactly did you find her?"

He jerked a thumb over his shoulder the way we'd come. "Walking from the east gate. Her truck was near there. Like she'd locked herself out."

She patted my shoulder. "Well, what if the guys put dog food and a bucket of water over there? Leave us a number where we can reach you if your dog turns up."

There didn't seem to be a better option, so I got up. Gabe passed me by and was away with a roar on the four-wheeler. The big Appy flicked an ear and held steady. Good horse.

Ivy walked with me to Ol' Blue where she took back her package. "Getting to town from the front gate is easy. Just follow the road, you'll see signs. You cannot miss it. You're okay to drive?"

"I'm okay." But I wasn't. The blonde vision and her perfect Appaloosa blurred in and out of focus. Still, I gave her my business card, which has the house number in Cowdry, same as Ol' Blue's door, but also my cell number.

I felt worse as I drove away, ever farther from my dog.

Chapter 5

THE SUN WAS TOO HIGH TO let me get oriented, but if town and the Black Bluff sale grounds lay west of the ranch as the woman with the Appy had said and I followed my nose past the first several crossroads to bigger roads, I hoped to get lucky beyond the strip of haze hanging over the interstate. The air's so much cleaner in Cowdry. I had to get back. I had to get Charley, get home, and get married.

With twenty or thirty minutes' driving, I cleared the town of Black Bluff and was on the west outskirts, where I pointed Ol' Blue back through the main gate at the bull sale and aimed straight to the commercial area behind the grandstand where the announcer's box was situated, beyond the dusty hot dog stand. In the main arena, everybody's attention was on a half-dozen rough steers challenging a tiny black-and-white Border Collie.

A pang of longing pulled at my heart as I remembered running Charley in the arena first thing in the morning, and how I'd hoped to do it again. I told the good old boy in the front booth that I'd been robbed and needed to talk to the police.

He adjusted his greasy felt cowboy hat and looked at me more than twice. "Are you all right? Where'd that happen?"

"Here."

"Just now? I'll call the security guard." He looked around, past countless parked pickups and tapped a radio by his announcer's microphone. "Hey, Bob, come on up to the booth."

"This morning," I said.

He said he'd tell the man called Bob that I'd be waiting by the announcement boards, then waved a hand toward a structure like the sort of little semi-weatherproof bulletin board used for trailheads.

A couple of cowboys stood there with their backs to me, fingers tracing over the posted placings of the day. One of the gawkers elbowed the other and jerked his chin my way as I joined them. I turned my back to the bulletin board and decided the police had maybe ten minutes to come talk to me or I was going right back to the ranch to look for Charley.

The two men at the board cast more looks at each other and me. One nodded, maybe looking at my bare left hand.

The thing Guy and I have been negotiating—whether or not he'll hang a bird band on my ring finger—well, maybe it ought to get settled his way. I'd had about enough of every cowpoke wanting to poke where he ought not. I never much cottoned to the way some guys yuckety-yuk each other into swaggering up to every gal standing alone for a moment. It's bad chess, the way they ponder, then make their moves. I've never been any good at games, indoor or outdoor.

Now the kind of chess a herding dog plays, there's a game I favor. The Border Collie in the arena had its head so low to the ground while he gave six steers the evil eye that the dog's jaw was almost in the dirt. The cattle gathered tighter together, then froze as though the dog had cast a spell on them. He might as well have.

My mouth felt dry and bitter. My temples pulsed with pain that drilled straight through to my ponytail, and I was three breaths away from throwing up.

One of the cowboys tapped my arm. I flinched.

He jerked his thumb toward Ol' Blue and nodded in a way that made his thick mustache and giant, joined-together eyebrows seem alive. "'Scuse me. You came in this morning? Brought that bull that used to go rodeo, did you? Charged a man in Salinas?"

I nodded, not seeing it necessary to say how I came to be hauling Dragoon. If the beast sold, he'd no longer be my concern.

The man bounced his unibrow and gave a crooked grin. It seemed one of us thought this might be the start of a beautiful daylong relationship. "That bull really unridden?"

I nodded again. So did the other fellow, a lanky wisp of a man, as he stepped closer to my rig and gave it a good going-over with his eyeballs. I still needed to hitch up Hollis Nunn's stock trailer to Ol' Blue but decided that could wait. Ol' Blue's much more maneuverable when not hauling.

My hope for the killer bull was that he'd be bought by someone who would be safe and maybe get him in a breeding program or at least a serious set of pipe corrals. Though I'd seen Dragoon's respect for a fence, it still gave me the creeps for him to be contained in anything less than could stop a truck. The bull's value was as wild as his nature. Whether Dragoon got tried again for rodeo—a deadly idea if ever there was one—used for breeding, or made into rank meat was for his future buyer to choose. It wasn't the nicest thought to wander through my skull, but then, I wasn't interested in ruminating on the bull. Right then, Charley was all that mattered to me. Maybe after I found my dog, I'd get serious about who hit me, stolen my tools, and moved my truck, then I'd deal with the bull. My head kept throbbing and I felt half-starved, but I would have barfed if I'd tried to eat.

The cowpoke with the face caterpillars was still staring at Ol' Blue. I guessed what he was thinking on. Dale's Horseshoeing, my out-of-state plate, and out-of-state phone number on the truck door. Ooh, he saw himself a real live woman horseshoer. Yippee.

After the hairy half-cowboy left, probably hoping to eye the famous killer bull up close and personal, I thought of what had been in the trailer, too.

Naturally, I swiveled my noggin and accidentally met the look sent my way, a dip of a cowboy hat that had been trained on me over a hundred yards away by the heavy pipe corral where my morning cargo waited. Dragoon swung his head, snot flying, then circled in the stunted freedom that didn't suit him. He took a mean lap around the dusty corral, pawing and threatening the world in a way that would have let me feel his power vibrating through the earth if I'd been closer to him.

"He farts sparks," one rail-sitting dude shouted to another as they studied Dragoon.

I didn't know if farting sparks was a good thing or a bad thing. Looking over at them didn't help me figure much out except that the sandy-haired one needed time in a barber's chair to keep that straw cowboy hat on better. He was eyeballing another couple of good old boys yonder who were checking out Dragoon.

The security guard for the sale showed up, blue uniform and all, and asked me what happened. He looked to be about thirty with an IQ of not quite triple his age. This grassy area by the bulletin board wasn't private enough to suit me. Though the cowboys had left to ogle Dragoon at closer range, I could still see the flirty one looking my way, and I was working to not meet his smoky, brow-and-mustache-framed gaze, lest he feel invited back over.

"My dog's missing, and some of my stuff was stolen. Someone hit me, truck-jacked me, and dumped me twenty-some-odd miles up the road." My hand went to the back of my head. It was tender, felt thick and mushy, but since the lump was in my hair, I didn't have a nice bruise to impress the security guard or a cop. I didn't have squat.

After I told him my complaint, he wanted a real good description of who hit me.

"I think he was wearing jeans."

Mr. Security Guard stared pointedly in every direction. I didn't need to look to know what he saw.

No one wasn't wearing jeans.

Finally, he tried again. "But you know it was a man, not a woman who hit you?"

I shook my head the two centimeters that didn't make my nausea worse. "I really couldn't say."

"Well, your description eliminates anyone in slacks or a skirt, which is no one around here. Follow me?"

"I think I might. You're saying you can't help me."

"'Fraid so."

"Then I have to wait for a real cop to come fingerprint my truck?"

"Trucks don't have fingerprints." He grimaced and shook his head, like a man who was standing before a most simple woman. Then he sighed mightily and said he could call for a police officer to come talk to me.

The security fellow used his cell phone, worked to convince a dispatcher that I needed a deputy then told them I'd be waiting by the corkboard at the sale grounds.

I stared at the board's older posts above today's standings of how the dogs exhibiting at the sale competition had placed.

Maybe it's just bad luck that my eyeballs happened to settle over a dog's picture on a weathered flyer for stud services. I wished he hadn't looked so much like a puffed-up, younger version of Charley. This was a yellow Aussie stud dog, Champion Beaumont's Wild Firestarter, C.D.X., H.D. II, blah blah. Crying wouldn't help, but this dog picture set me to thinking. Some stupid part of my brain—and there are a few—wondered what would happen if I couldn't get Charley back. Would he wander and wonder why I didn't come for him, why I'd left him and wouldn't be his friend anymore? Was he hungry and alone and scared like he'd been when I found him? We've had great times together, helped heal each other. He's family. He's the one who okayed Guy, for the sake of all that's good.

I got my day planner from Ol' Blue, ripped a blank page from the back, and scribbled down the date, my cell number, the phone number at home, and Charley's description. At the top and bottom, I wrote big.

Missing Dog. Reward.

I took five of my business cards and wrote an abbreviated version: Missing yellow Aussie. Reward. And I pinned it all to the weather-bubbled bulletin board next to offered flyers for hay sales and livestock of all kinds. Below the stud dog Aussie picture was a page about a missing teenage girl, a runaway who was considered endangered.

Would Charley be considered endangered? Brokenhearted, at least, like me. Beside the full-page flyer for the girl hung another, though it was not protected in plastic, not in color, and not official-looking with phone numbers for the local police who still hadn't showed up at the sale grounds to help me. The weather-bubbled flyer by my scrap note and business cards asked for information on a man, and the photo looked oddly familiar.

The security guard flicked a glance at the poster of the missing man.

"That case," he said, tut-tutting with a shoulder-sagging sigh. "Yeah, that Arriaga character's in town again, I heard."

"Arriaga." Was that the name of the fellow with the white rental car? He'd seen my truck go missing, which meant he'd been close to my disappeared dog. That joker had been way too handy to my being attacked, way too weird about where my truck had been driven off to.

He'd shushed me when I'd hollered for Charley. Had he been about to do something and I scared him off? Had he changed his mind just because I was yelling? What would he have done to me if I hadn't walked away?

"That fellow was there," I said, "after I was attacked or at least when I got dumped on a back road. He got me into his car when I was pretty out of it. See, I woke up on a dirt road a convenient half-mile or so from my stolen truck."

"You should talk to the cop about that when he gets here."

"What's the story with that Arriaga dude?"

"He pops into town now and again, pisses people off, leaves."

"That's his job, huh?"

"Seems to be."

"How long's that been his thing?"

"Oh, a year, year-and-a-half now. It's getting old."

I nodded. It had gotten old with me in a lot less than a year. "He's missing someone?"

"So he says."

"This place seems to be a Bermuda Triangle of sorts."

"Begging your pardon there, young lady. I don't know of any aircraft down in the area."

"No, I was thinking of my dog and my tools and, for a while there, my truck. And someone in that Arriaga dude's family."

If only the rent-a-cop had more enthusiasm. If only someone else at the sale grounds stepped forward as a witness to what happened to me. If only I'd taken note of exactly where Ol' Blue had been. If only the rent-a-cop hadn't muttered in Spanish to a man who walked up and interrupted.

After they had said their piece, He-Who-Hadn't-Helped-Me gave me one order as he moseyed off to watch steers or dogs or drink a soda and enjoy a hot dog or four while I hadn't had so much as a Milk Dud all day.

"You wait here," he said, holding up his palm for me to fully comprehend his *stay* command. "Don't leave. Wait by your truck."

I reconsidered the cluttered bulletin board. Just a thick cork veneer glued onto the plywood sheets. Some of the ads were yellowed and tattered, some leafed over each other and some were spanking new, laminated. Business cards were pinned all over, too.

Horseshoeing. Reasonable rates. Call now. Robbie Duffman.

The notice was fresh, handwritten on a plain sheet of paper. I wondered if Robbie Duffman was a new shoer.

New shoers need tools.

Only a shoer or at least a horseman handy with the tools of my trade would have stolen tools out of Ol' Blue. And whoever did that had first conked me in the head and stolen my truck and dog.

My morning sounded like a bad country song. Felt like one, too.

I wrote Duffman's number down and told myself to check on every single shoer I could find for however long I had to be here. And then I looked more carefully at the old photo of the missing man. Middle-aged, grinning in a meadow, a dog leaning against his leg. I wouldn't have remembered the name of the fellow who'd tried to show me that picture, but the same name was there, on the poster.

Arriaga.

Vicente Arriaga was missing, and any information would be rewarded.

I put my fingertips on the picture of the missing man, let my thumb slip off the photo. Swallowed and stared.

Charley sat beside him, leaning against Vicente Arriaga's leg, smiling up at him, ready to work woolies. My Charley.

No way was I going to stand here waiting for a cop.

***

A California Highway Patrol officer flipped on lights and siren as soon as Ol' Blue rolled within sight of the ranch.

The cop did not come up to the window like normal.

His PA squawked orders.

"Driver, exit your vehicle with your hands in the air, facing away from me."

Really? I sat there for a second, thinking about the unlikeliness of pretty much everything that had happened today. The cop repeated the command over his PA and added, "Do it now."

I unbuckled my seat belt, creaked Ol' Blue's driver door open, then stepped into the sun, making shadow puppets with my arms extended as ordered. Behind me, the black silhouette of a cop came up, gun in hand.

Chapter 6

ALARM ROSE IN MY CORE. THE sound of the cop holstering his weapon competed with my breathing. I'd never before had this experience, but I didn't move a muscle as he patted me down.

"What's your name?"

"Rainy Dale." Man, my head hurt.

"What's your real first name?"

"Rainy." I wondered if I should spell it for him.

"I.D."

A pause drew on while I ran his last comment around in my brain, then I happened upon the notion that he meant to be requesting my driver's license. I fished my Oregon state license from Ol' Blue's visor under the cop's close observation.

Right away, he impressed me by showing he could read. "Rainy Dale. No middle name."

When I said nothing, he added, "I stopped you because you have a taillight out."

Even in my dulled state, my hackles rose. His approach on a bad taillight was way too aggressive.

The cop stepped away back toward his patrol car and talked indecipherably to his radio while I waited to see if this was going

47

to turn into a fix-it ticket or one with a fine or if he was having the kind of day where I got to drive away with a promise to deal with Ol' Blue's old wiring.

When the cop came back, he said, "Do you have any objection to permitting my dog to sniff around your vehicle?"

"Huh?"

"Yeah, what I'd like to do is leave your truck doors open and just let my dog walk around to check it out."

"I guess that's all right. Is this usual?" I waved a hand in agreement.

But he was walking sideways back to his car, which was when I noticed the bouncing, pointy-eared dog in his back seat. He leashed it, all the while talking in a girly-high tone about what a good boy the dog was.

Tears for Charley flooded my eyelids, so I had to open them like saucers to not drip. "You want me to just stand here?"

"If you'll wait right on that line, ma'am." Twenty-four years old, I am, and the cop called me ma'am. I toed the white-painted line on the shoulder of the road where he pointed, right in front of Ol' Blue's open door, since the cop's dog apparently liked to sniff vehicles with the doors open.

The dog looked like a pared-down German Shepherd, yellow-bodied with a black face. From the way its tail was going, snuffling around Ol' Blue was the best part of his day so far. Absolutely no traffic came by in either direction, which was a shame, 'cause I thought we made quite a spectacle. The dog sped around Ol' Blue's tires and took a good long pause in the cab, wagging like crazy while the cop peered and frowned at the dog and my truck cab.

"He smells my dog," I said.

"My dog does not give a flip about other dogs."

Working dogs don't. They honor another when it's the other dog's turn to work, and they want their next chance to work, that is all. I started to say this aloud but skipped it for what mattered.

"As long as you're here rooting around my truck, I need to talk to a police officer about a theft and an assault. It happened this morning at the Black Bluff bull sale grounds."

The dog and cop both looked at me.

"Go on." The man waved to Ol' Blue's wheel wells and the space between the cab and the truck bed. The police dog shoved his nose everywhere the fellow pointed, wagging all the while, moving on, and sniffing.

I raised my voice unsure if the cop was listening. "A-couple-three hours ago, I was at the Black Bluff bull sale grounds, way off to the side, and someone hit me in the head. When I woke up, I was just outside that ranch." I pointed. "But didn't know where I was, 'cause I'm not from here. I was way over near the ranch's east side. A fellow said my truck had been driven onto the ranch, and that's where I found it. My dog was missing. Still is. I found my truck not too far onto the ranch."

"Your truck was jacked, driven onto the ranch, and abandoned there?" His eyebrows were up with surprise and interest.

"And some tools and my dog's gone."

He put his dog back in his patrol car and then came forward with a question. "What kind of tools?"

As I named the track nippers and nail cutters and crease nail pullers and whatnot, the uniformed cop repeated the words and wrote, but asked, "What is this stuff?"

"Tools of my trade." I cleared my throat so it was strong and sure when I said, "I'm a horseshoer."

His face did the surprise expression parade all over again. He muttered toward his dog like that was the only person he talked to in his day. "Tools. Track nippers?" His mind seemed to really be spinning.

I admit sometimes to a little part of me getting a kick out of the surprise most men show when they find out what I do for a living. I offered to show him my big nippers for comparison, but he said he didn't need to see them.

The cop asked to look at the back of my head, posed me more

questions about what happened at the sale grounds and when I'd woken up and if I wanted medical help. "Why didn't you call the police from the ranch house?"

"They said there was a jurisdictional thing. That I had to go back to the sale grounds where it happened."

He snorted. "I bet they did. Any law enforcement officer can write an informational report that gets forwarded to another agency." Then he gave me a card with a case number that he said would help me file a claim with my auto insurance, and the case wasn't likely to go anywhere since they had nothing to go on at this point. But he hoped I'd find my dog.

I couldn't go home without Charley. How long would I live out of my truck, calling and waiting for him?

And I'd miss my wedding in a few days.

"So," the cop said, "you don't work for the ranch or have any dealings with them?"

"Right," I agreed.

He left me with a verbal warning to fix the taillight. When I could no longer see him, I fired Ol' Blue up and drove on to the ranch through the main gate.

***

Barbie-Ivy was walking toward her showcase home when I pulled Ol' Blue up a respectful distance from the big house, next to the beat-up Ford Bronco, Nevada license on its bumper, resting close to the bunkhouse. The Appaloosa had been moved to the oak-shaded side of the arena, but waited patiently, still tacked up. And this time, I noticed several fancy, shaded, empty kennels by the triple garage.

"Back already?" Ivy called. "Did you go to the sale grounds?"

"I'm back." My voice sounded so weird. "What matters to me is my dog. I really need to look for him. I'd like to walk—"

"Gabe or Oscar or Stuckey could take you out on a four-wheeler."

Sitting sounded nice. I was beat, which isn't like me in the middle of the day, especially when I haven't done a single shoeing. But, no. I shook my head, just enough to communicate. Dang, this headache was making me sick to my stomach. "It's pretty hard to hear and to call a dog from those machines. I'd better walk."

The much faster way to get around this ranch would be ahorseback, but I couldn't ask Ivy to put a good horse under me. If I were home and some stranger asked to borrow my Red to go look for a lost dog, I wouldn't exactly hand my horse over.

"Dale's Horseshoeing," Ivy read aloud from Ol' Blue's truck door. "I didn't notice before. Is your husband a horseshoer?"

"I'm a shoer." And I wouldn't have a husband until the middle of the week, assuming I could find Charley and go home.

"No way! For real?" Ivy stared as I nodded, then she reread Ol' Blue's door. "A woman horseshoer. Imagine that. That's so cool. But it must be hard. Oh, you must be strong." She reached for my shoulder and bicep, fondling away. "You are a hardbody. Like you do weightlifting."

I don't work out, but I tested the headache with half a nod and a shake. It wasn't getting worse, but a couple of aspirin might be helpful.

"It's Ivy Beaumont, by the way. My husband Milt and I own this place." She waved in every direction, her voice the music of someone who's never had a bad day.

"Rainy Dale." I shook hands, which sort of seemed to surprise her. "I've got to look for my dog."

"So, you need to drive around to the east side? You were on the boundary road?"

I shook my head. "I think he's here, on this ranch somewhere."

"Wait, why would you think that? Gabe said they noticed you wandering by the back gate. The east gate." She peered hard at me. Maybe I was wavering on my feet.

"My truck was dumped on this ranch."

"Your truck was dumped on the ranch? Why? Oh, some people.

That's a hell of a thing. I hate that. We've had people throw trash over there, old refrigerators, junk. Someone even abandoned an old car over on that edge of the ranch. I'm sorry I didn't get the whole story before. Look, the pig hunt is finished, so you go ahead and look for your dog if that's what you'd like to do. I've a few ranch workers out there. If anyone stops you, tell them Ivy said it's okay for you to be here."

***

Glad I'd slugged down that water they gave me earlier, I struck off, farther and farther from the houses and barn, through one cross-fencing gate after another. The ranch had scrubby native grass that would be nothing but brown and dead-looking come summer, I knew, but greened the hills nicely now. I grew hoarse and thirstier from calling for Charley, saw pig sign, heard sheep. Scattered oaks gave shade, and there were plenty of little hollows in the hills. The ground was the kind that's good for horses' hooves, sandy, some rock, well-drained. One giant hill crowned the whole of the rolling land and would give me the best view, so it was my lot to climb and climb. After I'd been afoot a good hour and a half, I didn't have much spunk left in me, if I'd ever had any since it got knocked out of my head that morning.

A perfect vertical stack of rocks, maybe two dozen or more, marked the summit. Past that cairn lay a small, flattened mound of gold fur.

At a glance, it could be him.

I stared, swayed and stared some more, trying to focus. It couldn't be him. My Charley would come to me, wouldn't he?

If he was able.

But that body on the hilltop looked like my Charley, and he looked dead.

Chapter 7

IT WASN'T RIGHT THE WAY CHARLEY lay, his head and throat pressed into the ground, his whole body unmoving.

"Charley?"

No wiggle of greeting, no pushing himself to his feet as I called.

"Charley!" I ran to him, slid on my knees, ending up right in front of his nose and paws. "Are you okay?"

He crawled onto my lap. I stroked him all over, looking for a gunshot wound or fur turned red and wet with blood.

Nothing.

I caressed more gently, searching for the unstable crunch of broken bones.

He was whole. I lifted him from my lap, placed his body on the dirt at my knees, rose and stepped five feet away.

"Charley, come here."

He lifted his golden body, oddly, stiffly, head low, then slunk forward with a reluctance born of indecision. When he reached me, I stepped back again, ten feet, and called him. He followed. Again, twenty feet, then thirty. He wagged as he re-approached me each time. Hiking backward made me trip and stumble, but I kept this up until Charley trotted to me and whatever was broken inside his head got restored.

By the time we staggered back to Ol' Blue at the ranch house, I was beyond whipped. I wanted to crawl into Ol' Blue and sleep, snuggled with Charley. My best plan was to drink the water I carried in several old half-gallon jugs Guy buys apple cider in, sleep on the roadside, and get back on the interstate after some rest. I'd have to make the hundreds of miles home in spurts.

A four-wheeler came up behind me with a careful hum, raising no dust as it passed, shutting off and gliding in under momentum beside Ol' Blue. The driver wore a white full-face helmet and sunglasses. His black jeans and checked shirt were dusty. He was a smaller fellow than the one who'd escorted me from the far east of the ranch, probably shorter than my five-six.

He removed the sunglasses and addressed Ivy as she stepped out of her castle. "They only wanted the head and cape."

"Oh, nice. That's lucky for us—" She noticed me there and shrieked, then covered her mouth with both hands. She came around the four-wheeler staring at Charley, then froze. "Flame?"

Charley wagged and headed toward her. My guts clutched hard. "Charley, wait," I said.

He stopped.

"Flame! Oh, my God! For real?"

Charley wiggled his whole body, muscles vibrating to Ivy's excited, "Flame, Flame Flame, where have you been, darling?"

I cleared my throat hard. "He's been with me. He's mine now. Charley, come."

"I can't believe it," Ivy squealed. "What do you mean, he's been with you? How is it that you have him? How long have you had him? Do you know Vicente? What happened?"

Her questions were way too much for me. I blinked and opened my mouth, gears whirring in my head, but couldn't think where to start. Couldn't think.

Ivy grabbed my hand and jostled. "Where was he?"

"On the hilltop, near the rock cairn."

"He was at the stone boy?" Ivy's voice brimmed with wonder. "But, God, where's he been all this time?"

"I just lost him this morning."

"But I mean, wait, so you've had him with you, as like, your dog? No way! For how long?"

"Two years. He's been my dog for the last two years." I needed her to realize that whatever prior claim she'd had on Charley had evaporated, or I was going to be crying again. "He's seen me through a lot. He has a good life with me up in Oregon."

The man on the four-wheeler swung one short leg over and took a seat sideways as he watched the volley of conversation between Ivy and me. He looked to be a lot closer to Ivy's forty-something than my age. With the white helmet resting in his lap, he pulled a black baseball cap from his waistband, donned it, and cocked his head. Behind the four-wheeler seat, an open-topped cargo box held a grisly load. I smelled blood.

Really, blood has a stink all its own. I was way too young the first time I wandered into the slaughter barn on the west Texas ranch where my daddy had been working at the time. Excessive spilled blood makes a smell that stays with you, and it's not nice.

A sick feeling of dread banged on my brain, demanding to be recognized even as Ivy shrieked.

"I can't believe it! It's like seeing Fire, almost. Oh, I loved that dog like you can't believe. He was so perfect, my heart dog, you know?"

I pointed at Charley, fighting the sway that wanted to topple me to the dirt. "Flame?"

"No," Ivy said. "Fire. My dog, Fire." She too pointed at my Charley dog now. "Flame was small, and I gave him to Vicente as a puppy. Fire was mammoth. It was a two-dog litter. Very unusual. But Vicente brought Flame along and he became a really good sheepdog." Ivy turned toward the man on the four-wheeler. "Were you here then, Oscar?"

Oscar removed his baseball cap, ran a hand through his black hair, and tugged the cap on hard. "Perhaps that was before my time."

"This girl . . ." Ivy turned to me again. "I'm sorry, what was your name again, honey?"

"Rainy."

"Rainy? That's pretty." And boom, Ivy turned back to Oscar. "She's a horseshoer, visiting. And somehow, she's had Flame all this time."

That sure seemed to be the deal. My Charley used to be called Flame, used to live and work on this ranch where I was standing. I'd found my dog again, but I was afraid I could still lose him. My knees buckled, and I startled, trying to catch myself quick enough.

Ivy hugged my shoulders. "Are you okay? You're not okay, are you? I don't think you should walk around anymore. You know, I think you're concussed. I feel silly for not realizing it earlier. You shouldn't have been driving. But, Flame!"

"Charley," I said.

"I know, I know," Ivy said. "But the other thing, you know I've heard about the concussion protocol with athletes. You're not supposed to exert yourself. You're not even supposed to read a magazine. You have to rest, like for a couple of days. And you're not supposed to be alone. How about something to eat?"

A meal sounded purely wonderful. I realized I hadn't eaten a thing today, not once. And drunk not so much as a cup of coffee. I loosened my ponytail where the swelling was making the hairband dig into my scalp.

"Come on." Ivy steadied me with both hands. "And come on, Flame."

"Charley," I said.

"And shouldn't you tell your family you got conked in the head? Isn't there someone you want to talk to?"

A gasp slipped through my lips and my ponytail bobbed as I nodded. I wanted to talk to Guy, my Guy, so bad.

Oscar started the four-wheeler and headed around the back of the barn where a cinder-block building stub was attached.

"Wear the helmet!" Ivy hollered at his back, but her voice was lost over the engine's racket. They had some seriously beefy four-wheelers on this outfit.

I recalled that Gabe fellow had gone to fetch me some water at the older house however long ago and turned toward the wiggly-looking building, one step then another.

Ivy said, "There's no landline in the bunkhouse, but come on up to the house—my house—and you can use the office phone. You look woozy. Can you walk okay?"

The big house was some hundred feet away, beyond the farmhouse. I faked steadiness and followed her across the flagstone entry. Charley stuck to me like a true shepherd, but when I started to tell him to wait for me, Ivy said, "Oh, you can bring him inside. Don't worry about it."

Charley had stopped on the flagstone, knowing better than to walk into someone else's house, but when I called him along, he obeyed, chin tucked, entering respectfully.

Through the house's double front doors, a hearty scent of a fantastic meal hit us. Sunlight shimmered over the ceramic-tiled great room beyond the foyer, the light reaching us through massive, glass-block walls on the other side of Ivy's house. The white leather furniture making up a living room corner covered an area as big as Guy's whole house. The other end had several of those really tall dining tables and chairs, all in black. Wide hallways stretched away from both ends of the great room.

Ivy turned to me. "What would you like to drink?"

The obvious thing about Ivy was that she had real money. And some of these Money People eat their young. They scare me. And they know I'm poor and not their type. But Ivy radiated kindness.

"Well, I, uh, I—"

"Eliana?" The split second Ivy called out, a beautiful bird of a woman in an orange flowered skirt stepped out, towel in one hand, spoon in the other, gleaming white smile framed by long, swinging black hair.

"Some tea?" Eliana suggested.

"Please," Ivy said, "and a taste of that stew you've got going." She turned to me, squeezing my arm like we were best friends, and led me to a ten-foot-wide hallway that ran from the dining side of the great room. "Eliana's making boar and hominy stew. It's got poblanos and tomatillos and juniper berries. She thickens it with masa. It's from a Zuni recipe. To die for. Come on, you'll love it. She says it's best when it gets to simmer for hours—we'll have it tonight—but I'm sure it's already amazing."

Hungry didn't quite describe how I felt, and a heaping plate would go a long way to help my mood.

Ivy beckoned me down the wide hallway. The first door on the left was open to a giant office with plenty of windows, most of the available wall space decorated with dog photographs. I stood in the hall and stared. Ivy reached for the doorknob and started to pull the door shut.

"My office is always a mess." Then she paused and followed my gaze.

The biggest photo showed a full-body profile of a bigger and youthful version of my Charley, only with a blockier head and more developed shoulders.

The table under the framed two-foot photo held a bunch of hand-sized, identical packages of what I'd guess was some kind of food or supplement or beauty product with the same image under four words.

Give Your Dog Fire!

Ivy said, "It's a supplement I developed. I'm a businesswoman. You know how people give their horses all kinds of supplements? Vitamins and minerals and things for their moods and hooves and digestion and everything else? But there's less available for their dogs. I studied it and consulted researchers and veterinarians and nutritionists and created this line of supplements. Got a specialty store in town and we ship all over. Have you heard of my products?"

I allowed as to how the Fire supplements for dogs hadn't made it to little Cowdry, but we were rural central Oregon and maybe a good bit behind the front-runners in California.

Ivy squared off to her picture of the big beautiful dog. "You never heard of Champion Firestarter of Beaumont Hill? He was a famous stud dog and a ranked competitive herder. I was breeding herders here. He was my foundation sire. Oh, I'm sorry, honey, listen to me just going on and on. That's how I am. If it's dogs, I can just talk and talk. Listen, there's someone you want to call, right? Come this way. You can use Milt's office. Sadly, he's not here this weekend. Again."

I took the backward step necessary as she came forward, into the hall. After Ivy latched her office door, Charley and I followed her down and across to another nice room bigger than lots of barns I've been in. Ivy waved me toward a black leather desk chair behind a giant walnut desk. These people didn't skimp on the furniture.

Her man had not one dog or horse photo on his walls, it was red carpet shots at various Hollywood-looking fancy shindigs.

Doing a double take, I saw Ivy in one photo on the arm of the big bearded fellow in a suit right behind some movie star who looked familiar, but like so many others. Blonde, bony California wives. Maybe my mama's heard of Milt Beaumont, but he probably never heard of Dara Dale, whose last acting gig was being the mother of the neighbor of the sister of the star in a TV movie about what to do when intergalactic fighters move into your neighborhood.

Eliana carried in a tray with two towering glasses of dark iced tea, lemon slices wedged onto the sides, straws and stirring spoons next to a little bowl of sugar, cloth napkin padding a silver spoon next to a big low bowl of lively stew.

"Sit down, sit down," Ivy said. "There's something I want to talk to you about, but let's get you taken care of first. Get this food inside you and make your calls."

I parked behind the big desk, totally out of place except for the way Charley curled up at my feet.

Eliana lay the spread on Milt's desk and made for the door. Ivy took a glass of tea and followed, saying, "I'll give you some privacy."

She gave me the comforting smile of the big sister I never had.

***

I'd hoped huge to hear Guy's voice and wished it was his on our message for our home phone voice mail, not me going on to callers about what information they should leave regarding a horseshoeing appointment.

Guy Kittredge can't be the only man in captivity about to marry a woman who can't cook, lets her dog on the bed, shoes horses for a living, and is not going to change her last name, but he's a rare find, all the same. After dialing three alphabet letters with three numbers, I succeeded only in learning that we had no new messages. I called back, got our answering machine, and rattled away.

"It's me," I told the machine, imagining Guy's face as he played the call whenever he got back from his trip up to Washington. "I'll call back. Charley got lost, and some of my stuff got ripped off, but I found him." I stopped shy of saying I'd been attacked. Seemed wrong to worry him, and, besides, I wasn't as clear as I wanted to be on a few things. "I'll call again real soon. I sure wish you'd happened to be there, 'cause I want to—"

"Shut up," Melinda screamed on my house phone. "I'm here and I do not want to hear you phone-sexing Guy."

"Hey! What are you doing there?"

"Feeding your cat, who seems to not exist."

Dishing kibble to Guy's cat is not high on my list. We came up with a mouse problem this winter and if Spooky missed a meal now and again, perhaps he'd get motivated to honest work.

"Did you feed Red and Bean and the Kid?"

Melinda snorted. "'Course I did." She knows how important horses are to me, especially my horses.

"Spooky's probably hiding from you. Maybe you're being scary."

"I'm not scary!"

Melinda's hollering does not a convincing argument make. It seemed like there was more I could have talked to her about, but I was sort of on my back foot, so to speak. Hadn't been thinking I'd be talking to my girlfriend when I tried to call my boyfriend.

"Would you tell Guy that I—"

"Damn it, why don't you two just talk to each other? I just had to la-la-la with my fingers in my ears for a minute-plus because he called and left you a lovey-dovey about what he's going to do to you to make up for not getting home tonight."

"Guy's not getting home tonight?"

"Apparently not. Still in Seattle. Something about a market he wants to hit in the morning for the best clams ever and then he'll head home."

"Would you leave a note for Guy so he knows where I am in case he gets home before me?"

"Yeah, I'll scribble something down," Melinda said, "and stick it on your fridge."

"Leave it on his computer screen." I rambled about getting Dragoon to the sale, getting to exhibit Charley at herding, and then my day going severely downhill, losing my dog, and finding him again after returning to the ranch after the cop stopped and ordered me out at gunpoint.

It was that last thing that Melinda made me run through twice. Then she said, "That was kind of a felony traffic stop. What else did you do?"

"What did *I* do?" I echoed, full of defensive wonder. "I didn't do anything."

"Rainy, that cop had a reason for stopping you that way. He had information on you."

"On me?"

Melinda sounded like she knew what she was talking about, like all police people have some kind of inside stream they fish from. "Maybe your truck matched a suspect description, maybe another agency requested you be stopped. But something gave him a high index of suspicion that you'd be trouble. What in the world are you in the middle of?"

Chapter 8

I VY'S OFFICE DOOR WAS SHUT, so I didn't get to see the picture on her wall of Charley's magnificent brother, Fire, when I left Milt's office.

"I take that." Eliana was suddenly with me in the hallway, reaching for my cleaned-up stew bowl and empty tea glass.

I felt a blush creep across my face. Guy often serves me food at home, but I don't expect him to adios my dirty dishes. I pull my own weight.

Eliana saw my hesitation, my lingering glance at the empty bowl. I'd hardly tasted the stew, truth be told.

"You like more?"

I was no doubt crimson in the cheeks now. "I sure wouldn't mind another bowlful," I admitted.

"I bring for you. Go sit." She waved to one of the tall dining tables and I took a seat. My dog was my shadow, curled up by my left boot.

"Do you remember Charley?" I asked Eliana when she came to me with another tall glass of tea and a full bowl—this time I smelled and tasted the softened, strong peppers, the perfectly

63

braised game meat and spice. "Maybe you remember him being called Flame?"

"Pretty dog." She flashed her perfect smile.

Bells sounded. It took me a few seconds to realize it was the doorbell, though Eliana turned away in an instant, making her flower-printed skirt swirl around her knees.

"I had to close the store to come up here." The gal who said this headed right for my table.

She wore inch-long dark eyelashes and skin-tight, neon-colored yoga clothes, looked to be my age, and weighed about ninety cents. She drummed her fingernails—each with a different tiny decal of some sort: peace sign, yin-yang symbol, lightning bolt, whatnot—on the table and tossed her long, straight blonde hair while I wolfed my second bowl of stew.

"You're new," she told me. She brought one tiny ankle up to her palm and stretched, extending the whole leg straight up, perpendicular to the ground until she was standing there with arm and leg pointing to the ceiling, like that was normal or something.

"I'm Rainy."

"And you're new."

She hadn't even acknowledged Charley, who gave her a polite glance. We were not going to be best friends. When she ignored my dog, he set his head on my boot toe and got to work cleaning under his dewclaw. I smiled and leaned down to inspect Charley's work. He grew the world's longest dewclaw. A few months back, I'd cut off one front thumb hook after it reached a full curl. It makes a different-looking necklace. Guy said he wanted a matching charm to put on his keychain, so Charley's growing one for him.

"Oh, Solar," Ivy's office opened up down the hall and she burst forward with a green tote bag and a handful of samples. "Good. You made it. So, this to the private delivery and here are some freebies for giveaway."

"That's it?"

"That's it," Ivy said, then gestured a mannerly palm toward me and added, "Did you meet Rainy Dale? She's a horseshoer."

"A what?"

Ivy laughed and waved Solar away. The girl gathered up the tote bag and dog supplement samples, then headed for the foyer.

I picked up my empty bowl and drained my glass.

"Oh, leave that," Ivy told me, following Solar to the door.

Eliana came for my empties again. I followed Ivy. Charley followed me.

On the flagstone outside, Gabe was striding up from the right, and he tipped his hat to Solar. Charley swung around, plastered to my left leg in a heel.

Ivy asked, "Did you find Stuckey?"

"Yes, ma'am," Gabe said. "He's checking the flock. Thinks they're all down in the lower part now, but a few might have wandered the hill. I told him to get a count. It's not looking like all the geldings are going to get ridden. Oscar's butchering."

Ivy cast a glance to Solar as though Miss Yoga should grab on to the idea that there was more than horseshoeing that the girl didn't get about life on this ranch.

Solar shook her head and got into one of those super-quiet electric cars and turned around using more space than I'd need to one-eighty Ol' Blue. Gifted as a driver, Solar wasn't.

"We wanted to get some exercise in all of them," Ivy said.

"Yes, ma'am." Gabe sounded like it had been his idea, but now she was making it hers.

Horses were needing riding? I perked up. Ivy had brought me into her home, let me use her phone. They'd fed me and rinsed me out with plenty of tea. I'd had the thought, of course, to offer to shoe for them—the Appy mare was close enough to due—and I'd been on and off their ranch for some bit of the day. I owed these people.

"I can ride for you."

"Hmm," Ivy said, starting to shake her head, then hesitating. "Okay, I'm going to ask you something, and please don't feel insulted. You have no idea how many guests we get who say they can ride and what they mean is they have sat on a walking horse that needed no guidance in an arena. Riding out loose on the ranch is totally different. Things can spook a horse, and it's hilly, and the horses can slip anytime. And you have to be careful of wire fences. And you have to duck when the horse goes under a low branch. If you can't really ride—"

"I can really ride."

"I'm not sure. I don't think you should have been driving. I'd feel terrible if you got woozy again and fell off a horse."

"I'm not going to fall off. I'm feeling so much better." It was true. "Really, I'd like to repay your hospitality, and if you have horses needing wet saddle blankets, that'd suit me fine as a way to help you out."

Ivy looked at me in silence then smiled. "Okay then."

***

Oh, stepping into a stirrup after checking the cinch, swinging aboard a fine horse, feeling all the power and goodness at the ready, it's the best. With Ivy's okay, Gabe directed me to a blood bay in the second stall, a gelding called Decker who told me he was more than ready to get out for a ride. The bay had good shoes, but I couldn't help noticing a flashy chestnut gelding across the wide barn aisle was bare, overgrown, and needing a full set. Gabe took a burly buckskin—its shoes clipped all the way around—from down the aisle and we headed out with Charley holding point like the header of a herding dog he was born to be. It was a fine thing to ride out on the Beaumonts' ranch. Halfway up the big hill, the sound of a sheep's bell rang below us. I figured they had it hung on a ewe or a wether. Leaving a bellwether, a castrated ram, as a good-sized and noisy bachelor to help mind the ewes and lambs is one more piece of protection to afford a flock.

Sure enough, with more height, we spied Stuckey in the bottomland far to the east, counting sheep amid the oaks. Gabe checked cross fencing and I noted the coyote scat on a scrubby knoll overlooking the field where the ewes had apparently bedded down the previous evening.

Gabe reined up and studied the coyote tracks with Charley and me.

"Varmints need bullets in their heads," Gabe said.

"Is it legal here to kill them outright when they're not bothering you or any stock?"

"Ever heard of the three Ss?"

Actually, I had. "Shoot, shovel, and shut up."

He grinned. "That's right."

"Should we go up the hill all the way?" I remembered now what he'd said about the summit having cell reception and wished I'd thought to grab mine out of Ol' Blue. I could have called Guy's cell.

"No reason to go up there."

"Wouldn't it be the best view of the whole place, if we want to see stray sheep?"

"If there's any stragglers, they're probably over the low hill to the east. Some of them would have moved that way during the hunt."

"We could split up," I suggested. "If I find some, Charley can bring them in, push them down to the others."

Gabe shrugged. "Reckon you can go wherever you want."

I broke away from him, cut the bay gelding he'd assigned me straight up the slope, urging him to work.

Climbing that hill—the second time that afternoon—was a sight easier ahorseback than afoot. Decker wasn't in great shape, but the thrust of his hindquarters lurching us up the slope felt wonderful.

Even though Gabe was pretty sure he'd be the one finding sheep, I hoped to score, to be doubly useful to Ivy. In one glance over my shoulder, I glimpsed a lone old cowboy on a small, sturdy horse, descending a ridge way off, across the Beaumont fences, at a neighboring ranch. The horse was tailed by a small, fluffy dog, but when I looked back again, the brush had swallowed up the threesome.

At the summit, my horse Decker got a good rest while I looked in every direction. Amazing how much better the view is from the saddle. A few feet higher makes a difference. I saw more ranch land to the east. Haze to the west and bits of town. Maybe even made out the Black Bluff bull sale grounds. Somewhere in that little town was Ivy's specialty shop where she sold her supplements for dogs. I heard distant traffic noise and realized good old Interstate 5 was down there at the bottom of the hill's super steep west side. The north seemed to be a kinder slope but was fenced off.

The bay blew the wonderful noise of contentment that horses make. The honest scent of horse sweat drifted up. I smiled down at Decker's russet face, then frowned. Below the horse's black-tipped nose lay Charley, pressing his head to the ground in the same spot he'd been when I found him earlier in the day.

I backed Decker up a stride, then another.

So odd, the way my dog lay, his front legs a little spread, hugging the earth.

"Charley, get up. Come."

Decker pawed and stamped a front foot while I made him turn on his haunches to let me see Charley from all angles.

Weird.

I had to ride away and bark the command to get Charley's cooperation. And we didn't find any sheep as we forced our way down through the rocks, brush and oaks, bushwhacking blind until we could see the houses and arena.

Back at the barn, Gabe loped up on the buckskin and said all was cool, the sheep were all accounted for in the low part where he'd expected. I was still glad to have had the ride and been a little use to Ivy. I set to work untacking, got my bay taken care of faster and better than Gabe did the horse he rode.

Gabe kept walking out the barn aisle and peering away from the houses, deep into the ranch or down the back road, the way he'd brought me in when he escorted me across the property in the morning. He went for a look-see after he carried his saddle to the rack, when he fetched a bucket of water to sponge our horses down, and once in the middle of brushing his out, banging the bristles absentmindedly on the heel of one hand as he strode the aisle.

Every stall had a nice run-out paddock and there were at least eight stalls on each side of the barn, plus open bays of hay storage before the stalls even started, but there were only four horses at this outfit.

"How long have you worked here?" I asked when Gabe came back and put the buckskin in a stall. "Long enough to remember Charley back when he was called Flame?"

Gabe nodded. And I realized why I'd wanted to ingratiate myself to Ivy.

I wanted to win favor here because I didn't want this ranch to try taking my dog away from me. How was I going to deal with it if they tried to keep Charley, call him Flame again? I could have cried at the thought. Charley circled me in that way herders can't help but do. When I stroked his fringed ears, he pressed his throat to my thigh. I wanted to fall on my butt and haul him into my lap. Maybe Ivy was right, I was concussed.

"He sure is loyal to you," Gabe said.

Shepherds are special. They see you to the end and beyond. I couldn't keep the hoarseness out of my voice when I asked Gabe, "And what happened to his brother, Fire?"

"Well, honestly, she thinks he was stolen by her old herdsman. Figured he got both dogs."

"Was that the guy I saw on a flyer on the bulletin board at the bull sale? Vicente Arriaga? He disappeared?" I faced Gabe and almost told him that I'd met the man's nephew but paused and thought better of it. Things were fuzzy, but the contradictions were waving at the back of my brain. "Just up and moved off one day?"

Gabe looked up, above me. Another man's voice whispered something behind me, from the back of the barn where I remembered the cinder-block building snugged up. I turned but saw no one there and had caught nary a word. Gabe strode past me and disappeared through a narrow doorway at the back end of the barn.

Curious, I put my horse away and started to follow him but then Ivy appeared at the open end of the barn aisle, her Barbie-doll silhouette reminding me what an eyesore I am in the state of California, where so many women weigh a buck ten or less.

I stood there trying to make sense of things and musing on the good fact of life Gabe had observed when he noted Charley's loyalty. Then the truth struck me so deep inside I almost choked.

Why hadn't I seen it before? And what should I do about it? I knelt to stroke the reassuring warmth and softness of my good old Charley.

"I get it now," I whispered to him.

Nothing had been broken inside Charley's head when I'd found him at the summit either time today.

It was his heart.

My good dog knew something, I realized. And he'd known for nigh two years.

Charley knew where the body was buried.

And now, so did I.

Chapter 9

I N THE WORST OF WAYS, I wanted to be home. Even if I could
get home—though I couldn't possibly drive all the way back to
Cowdry tonight—Guy wouldn't be there, according to Melinda.
But now I was having a hard time keeping my eyes open. I needed
to bed down. Where should I park Ol' Blue to sleep? The Black
Bluff sale grounds probably still had people overnighting, but
given what had happened to me there this morning, the option
wasn't appealing.

"Gabe? Oscar? Stuckey? Rainy?" Ivy pirouetted where she stood,
just outside the barn in the last of the daylight, staring hard. Took
me a while to realize that she was having trouble seeing me and
Charley in the dark barn aisle.

I came forward and made my tone as friendly as she'd been
toward me, which was plenty. "You said there was something you
wanted to talk to me about."

"Oh, Rainy! You were so quiet. What were you doing?"

"Just putting the horse away."

"I do want to talk to you about something. Where's Gabe? Did
you guys check on Stuckey? Oscar finished his work and is cleaning up at the bunkhouse. We all have dinner together here."

71

"Gabe went that way." I pointed down the dark barn aisle.

"Oh, he's in the smokehouse? Come on." Ivy sashayed away, Charley and me in her wake.

We ducked through the narrow doorway that Gabe had disappeared in and stood in the cold, cinder-block room that I now realized predated the barn. There was another dark doorway at the back of this little fifteen-foot-square building, but we were obviously in the main room. And this was no smokehouse, no matter what Ivy called it. A truly crappy, dinged-to-pieces old anvil sat on a stump next to the room's main feature, a cinder-block open-burning forge with a fire bed almost as wide as Ol' Blue. The old bellows off to the side had brittle, scarred leather. This had once been a true blacksmithing shop.

Ivy lowered her voice. "Now, what I wanted to talk to you about—"

I pointed behind her. "That's quite a forge."

Ivy turned and we both studied the old open forge. The hip-high burn bed was within reach, and I ran a finger through its dust. It had been a long time since this forge had seen a load of coal coke. The coke shovel hanging by the bellows was dusty, too.

"Oh," Ivy exhaled, letting her shoulders drop. "I wasn't thinking about how you're a horseshoer. Have you used this kind of forge?"

Precious little, but I had done so. My first internship was with a ranch shoer in Texas, and he'd used an old-fashioned open-fire forge like this. I told Ivy all about it, but I could tell she was only half listening.

"Okay, now, Rainy—"

"And I sure never had a sink right by the forge. That's real nice." I stepped to the room's corner where a laundry-tub-style sink occupied most of a little three-foot counter. A giant pump jug of hand soap, a towel and—of all things to be in a smithy—a microscope under a plastic cover took up the rest of the counter space.

Red wet stains in the sink, rinsed but still there, made me

remember Oscar heading to this end of the barn with his grisly cargo on the four-wheeler, back before I'd found Charley. Another sick thought arose.

As Ivy stared with raised eyebrows, I stepped to the other little doorway and confirmed my suspicion.

A dead pig hung in the cinder-block anteroom. The air reeked of blood and death.

Ivy waved toward the sink. "My old herdsman talked me into buying that."

"Huh?" I turned back to the sink and then realized she was pointing at the microscope.

"He was learning about parasitology, you know, so he could do fecals for us. Do you do that, or do you just worm your horses?"

Deworm, I thought, but didn't say. How to do a fecal—a count of the number of worm eggs in a sample of horse's manure—was on my list of things to learn. I'd read up on it some but didn't exactly have the spare money for a microscope, so hadn't nailed down the procedure.

"I've used those mail-away fecal tests, so I can target the *de*worming right." I felt myself redden with being unable to stop myself from fixing her terminology.

"Oh, good." If Ivy felt slighted over my correction, she didn't show it. "I've learned so much about ranching stuff since I started staying here more, taking more responsibility for things. There's so much to learn and I just love it. Milt thinks I've gone native on him. I'd rather we spent all our time here. I'm so done with LA. Anyway, I encouraged Vicente when he wanted to learn to do fecals. I really want everyone here to feel empowered."

I imagined how the menfolk on this ranch would roll their eyes, hearing her talk. Of course, they'd heard it plenty more than me. I stiffened as Ivy reached for my arm.

"Listen," she said, "I want to ask you something and I didn't want to say in front of a strange man." Ivy had both of her warm palms on my arm now. "Not that Oscar's strange. He's a good man.

Sends every dollar back to Jalisco. But, you know what I mean. I didn't want to put you on the spot when you drove back, but he was there on the four-wheeler, and you'd just found Flame."

She fondled Charley's head who took it good-naturedly.

Here it comes, I thought, bracing myself for the fight. She was going to make it plain that she expected Charley to stay here on the ranch now.

Ivy inclined her head with sympathy. "When you were assaulted, did that mean something worse? Do you need to go to the hospital? There's a special exam that they do for those cases."

I blinked and shook my head just enough to convey the negative. "Not that kind of assault."

Ivy sighed with such satisfied relief that I could have teared up at her caring. She narrowed her gaze, looking me up and down. "I was going to offer to call my doctor, but then I thought about the exam thing, and I think it's got to be done in an official way."

"I'm okay," I said.

"Oh, good. I'm so glad to hear it wasn't worse. It happened to me, and I wouldn't wish it on my worst enemy. No woman should be—oh, honey, I do go on, don't I? Look, I still think you should report what happened to you. You got hit on the head, right? Can I see?" She reached for my hair, and only then did I realize I'd been holding the back of my scalp. "Oh, wow, you've got a big lump there. Maybe you should go to the emergency room. Or I can call my doctor. Really, he'd come out here on a weekend, no problem. Do you want me to call him?"

Maybe I did have a concussion. Maybe that would explain a whole lot about feeling so tired and sick to my stomach and even being weepy, which is not like me at all. And now I was super distracted, scared she'd try to keep Charley, plus needing to think about what I'd realized Charley had been telling me.

It would seem so outlandish to say it out loud, I just couldn't.

Ivy was waiting for a response. I shook my head. "I don't need a doctor, but thanks for being so nice."

"We women have to stick together, lift each other up," Ivy said. She invited me to dinner and, when she heard I was going to push out and find a place to sleep in my truck, she offered me the night in the big house's spare bedroom.

***

Oscar and Gabe exited the old farmhouse that everybody around here called the bunkhouse just as Ivy and I walked out of the barn. A third fellow in a straw cowboy hat, jeans, and a work shirt, more than good-sized, tucked in behind them, like he was trying to hide himself behind the smaller men.

"I got pulled over on my way out here," I said, "but the cop didn't write me a ticket."

"Ah, they harass us all the time," Gabe said. "Means nothing. Like my old man always said, be respectful and get out of there, then it's no trouble."

My daddy would have said the same, did many a time. He'd been a ranch hand many years and now drives truck, usually on I-10, but is supposed to be hauling up I-5 to get himself to his only child's wedding this Wednesday.

"Come on, everybody, Zuni stew," Ivy said.

"Aw, no, the peppers make Stuckey stinky," Gabe said, grinning himself silly.

"Gabe!" Ivy and the third fellow said together. Then Ivy's admonishment turned to laughter and she asked Stuckey about the sheep count and if the ewes seemed peaceful, not disturbed by the hunt earlier in the day.

"Yeah, they're good," Stuckey said. He looked a few years older than Gabe, but acted younger, acted like the low horse in the herd. "Ain't seen any coyotes. Jack and Joe are down there."

I looked over my shoulder from one fellow to the other, counting, remembering names, trying to keep track of the employees Ivy had on the ranch. "Jack and Joe?"

Gabe read my wonder and explained. "Joe's a john. Jack's an ass."

Stuckey honked with laughter that drowned out Ivy's light tinkle of a half-giggle.

I was confused and asked, "You don't like Jack?"

"No, no, the guys are being goofy," Ivy explained. "Jack is our donkey jack. He lives with the sheep. And one time, he bred my best mare, which gave us Joe, who's four now."

I said, "My best friend has her heart set on finding just the right mule."

Oscar removed his baseball cap and tucked it in his waistband as we crossed the flagstone and entered the big house. The tall square dining tables had been pushed together to form one long table that was set with big bowls under charger plates, plenty of glasses, and silverware on thick cloth napkins. Ivy took the head of the table and I found myself in the middle of one long side between Gabe and Oscar, across from Stuckey and the chair Eliana would take after she served us. I figured the empty spot at the other end was reserved for Ivy's man, Milt, even though he wasn't there. Gabe turned his cowboy hat upside down and slid it under his chair then gave Stuckey a look that resulted in Stuckey properly un-hatting himself.

Ivy passed out white envelopes to the four of them. I could see it was greenbacks, not a check, in the envelopes everybody pocketed. Served, they all gabbed, numerous conversations going at the same time. They were like siblings, these ranch hands, and I found myself smiling, relaxing. My growing-up years were lonelier than they had to be. I was an only kid, and so was Guy. Not until this winter, when Melinda and I became good friends, had I gotten to enjoy having a friend who felt like a sister. Guy's poker and rugby buddies are starting to feel like an extended family, too. I was happy for these hands on the Beaumont ranch. Gabe and Stuckey and Oscar and Eliana had a good setup. Lots of ranch owners don't open their homes to the help like Ivy and Milt did.

But as the minutes ticked by, I observed some sketchy vibes. Eliana had served Oscar last, and least. She ignored his nod of thanks though she gave Stuckey and Gabe and Ivy and me big smiles.

And Stuckey couldn't look me in the eye, while Gabe grew so boisterous, it rang false.

While Gabe talked loudly across the table, joshing Stuckey about being lost all day, I asked Ivy something that I couldn't get off my mind. "Ivy, about that fellow Vicente . . ."

"Oh, Vicente. He was terrific. He was Basque. He minded the flock, moved them as needed. Checked fences. Kept the brush down where it could provide cover for coyotes. Never got drunk. Never. He was lovely. I really miss him." Ivy gave a shrug. "He just moved on one day. That's how it can be with ranch hands. Maybe he got a letter from home, maybe he decided to see more of the country. Maybe our summers had gotten too hot for him. It happened back when I wasn't at the ranch much, so I'm a little fuzzy on when he and Flame left. And he took Fire when he left. I had to make peace with the loss. But I still don't get how you came to have Flame. Tell us all about that!"

The others fell silent. I had nothing to hide, so explained how I'd found him hungry and looking for company two years back when I'd been on my way to Oregon for the first time, hunting down my childhood horse. That was a life-changing effort that led me to my new hometown and love. I told her that in a matter of days, Guy and I would be married, and that pretty well brought the house down with wide-eyed hollers of congratulations.

"Thanks," I said, turning back to Ivy. "So, you don't know how Charley or Flame and Vicente—"

Ivy waved me off. "I used to get here about once a month and then I started coming every weekend but after I got the Fire supplement business going, I'm here a lot more. It's great."

"Well, the hunts picked up," Gabe said.

"Right," Ivy agreed. "That side of the business really took off."

"Wild pigs?" I asked.

Ivy nodded. "They're a hybrid from generations back, like a hundred years ago. Domestic pigs had gone feral, then European boars were released and interbred with the feral pigs."

"Huh," I said. "Pig mules."

Ivy's laugh was like ringing one champagne glass against another, a quick musical toast. "Result is there are these wild pigs running around most of California that hunters are happy to hunt, and ranch owners are happy to have hunted. Everybody wins."

Except the pigs, I figured, but chose not to say out loud.

Gabe smirked all around the table and elbowed me. "When I found her this morning, she was worried that someone would shoot her dog. I told her how people have to be careful of what they're shooting at."

Stuckey studied his stew bowl.

Ivy gave all a quizzical look, but said at last, "We have safe hunts. We make sure to inspect the guns—no twenty-twos or other inadequate calibers—tags, everything. They're accompanied all the time by Gabe or Stuckey, or even Oscar or Eliana."

Trying to picture Eliana following a hunting party around, telling city folk in her limited English when and where they could shoot, made me smile. Ivy tipped her wineglass toward Eliana and gave one quick nod.

I thought she'd been toasting her female guide, but I realized, when Eliana jumped to refill Ivy's wineglass, that I'd misread her gesture. What else was I missing? "But your main business is sheep? And you had a real shepherd, a human one. And now, what do you use since you don't have a guardian dog for your livestock?"

Ivy sighed. "We've tried different things. Fencing, patrols, scent. Jack is a help. We wanted to use the livestock protection collars. You know about them?"

I dipped my chin in affirmation. "They come from Texas, like me."

"You're from Texas?"

"Originally." The collars she was referring to consist of two black rubber bubbles of poison that are strapped to the throat of every lamb and ewe. The coyote that bites the sheep's neck dies.

"They're not exactly legal around here anymore," Gabe said.

Ivy explained. "California banned them."

"They're banned in Oregon, too," I said, "but M-44s are still legal back home last I heard."

Ivy frowned and leaned forward like an eager student. "M-44s? I don't know about those."

"Spring-loaded cyanide devices," I explained, "that a predator bites or tugs on. Kills 'em fast."

The battle between wildlife protection and livestock protection will never be over.

Ivy looked around the table and frowned again. "How do they know only the intended predator activates the M-44?"

"They don't," I said. Gabe nodded. Oscar and Eliana looked bored, and Stuckey looked at his stew, the bowl still half full, which was amazing. The braised boar meat and poblanos of this Zuni stew, melding for hours, it was a delight to the tongue. Even my Guy, the culinary wonder of Butte County, Oregon, would have been impressed with Eliana's Zuni stew.

I was real glad when everybody got up and Eliana was going to show me to the guest bedroom, down the other wide hallway. Charley of course stuck to my side, pleased with the joys of best-house-living while men were banished to the bunkhouse.

The men milled by the open front door now. It was just too awkward to tell Ivy what I figured Charley had been trying to say, but I managed to ask if I could borrow a horse in the morning to take a goodbye ride. Ivy had been more than kind to me, and she was willing yet again.

"Yeah, Gabe said you were great on a horse, said you untacked Decker and brushed him down and everything. Help yourself." She said she had some work to do in her office, apparently forgetting, thank all, about her earlier need to have a serious talk with me.

As the three men filed out, I heard Stuckey mutter in a surly tone. "You don't got to needle me like that."

"Just funning," Gabe laughed as they walked away in the dark, followed by Oscar.

Eliana shut the door and went to the kitchen. I headed for the spare bedroom and soon heard her on the other side of the wall. As I fell asleep, it occurred to me that someone else knew what Charley and I knew. And likely as not, that person who knew where Vicente Arriaga lay dead and buried had been at Ivy's dining table tonight.

Chapter 10

D<small>AY BREAKS EARLIER AND A SIGHT</small> smoother in Northern California than up in Butte County. Good weather for a goose was all we'd had for a while in my part of Oregon. That's how our winter starts, stays, and ends.

I creaked open Ol' Blue's door, fetched my cell phone, then eye-balled the farmhouse by the barn. All lay Sunday-morning-quiet in there. Given the odd task I'd assigned myself, it was a good thing Gabe and Oscar and Stuckey weren't around as Charley and I stepped into the dark barn aisle. Back in the house, there'd been not a sound from Ivy or Eliana when Charley and I slipped out into the sunrise.

A heaviness like wet sand seemed to slow all my limbs. The nausea and headache were back, if they'd ever been gone, and the reality of what I was aiming to do settled in to haunt.

Charley followed me all the way down the barn aisle and through the little end doorway to the cinder-block room that now served as a slaughterhouse. I couldn't help standing and staring at the magnificent old open forge, the hand bellows meant to coax fire that had lay dormant too long, the racks that should be housing farrier tools. This was not supposed to be a place where fresh-killed wild pigs got prepped to become stew, but rather where metal was made hot, malleable enough to shape into horseshoes or good tools. I tried to ignore the scent of blood seeping in from the next room but couldn't help imagining the hanging carcass of the pig shot the day before.

The coke shovel was the best I could lay my hands on. I considered the horses. Gabe had ridden the buckskin. Maybe it was his horse. The flashy, powerful chestnut colt with four white stockings and a bald face was unshod, with long, chipped hooves. The big black Appaloosa mare was due for a shoeing. Again, I pulled the blood bay from his stall and asked him if he'd like to go back up the hill. Decker's wide-eyed look of wonder was good enough to take for agreement.

As I saddled up, I shot a thought at Charley so hard he turned and blinked at me. I'd do whatever it took, I told my good old dog, as I mounted up and we rode away from the barn in the quiet of early morning.

"You honored him. And me. I will honor you."

***

Decker trotted in silence, climbing in the early sunrise. I wanted to enjoy the pleasant sound of his hooves crunching dirt in thuds, but my dread of the summit was distracting. Halfway up the highest hill, I turned the gelding slow on his haunches, a full three-sixty, taking in the view to the west, the Black Bluff sale grounds on the edge of town, then east, where another ranch—a cattle operation—bordered the Beaumont outfit. A small canyon paralleled the fence line on the other ranch, leaving them just a thin slice of useable land along the fence, though untold acres lay east and north of the canyon. South was just more California. Far north was where I wanted to be, but I was about to kick a wasp nest and it might take some time to set things to right after I stirred the dirt.

In the distance off to the east, a lone rider rounded the top cut of the canyon and began to descend along the fence line.

Riding fence, in my view, is one of the best chores in all of ranching, just you and a few hand tools, on a good horse, especially if followed by a good dog while checking and mending the property's borders. Good work. I let Decker drift farther and farther east, on a course that would intercept polite hollering distance with the rider.

If he was a horse, the old cowboy would be an old-style Quarter, plain-colored, but rim-rocker solid for a day's work, just like the one he rode. Both looked full of patience and smarts that lasts even when the body is giving out. Clearly, the gelding had been athletic back in its day but was worn, looked to be well into his twenties. I wondered if he was a hand or the ranch owner. He didn't seem to have noticed my dog, but I sure studied the little one following him, a small, gold Aussie, young and full of eye. Well, he was the spitting image of my Charley, is what he was.

"Morning," I called.

"Morning."

I reined in when he did likewise on his side of the fence. "Was your dog sired by Fire, the stud dog they used to have here?"

"S'posed to have been. She still have Laurel and Hardy working the place?" His unshaven jaw worked the Snus that pooched out his lower lip. His cowboy hat was filthy, packing probably fifty years' worth of work dust.

"Who?"

Decker pawed the ground, impatient under me. I tapped my fingers on his neck to remind him to be patient when grown-ups talk.

The old cowboy spat over his right shoulder then turned his face back toward me. "Maybe George and Lennie is more like it."

"I don't know who you're talking about."

"You're new." He nudged his horse to a walk.

I kneed Decker, matching his stride to the rancher's horse. "I don't work here, mister. Would you tell me what you're talking about?"

"Not my place to say, but someone should have told her." Then he goosed his horse hard away, creating enough distance between us to end the conversation.

There was more than a fence between us.

***

Talking to Guy at the summit would have been way better than getting his voice mail. But he didn't pick up. I had way too much to explain—so I tried to keep the stress out of my voice and left it at I'd call him again as soon as I could. I sent him a text that said I was thinking about him. What else could I say? Then I took a deep breath to tackle this hideous job.

The thing with digging of the kind I was fixing to do is my mind grew more wrapped around the creepy goal than it usually gets in a purely non-horse-feet-related matter. Before I even dismounted at the summit, Charley again pressed his body to that same spot in the dirt.

"Right there? Okay."

I tied Decker to a shrubby juniper and freed the coke shovel from the saddle, wondering now if the old rancher might have seen my odd baggage, as I'd strapped it on Decker's near—left—side. Only my off side—my right—had been visible in the cross-canyon greeting, but when I'd turned Decker to continue the conversation, the coke shovel would have been visible if he'd cared to look back. It's not a tool for riding fence. The old rancher would think I was a loon or something worse.

It's not crazy to trust a good dog. Charley had a reason for his strange behavior. And my gut told me what that reason was.

I dug around my dog, beside him, and as he shifted on the dirt that I scraped off that hill, I dug under him. It wasn't fast work, but I kept at it.

When the shovel's blade hit something that wasn't dirt, I was real careful, scraping the ground with a timidity born of respect and squeamishness. It got so I had to use my hands, and I wished I was wearing gloves as I scooped dirt away.

Blue fabric is what I exposed. I gulped and brushed more dirt off, not sure what part of the body I'd unearthed. Had to make myself keep at the chore as the scent of the dirt changed.

The body didn't smell as bad as I feared, and it wasn't even quite as scary as I expected, though I only uncovered enough to show the obvious. I left the head and face alone, not wanting to see.

On the dead man's torso was a dirt-crusted solid dark blue shirt, buttoned, intact but a bit threadbare, though maybe that was due to the way wool decays after it's been buried for a couple of years. His arms lay at his sides, long sleeves buttoned down. I brushed a bit more dirt off, then hesitated. The outline of his legs extended beyond his jeans-encased hips in more dirt, but I'd had enough. Enough that I didn't expose the man's face, which I was afraid bugs might have got to.

"Is this Vicente, Charley? Was he your person?"

What reaction I expected from my dog—Vicente Arriaga's former dog—I don't know exactly, but it wasn't the indifference he displayed now, flicking a glance of the barest interest since I'd exposed parts of the dead man.

Made me wonder if I was digging up the wrong grave. The Beaumont ranch was sizable enough that it could surely harbor more than one unclaimed body.

Chapter 11

H ADN'T IVY TOLD ME THERE WAS some sort of weird jurisdictional question about this property?

Chewing the edge of my lower lip didn't help me decide what to do. Finally, I pressed the personal number stored in my cell phone for the new probationary deputy in the Butte County Sheriff's Department back in Oregon.

Right as I thought the rings were going to take me to voice mail, Melinda said, "Hey. I talked to Hollis Nunn this morning—"

"They're back?"

"Yeah, and he's not happy."

"Because I hauled the bull for him?"

"He said you shouldn't be at the Black Bluff sale grounds. What's that all about?"

"Beats the hooey out of me. Ask him," I said. "I did get ripped off when I was there, but I think it's unusual—"

"Ripped off?" Melinda asked.

"Someone ripped off my truck and—"

"Your truck got stolen? You didn't say that before. Oh, man—"

"I got Ol' Blue back. And Charley . . . you know what? Never mind that right now. Not why I'm calling. Listen, I've got a po-lice

87

question for you." I pronounced po-lice in the Texas-proper, two-word-sounding way. "I've sort of found a body. You know, like a dead person, and I'm wondering what exactly is the right next step."

There was a good three second pause.

"You just filled me with questions," Melinda said, speaking slow enough to be suspected of talking to a moron, "but I'm going to cut to after the chase and tell you to call the police, Rainy. We hang up and you call nine-one-one right now."

"Yeah, but what do I say?"

"Do you know where you are?"

"'Course I do."

The doubt in her voice showed she knew me well. "Then you give the person who answers your call the address."

"See that's the thing that's maybe a little tricky. Will they just get the location off my cell call somehow? Or will they have to look up where to go when I say I'm at Ivy and Milt Beaumont's ranch, out east of Black Bluff?"

Melinda exhaled like she was showing me all kinds of patience. "So, you're at someone's house? Beaumont. You're on these people's place? There's a building with a house number?"

"Well, no, I'm way up on a hilltop. I wouldn't be able to use my cell back at the house. The signal's bad there. It's bad most places on this ranch."

"And this body you've found," there was a pause as Melinda took another big breath and then only half-stymied a scream at me, "it's on a hill on the ranch? That's where your dead body is?"

"I'm looking at it."

"So, if I was at the ranch house, how would you tell me to come meet you at this particular place on the ranch? Can you give directions to where you're standing right now?"

"Sure, but do I need to worry about the jurisdiction thing? Like exactly what part of what county I might be in? I'm not real clear on that."

"Just call nine-one-one and tell them where you are. They'll send the closest people to you right away. Don't worry about jurisdiction, all right?"

My, Melinda does go on like I'm four-fifths stupid.

"Okay, I get it. Hey, since I'm a bit out of touch and might not get back for the evening feed, could you check in with Guy and take care of the horses again tonight if he's not around? And maybe same in the morning, since I've no idea when I'm going to get on the road now?"

Of course, Melinda agreed, so with that settled, I quick called Guy's cell phone but got his voice mail. I left him a good one, the cleaned-up version of what was going on, how I'd had to find Charley, finishing with, "I really miss you." And I texted the same after reading texts from him that were composed of a lot of question marks.

Getting home to marry that boy was competing for the high spot in my mind, even with a corpse at my feet. Picturing Guy, home, a memory, a weird from-nowhere thought came to me. Something that happened months ago at the Buckeye ranch, when Hollis and Donna got married. They sort of act like parents to Guy and me. Hollis had fondled my dog, and looked at me strange-like. They'd just been talking about what to do with Dragoon, Donna's daggummed killer bull, and someone threw out the notion of taking him to Black Bluff. The idea had excited me, as I'd long wanted to see the sale and work my dog there. Then Hollis had told me that I ought not go to the Black Bluff bull sales.

I remembered his words *You and yours ought to stay clear of there.* Seemed a busybody bossy thing to say and I'd paid it no more mind, hadn't put it together with the startled look he wore when his hands went over Charley.

***

"Nine-one-one, what is your emergency?"

I still wasn't sure about Melinda's advice that I call the emergency number, since this didn't really seem to be a life-and-death situa—okay, it was a death situation, but an emergency? No. Still, I followed my best friend's directions, only to end up stumped too long by the first question.

"This is the nine-one-one center. What is your emergency?"

"I'm calling because I found a body."

We worked on getting through the part about how the dead person didn't need CPR. I've never taken a CPR class, but this turned out to be a training opportunity, because the dispatcher was willing to teach me the technique right then, over the phone.

"No, he's real dead. I dug him up."

Why she asked if I had any weapons on me, I don't know. It's not like I killed anybody. And when she heard I had a little shovel, she told me to put it down, like I was some kind of crazed maniac.

"Yeah, I'm not holding the shovel right this minute."

"That's fine, ma'am. Don't pick it up again. Keep your hands where the deputies can see them. Do you understand, ma'am?"

Ma'am again. Well, the dispatcher was raised right, I can say that for her.

We chitchatted until I could see a spread-out batch of official-looking white SUVs with door decals speeding toward the ranch, though I never heard sirens. I lost sight of them as the low hills, curves, and oak trees swallowed up the view of their approach.

"I don't know that the ranch folks are going to be pleased about all this. Maybe I didn't think this through." With no direct trail, bushwhacking and switchbacking up to this highest hill's summit could take the police maybe an hour unless they took horses or four-wheelers or were amazing runners like Guy. "I'm going to ride down to the barn. Just make sure you tell them the dead guy is at the top of the hill. There's a pile of rocks near the gravesite. They can't miss him."

I didn't want to be here anymore. While I talked to the police dispatcher, I untied Decker, sorted out the reins, and hauled myself into the saddle one-handed, and set the horse to trotting.

The dispatcher didn't want me to hang up. "Ma'am, you need to stay on the phone with me until the first deputy makes contact with you."

I explained how we'd lose the connection as I rode toward the responding police. Ending the call gave me a free hand to slap my thigh, urging Charley to come with me as Decker carried me down the hill. After a hundred feet, Charley tagged along in his panting way.

***

As I rode Decker down the hill. I could see the line of silent police cars clearing the ranch's front gate. I would have liked to lengthen my ride, enjoy the saddle's leather creaking, maybe find a way onto the neighboring ranch and see just how far I could go, but I took a switchback toward the barn, ready to find out how it goes after you dig up a dead body on your host's ranch.

Chapter 12

DECKER AMBLED ON A LOOSE-REINED WALK. In the distance, the first brown-uniformed, potbellied cop went toe-to-toe with Ivy, who seemed to be the only person on the ranch up at a semi-decent hour on a Sunday morning.

The temperature wasn't the only thing heating up. A second white police SUV rolled to a stop behind the first, the driver's door opened, and another uniform spilled out, this one with a sandy ponytail.

Ivy whirled right there on the flagstone entryway and bolted into her house, brushing off the pudgy cop. He hollered something at the woman with a ponytail. Ponytail's back was to me, but as Pudgy pointed behind her, she turned and faced me.

She pressed a button on her shoulder mic—the patch there read Tehama County Deputy Sheriff—and pointed up the hill I'd just descended. A third cop car spat out a uniformed fellow built like a whippet. Whippet started springing the route Decker and I'd descended. I looked left and right in this wake, girding myself for talking to the cops in about forty seconds. From the ranch's main entry gate, another police vehicle approached in a cloud of dust.

"Are you the caller?" Ponytail hollered toward me.

"Yes, ma'am, I—"

"We need to talk to you."

"Understandably." I closed the distance with Decker at a trot. Remembering the cop traffic-stopping Ol' Blue the day before, I realized the little card he'd given me was still in my right rear pocket. I fished it out and handed it to her. "I talked to a fellow yesterday who gave me this."

She glanced at the card, then said something into her shoulder mic in fast numbers and code that I didn't understand. She waved at the pudgy male cop. In seconds, she confirmed who I was and what I'd told the dispatcher. The fourth car pulled up hard while she squawked something into her radio.

Ponytail nodded at the next batch of cops, a twofer, rolling out of their vehicle some distance away from us. "We need to talk now, Ms. Dale. Get off the horse."

"Let me just put him in his stall."

As I rode Decker toward the barn, Ivy threw her front door open and saw the uniformed cops trying to stop me for a chat. She had other ideas.

"Rainy! Don't!"

I nudged Decker to a trot, past the pudgy male cop, who told me to wait.

"I already told the other cop I'm just going to put the horse away."

Decker stopped at the barn without any aid from me. I hate barn sourness, but in the horse's defense, I had just trotted him the last hundred or so yards home. And this wasn't a great free moment for me to school the horse on not stopping when he hadn't been asked to stop. I hopped off and led him in with one rein. Charley was my ever-present shadow as the dark barn aisle swallowed us up.

The male cop asked someone outside the barn, "Did you locate your identification, ma'am?"

Belligerence boiled out of Ivy's voice. "No, I refuse."

His reply was too calm for me to overhear. Footsteps crunched on the pea gravel beyond the barn. Ponytail joined Pudgy. I caught glimpses of them as I undid Decker's cinches, swapped the bridle for a halter, and grabbed the nearest dandy brush.

"You can't be here," Ivy screamed at the cops as she came into the barn aisle with them on her heels. "I have not given you my permission. I do not give you permission to be here."

To say that the woman cop was not impressed by Ivy's tirade would not adequately describe the response.

Ponytail yawned, with a big open mouth, full dental display, and lazy palm wave over her gaping choppers.

As I unsaddled Decker in the aisle and thanked him for carrying me up the hill, I realized I'd left the ranch's coke shovel on the summit. Ivy flounced down the barn aisle just in time for me to explain everything.

I took a breath. "Ivy, remember how you said yesterday there was something you wanted to talk to me about? There was something I needed to talk to you about, too. This morning I—"

"Something's going on," Ivy whispered, cutting me off with a finger held up near her lips. "The police say they got a tip. They're here with no warrant. Something about exigent circumstances—"

Footsteps crunched near the barn's open entry.

Ivy clapped her mouth shut and rolled her gaze hard to the side, but carefully didn't look over her shoulder at the cop behind her.

Ponytail stood just outside the barn, visible from the center aisle, hair swinging as she scanned every direction. Ivy's posture changed, one hip leaning against the stall door, a sweet smile fixed across her expression behind a palm that covered a dainty little cough. She tickled Decker's nose.

"Gosh," Ivy said, her voice loud and cheery, "you really meant it when you said you wanted to take an early morning ride."

I hadn't worked Decker into too bad a sweat, but a horse warm from exercise does add a nice aroma to the surroundings. But Ivy's weird pretense, for whatever reason she had going, was unsettling.

I don't do fake, and it's a thing I'd likely mess up anyways. Start with the smallest mistake, I decided.

"I left your coke sho—"

"Did Decker get enough exercise? Did you lope him?" Ivy's frozen stare iced me good.

Ponytail strolled into the barn, would be on us in a second. Ivy whirled.

"I have not given you permission to be in here. Please leave immediately. I've called my attorney. That other officer said that you guys were going up the hill. So your emergency business is out there. Not in here. You can't come in my barn or either house."

"I'll step out, ma'am. Will you please join me and just give us some very basic information? We just need normal cooperation."

"Of course," Ivy said. "We'll be there in a few minutes."

"Great. Perfect." The cop walked back out to the daylight, ending in a sideways stance, forty feet away, barely outside the barn. Her pose might have been meant to look casual, but passed for ready to brawl, too.

I felt like I was unraveling a knot I hadn't been the only one to tangle, and I spoke slow, low, with something like apology in my tone. "Ivy, I—"

She cut a hand between us and whispered. "I told Eliana to stay inside. I need to tell Oscar. I've called my attorney, but he hasn't answered me yet. He's on retainer. He should get back to me right away even though it's Sunday."

If Ivy were a horse, she'd be one of those super flighty, show-bred Arabians with the overexaggerated, carved-face beauty, big eyes, and skittering panic-mode of the too beautiful. All reaction, no responsiveness.

I took a mighty breath. "I've got to talk to you about—"

"Go tell Oscar for me, will you? Tell him to stay inside. He's not to come out at all. Tell him to stay in his bedroom and not answer the door. Tell them to lock the bunkhouse. And tell Gabe and

Stuckey to come up. No, tell Gabe to stay inside with Oscar, and tell Stuckey to come up to the house."

"I'll do that," I agreed, "and then—"

"And then come up to the house."

"Yep."

Ivy speed-walked toward her house, hollering something at the female cop, who asked her to wait for one minute.

I closed my eyes, counted to five, kissed Decker's nose, and popped him back into his stall.

Horses are so much more reliable than people.

***

On that stroll from the barn to the bunkhouse, I wondered if Ivy was watching me from the big house and why in the world she was acting the way she was. I missed the healthy scent of horse I'd been enjoying in the barn. I counted four police cars lined up on the driveway that separated the arena from the barn and houses, and I remembered the skinny cop speed-hiking for the summit. Two uniforms—the woman with the ponytail and the heavy fellow who'd started at Ivy's front door—were talking by the police cars. Both watched me as I knocked on the bunkhouse door and waited until Gabe cracked it open.

Bare-chested, barefoot, and stubble-jawed, jeans zipped but the button undone, Gabe rubbed his tousled hair while I passed on the message about Ivy wanting to see Stuckey and wanting him and Oscar to stay inside.

Gabe ran a hand through his dark hair like his head was lonely for the cowboy hat. He spoke under his breath. "They have these semi-absentee ranch owners where you live? Blow in for the weekend to enjoy the big house and an arena ride and think they—"

He shut up good and fast as Ivy waved from the flagstone entry of her house and hollered past the cop.

"Rainy? Stuckey? Come on up to the house now. We have a lot of stuff to do today."

Gabe blinked, stepped out onto the porch, bare feet slapping the boards, and noticed the police cars.

Another car—one of those fake undercover things that's obviously a police car but a plain sedan with antennas—pulled up behind the nearest marked car.

I said again, "Ivy wants you and Oscar to stay inside, and she wants Stuckey to come up to her house." I was getting my first look inside. This was no bunkhouse, it was a real house, with closing bedroom doors—probably the original farmhouse. The front door opened into the living room, which had a big-screen TV and a full works entertainment center. Above the stone fireplace, a small rifle rested in an open single gun rack. Across the living room was a dinette in an open kitchen bigger than the one at home in Guy's little house. Gabe and Stuckey and Oscar had a pretty sweet setup on the Beaumont ranch.

"Wow," I couldn't help saying.

"Yeah, wow," Gabe said, frowning at the cops and cars behind me. "What's going on?"

The pudgy policeman got back out of the first marked car and pointed at me while saying something to a man in a plaid shirt, straight hair down to his collar, who'd just pulled up in the unmarked sedan. Then Pudgy raised his voice enough to call out to me. "You're the caller, is that right, miss?"

"Yessir, I was up on the hill and I used my cell phone."

He closed the distance between us. "And you talked to Officer Steinhammer?"

Gabe stepped backward into the bunkhouse, pulling the doorknob as he went.

I faced the cop. "Um, I talked to a police fellow yesterday, and he gave me that card I gave the other officer."

Hearing real well is one of my gifts, though with enough pounding of steel, the daily ringing will make me deaf before my time. At this point though, I can hear a loose nail in lots of horses' hooves. I hadn't heard the bunkhouse door latch shut. It was a safe bet Gabe was listening on the other side, and I didn't blame him a bit. Must be quite something to wake up on a Sunday morning and there's police crawling all over the ranch.

"And that," Pudgy said to me, "was regarding an assault, theft, looks like a joyriding-slash-kidnapping that started at the stockyard sale grounds? Odd complaint."

"I don't know what the police officer called it. I just told him what happened, which was that someone hit me on the head when I was at the Black Bluff bull sale yesterday morning, and when I woke up, my truck had been moved and some of my tools and my dog were missing. I found my dog. Anyway, he gave me that case number on the card."

Pudgy glassed over a bit as I jabbered but said, "We need to take an official statement from you, Miss Dale. Can you come over to my car?"

Just as he asked me this, the woman officer hollered at him, and he gave a shout and nod in return, then said something I couldn't catch into the mic on his shoulder, followed by a "Ten-four." And he beckoned for me to follow along as he strode to his patrol car.

"Right now, Miss Dale."

"Yessir," I called.

But a stride before I cleared the bunkhouse porch, the smacking sound of a closed fist punching flesh made me freeze.

There'd been a time in my life when I was on the receiving end of that kind of treatment, and I wouldn't wish it on anyone. I turned and looked back. The bunkhouse's front door was slightly ajar. The door's glass offered a reflection from the living room window, thus displaying a sneaky view of what was going on inside.

Stuckey lay sprawled across the bunkhouse living room. Gabe stood over him. Stuckey's straw cowboy hat had been knocked off. I realized Gabe had sucker punched him.

I stayed frozen, breath held, waiting for one of them to make enough noise to cover my presence on their front porch.

Stuckey rolled onto his side, then his knees, grabbed his hat, and stood. His reflection wavered in that uncertain way of glass windows serving as mirrors.

I managed one good step with my right foot and two breaths. Two wooden steps remained between me and getting off this porch, then fifty yards from the cop who was looking at me from his front seat.

"Gabe! Hey! What'd you do that for?" The reflection of Stuckey rubbing his jaw glimmered ghostly before me.

"You fucking idiot, what did you do this time?"

"But Gabe, I—"

"Shut up!" Gabe's voice was low but boiling with fury. "I know it was you, Stuckey."

Chapter 13

A VAN PULLED UP BEHIND THE little police parking lot that had
formed up on the Beaumont ranch. Jumpsuited men and
women took their time getting out. Their van's door was plastered
with a police shield on the door and three words across the side.

Crime Scene Team.

Someone speedy from the police department must have made
it to the summit and confirmed what I'd told the dispatcher lady.
None of the police were looking my way that second, so I crossed
the flagstone and knocked on Ivy's front door. Charley stuck to
me like glue but still had that brief hesitation before crossing the
threshold when Ivy let us inside.

"I've called Milt and I called my lawyer, told him to get here
ASAP. Where's Stuckey?" Ivy shoved the door shut behind me
and turned the deadbolt.

"I reckon he's coming. I did tell them you wanted Stuckey to
come up to the house. Talked to Gabe, anyways."

Three knocks sounded, placed high and in the corner on the
door, two quickies, the briefest pause then a third rap. Ivy opened
it immediately and let Gabe inside. He'd gotten properly dressed
in a white western shirt tucked into his jeans. As he came in, he

removed his cowboy hat, slipped his right hand into his hip pocket, and told Ivy there were cops outside.

Ivy paced a tight circle in the foyer and gave a brief smile as Charley curled himself in front of the western fireplace far from us and our tizzy. "That big guy said they got a tip that there's been a body found on the ranch. I've called my attorney." She was breathing fast and hard. "I think what we all have to do is act normal. Like we have nothing to fear. Because we don't. We haven't done anything wrong. We should just go about the day like it's a normal working day. That will make the cops realize that everything's fine here."

If they wanted to have a normal working day, there were certainly things to do. There's always work that needs doing on a ranch.

I cleared my throat hard. "Listen, Ivy. I've got some things to say. For starters, I'm real appreciative of your hospitality, and, I'll tell you what, you've got horses due for shoeing—I saw the overgrown feet on that gelding in your barn, and your Appy mare is about due—and I can take care of those shoeings for you. Now, the thing is—"

Ivy held up a hand and cocked her head. I figured I was dealing with the same kind of accidental prejudice that often comes my way. She wasn't to know I'd gone to Cornell, I'd apprenticed twice under very good shoers and worked my tail off, that I know all the anatomy and physiology of the equine limb and can hand forge therapeutic shoes.

"I'm a good shoer," I promised. "Let me start with your Appy mare. I'll do her fronts and you can decide if you want a full shoeing." Couldn't believe I was talking a non-client into letting me shoe her horse for free, but I had debts to pay here.

"If she can really shoe," Gabe told Ivy, "I'd sure say yes."

Ivy nodded, eyes eager. "Well, that would be great, Rainy. Stuckey is going to be our horseshoer. You could mentor him along if you don't mind. He went to school for it and everything, but it takes a while to get the experience. And he knows another shoer, Robbie Duffman." She faced Gabe again. "Would he work for double time?"

Gabe nodded. "I'll call Duffy. Maybe you want to order a load of hay delivered? Be good for the cops to have some comings and goings to keep them on their feet. Eliana and Oscar can just stay shut in."

"I'm not sure how long I can hot shoe," I said, distracted with what I wanted to say and confused a bit by the whole pieced-apart situation. "I'll need to get a propane refill in a bit, unless you want to order up some coke."

Ivy stared at me like I was the weird one, her expression pinched, shooting me daggers with her eyes. "What did you say?"

"You need some coal coke," I said, "for that forge at the back of your barn."

"The forge. In the barn." Her face changed, relaxed one or two levels, then she nodded slowly, obviously thinking and deciding even as she spoke. "Coal coke? That's what it's called? Okay, then. How do you order it?"

"The heating oil place might have some," Gabe said. He pulled his hat on and headed for the door. "Since Oscar's shut up inside, I'll see to the morning feeding."

"Good," Ivy said. "Let's find a way to get him in here. It's safer."

The second Gabe was out the door, Ivy turned to me. I took a breath, set to clear the way, but she beat me to it with, "Did you talk to the cops out there?"

We could hear Gabe's voice through the door. Sounded like he was fending off the cops outside right that minute.

"A little." I sucked in several more giant breaths and exhaled. Where to start?

Pounding on the front doors made Charley duck his head flat on the floor and eye the entry. Ivy opened the door, ready to dispense a mouthful of sass, but the ponytailed woman cop beat her to it and pointed at me.

"Outside, Miss Dale. Right now." Ponytail held a tape recorder in her left hand.

Openmouthed, I felt it all pile on me, the full awkwardness of how things had developed, combined with confusion. I stood up straighter, and had to use some forceful air to keep myself from whispering.

"Ivy, I called them. I had a hunch from the way Charley was acting, so I went back up the hill with him and dug where he showed me, and sure enough there was the body, so—"

"The body!" Her shriek made Charley cringe. "What do you mean the body? A dead body, like the police are saying? You found it? Here? On my property? Who is it? How'd it get here?"

"Well, don't you know? It would have to be Vicente. Who else would Charley point out?"

"Turn that thing off," Ivy snapped at the cop who waved the tape recorder between us like some kind of news reporter.

Ponytail said, "I need to talk to Ms. Dale, now. She needs to step outside if you won't let me in."

"She'll be right out," Ivy said and slammed the door.

"Oh, my," I said. "I'm sorry for the ruckus. I didn't think this through, but I really don't know what else I should have done."

"Wait a minute," Ivy snapped. "You . . . Who are you, really?"

My jaw moved without words for a while as I considered her question. "I, uh, I'm me. Just me."

"There's a body buried on my ranch? And you dug it up? And you think it's Vicente?" Ivy's hands left her hips and spread in aggravated wonder between us. "Why are you really here? What happened to Vicente?"

"I don't know."

"What do you mean, you don't know? You just said you found his body on my ranch. You knew. You knew something."

"I didn't know. It was Charley," I said. "He went and laid down on that same spot. It's a shepherd thing. And I realized that down the steeper side of the hill is the interstate. It's where I found him, two years ago. I figure that sometime after Vicente was gone, Charley came on down—"

"What happened to Vicente?"

I held up two fingers. "Couple things. Why would he be buried if he died naturally? And B, I don't know what happened to him. I just unburied him."

"Who buried him?" Ivy whispered her question at me in an urgent way that made me realize she didn't want the police on the other side of her front door hearing this as she learned it. "And how did he die?"

"I don't know the answer to either of those questions," I said. "That's what the police are for. But I think I stopped at that same spot on the interstate on my way down here Friday night. Charley was staring up the hill. The spot calls to him. And that's because it's where his person was buried. I figure that after Vicente was buried up there, Charley waited some time before he came down to the interstate . . ."

Whether I shut up because Ivy waved me off or because I'd said enough to last a little while, I don't know. Ivy stepped across the great room to the righthand hallway.

"Eliana?" She hissed the name in a demand, smothered by an attempt at whispering.

The bedroom door next to the guest room I'd spent the night in cracked open.

"Did you know about any of this?" Ivy asked her. "Anything?"

"I don't know."

Eliana was teary-eyed and sounded like I felt. Physically, I did feel some bit better than the day before. I'd slept like the dead, and I had Charley back, after all, but mentally, things were just getting stickier. I could hardly take it in.

Ivy waved Eliana back into the bedroom—I gathered there had been a stern talking-to about the girl staying put—then took a series of hard breaths and started pacing. When she stopped, her hands melded to her slim hips, and she faced me hard.

"Damn, Rainy, you suspected Flame was trying to tell you . . . that? Why didn't you say something?"

"Guess I felt a little silly, if you can understand." Really bad, I was looking forward to the part of the day when things would get smoothed out. "We'd both been saying we needed to talk to each other."

"Not about this! I had no idea."

Knocking at the door went on for a good thirty seconds and Ponytail's voice called out, "Ms. Dale, we're not going away. You really do need to come out and talk to us. Come explain to me what the problem is."

I didn't know what the problem was. "All this time, you thought Vicente just packed up and left? Made off with your stud dog, too?"

Ivy nodded, a sad smile flickering across her face. "It's happened before. You feel like you've got the help all figured out, then one of them moves on. Or brings in drama, wants you to hire their wife and kids and grandma and everything."

I thought of her hired help, Gabe and Stuckey and Eliana and Oscar. Did they want Ivy and Milt to hire their families? Would they just move on one day? People are so complicated. Dogs and horses are straightforward, keen, biddable, and sure. My kind.

Words spilled out of me in a splutter that threatened tears. "I was afraid. I was scared that what you wanted to talk to me about was you keeping Charley." I squinted and forced myself to not wipe my eyes or let the hiccupping sniffle exit my gullet.

Charley came and pressed into the back of my leg again. I started crying, though I still tried to stem it. The way my shoulders shook gave me away.

"Oh, Rainy, that was it? You're worried that I'll take him from you?" Ivy hugged me, quick and hard. "No. I wouldn't do that. He's obviously yours now. Just look at him."

Wiped those tears up double quick. I hadn't realized the threat of Ivy taking Charley back had grown such tentacles of dread in my heart, like bad weeds. The second that Ivy told me it was never going to happen, the icy threat melted away to nothing.

"He's mine," I said.

"He's yours."

It was the most peaceful and relieved I'd felt since crossing back into this godforsaken state.

And Jeez Louise, I was ready to go home. I was getting married in three days.

Unrelenting knocking thrummed the double front doors.

Ivy let loose an impressive string of swearing that showed a whole 'nother side of herself. "How did Vicente die? And who in the fuck buried him?"

Outside, a four-wheeler roared to life and motored away.

Another string of curses flew and then Ivy asked, "Rainy, would you please tell the men to come in here? Now."

"The cops?"

"No!" Ivy's eyes went wide. I'd seen Eliana cast a similar, frightened look when she poked her head out of the bedroom.

"Oh." I got it, but felt late to the party again. "You meant Gabe and Stuckey and Oscar. Yeah, I'll fetch them."

Judging from the vibrations on the front door, I'd be bumping into cops on my way out.

"Oh, God," Ivy said. "I have to figure out a way to get Oscar in here. He usually does the barn chores on Sunday. Gabe and Stuckey get the day off, but that's not going to work right now. Oscar's a good man, Rainy. I know Eliana doesn't like him, but he's a good man. Sends everything he earns back home. He could stay in my guest room just for now, which means that if you stay tonight, you'd have to use the bunkhouse. There's a fourth bedroom in there. Would you mind? Gabe and Stuckey would be out there, but they'll be gentlemen, I promise."

I didn't figure on staying the night, but now didn't seem the time to say so. I planned to do one thing at a time—facing the cops being the first priority—but I wanted to consider all the stray bits of odd information.

"What's the deal with Oscar and Eliana?" I asked.

"Are you serious?" Ivy hissed, barely audible. "They don't have green cards. My ranch is a sanctuary."

The ranch wanted the cops gone so that Eliana and Oscar didn't get deported.

Chapter 14

IT WAS SUPPOSED TO BE THE fellas' day off, but Stuckey and Gabe were lined up like schoolboys on the bunkhouse porch in front of the pudgy cop, who held a tape recorder. Gabe and Stuckey both had their cowboy hats snugged down hard. Stuckey looked half-whipped and plenty scared, in jeans, a denim shirt, cowboy boots, and the beginnings of a good bruise on the left side of his jaw. Gabe wore an openmouthed stare as he listened to the cop. It occurred to me that just rolling out of bed, they'd both been caught unawares by police on the ranch.

I wanted to observe them but had no time. Another police SUV had joined the cluster of vehicles, this one towing a small, open, empty trailer with two ramps coming off the back. I realized the four-wheeler we'd heard from inside Ivy's house had been a police machine, not one of the ranch's rigs.

The ponytailed woman cop was leaning in the driver's window of that unmarked car, talking to a man in a plaid shirt behind the wheel who was holding an extra-large cell phone in his right hand. He was looking at me through the windshield and obviously mentioned my presence to the uniformed cop. Ponytail pressed the button on her shoulder mic and whatever it was she said made

Pudgy, over on the bunkhouse porch, press his radio button and say, "Ten-four."

I caught parts of what Ponytail and the plainclothes dude in the unmarked car were debating—whether to have me go to the station for a video interview right then.

Plaid Shirt said, "Let's do the preliminary in one of the residences if we can."

"I was going to put her in my front seat," Ponytail said.

He shook his head half an inch. "Not in a police car."

I cleared my throat hard and walked toward them. "Y'all wanted to talk to me."

A look passed between them, then Plaid Shirt started talking on his bulky phone again. Beside him on the front seat was a machine our local vet back home carries into a few barns on special call-outs—a portable X-ray unit. These were not the kind of people who looked at horses' bones inside a hoof capsule. I hadn't figured on them using an X-ray machine for anything.

Ponytail gave me a big smile and jerked her head toward the three men outside of the bunkhouse's front door. "I'm going to grab something from my car. Meet you over there."

I toddled to the bunkhouse. On the porch, I said, "Um, fellas, Ivy wants you up at her place."

Stuckey ducked his head down an inch as he asked Pudgy, "Can we go?"

When the cop gave an okay, Stuckey pretty well bolted for the big house.

"There's no one else inside this house?" Pudgy asked Gabe.

"Nope."

"Mind if we look, just for our safety?"

"Fine by me."

"Well, do you live here, sir?"

"Yeah," Gabe said, "I live here."

"Great, then you can give us permission to go inside. And you're giving that consent now, right?"

Gabe leaned without moving his feet and swung the bunk-house's front door wide open. "Be my guest."

I looked from Gabe to the cop and back again. All sorts of con-flicted feelings rose in me. I didn't have a dog in this fight. I didn't want to interfere with the police and whatever lawful doings they had on tap. Ivy had been good to me and she wasn't inclined to have the police tromping through her property. Oscar seemed like a real good fellow.

Pudgy walked in and kept going, room to room, with momentum.

In front of the open door, barely moving my lips, I said to Gabe, "Ivy didn't want the po-lice inside at all."

"Zoo monkeys having a shit fight are more organized than these cops." Gabe matched my super-quiet speech, eyeing the police inside, all the cars outside. "It would only make them suspicious to keep them out."

"But what happens if—"

Gabe walked into the open living room of the bunkhouse, removing his hat. I followed his lead.

Pudgy strolled back from his wander around the rooms and spoke loud into this radio. "That's a ten-four. It appears unoccu-pied in a quick search."

Then Pudgy turned away from us, fading back into the bunk-house living room and turning down the volume on his radio when a couple of different voices came back on the channel. I didn't catch a word of that static-clipped code. Ponytail stepped onto the porch and joined us, walking in through the open front door like it was an invitation.

Pudgy pivoted in front of an open bedroom door and asked Gabe, "What's in the trunk, sir?"

"My personal stuff."

"That's your bedroom?"

Gabe nodded and folded his arms across his chest, then imme-diately unfolded them and tucked his thumbs in the front pockets of his jeans.

"And the other rooms?"

All four of the bedroom doors were open, revealing small rooms, each with a twin bed, a footlocker, and a small dresser. One looked so clean and tidy, it had to be the unused bedroom that I'd been offered for the night. A fifth door showed a plain, single bathroom.

"Other hands stay here," Gabe said. "Some seasonal workers, some more permanent, like myself."

"I'd like you to make a list of all the people who work here."

Gabe did an angled tilt with his head. "Respectfully, officer, that's something you should see my boss about."

"I'd like your cooperation."

"I feel like I gave it to you, sir." Gabe redonned his cowboy hat. "If you'll excuse me now, I've got chores to see to."

With Pudgy's curt nod, Gabe headed for the front door and was out in a flash. I started to follow him but heard the mutter behind me.

"This could work," Pudgy said.

"Yeah," Ponytail agreed. "Noncustodial. That's how they want it done."

I wondered if I'd remember what they said long enough to ask Melinda about it the next time I had a cell connection or a landline. Or the next time I was home. I stepped out the front door and ran into Gabe, who was suddenly striding back across the porch, hatless. Almost touching him, I leaned in and asked, "Where's Oscar?"

"In your truck." Gabe's comment was so quiet, so low, only I heard, especially over his heavy footfalls as he continued stomping across the bunkhouse porch, jumped off, and made for the barn.

Between the two houses sat Ol' Blue. I realized how close my truck was parked to one of the bunkhouse windows and that Gabe and Oscar had made use of the convenience.

Now the creak of one of my truck's cab doors opening caught my attention. I was looking at the driver's side. Its door was closed, so the passenger side had been used this time. Over the topper,

I barely made out the back edge of a cowboy hat slipping away, making for the flagstone entry to the big house.

"Excuse me, sir? Ma'am?" Gabe's holler made both deputies come to the door and look his way as he headed for the barn. I walked a couple steps back on the porch to give them room. And I suppose my body blocked their view of the big house.

Gabe waved toward the barn, the opposite direction from that flagstone entryway to safety, the other side of Ol' Blue. "I have to go into the barn to feed the horses. I can be quick about it. Just throwing hay. And of course, you're welcome to come with. Is that okay?"

"That's fine, sir," Ponytail called then shot the potbellied cop a look.

"Yeah, I'll go," Pudgy mumbled to her, and followed Gabe to the barn.

That hadn't been Stuckey ducking for Ivy's house, I decided. It was Oscar, wearing Gabe's hat. I didn't like the feeling of deception, of taking sides, of conflict, but I didn't know where I stood in all this mess.

***

"So, Rainy Dale." Ponytail held a palm-sized recorder between us. "Can we sit down and talk? Maybe in here? Because your nine-one-one call this morning is a little unbelievable."

She stepped back into the bunkhouse. I hesitated only a second before following. Ivy had as good as invited me to stay there tonight, after all. I could be in the bunkhouse with the cop.

Ponytail plugged an ear bud into her left ear and her radio. The irregular squawks of police radio communications stopped.

She started her recorder and said some official-sounding stuff about how I was free to leave and that I was there of my own accord, then said, "I'd like to understand exactly what happened this morning that led to you calling nine-one-one."

"Oh. Right. Well, like I mentioned I figured out from the way my dog was behaving . . ." Again, we fleshed out what I'd quickly told the nine-one-one operator and the cops as they arrived on the scene when I'd been riding down from the hill, what, a half hour ago? I told again how it came to pass that I'd dug where I had and unearthed the body, just like I'd explained it to Ivy a few minutes ago, a hundred feet away.

My cop rolled her eyes, pointedly looking at Charley curled up beside my leg. "Should we dig up the floor where he's laying now?"

"Um, no I don't reckon so."

"I have a pit bull," Ponytail said. "Sometimes he lays down in the same spot in my backyard. I've never thought that maybe I should dig up the ground underneath him just in case there's a corpse where he lies down."

"Well, a pittie isn't a shepherd, is all I can say. If you're not into sheepherding, then you've never seen that painting of *The Old Shepherd's Chief Mourner*."

She exhaled, inhaled, then blew out a long time again. "You're serious? You figured out that this dog of yours, that you found two years ago off the interstate, used to belong to a Vicente Arriaga who worked on this ranch, and the dog lay down yesterday a couple of times on one spot at the top of that big hill, so you decided that his previous owner was buried there and today you dug him up?"

I nodded, whole and honest. "That's how it seemed to me."

Her gaze attained a canny glint. "Suicide, you think?"

"I guess I don't . . . well, I mean, someone must have buried him for him to be buried."

Her expression dulled as I finally articulated the point, apparently trying her patience. "How do you think he came to be buried up there?"

"I have no information or knowledge about that," I said. "None."

"Are you willing to sit down with our detective and also take a polygraph on your story?"

"Sure," I told her. "I'm not lying."

"What can you tell me about drugs here?"

Whoa, I thought. "Drugs?"

"As in illegal, recreational drugs."

I'm not brilliant or experienced on such matters, and I said as much with, "I don't know anything." But something pestered at the back of my brain. What had I missed?

"It's okay to tell us what you suspect," Ponytail said. "This is between you and me right now."

"I don't know anything about drugs. Why are you asking me that?"

"Oh, you know," my ponytailed chatty new friend continued, "you had a traffic stop yesterday, talked to a CHiP. We share information. He was aware of a couple other interesting issues."

"Like, drugs?" I asked, because I am so very quick on the uptake if it has nada to do with horses.

Ponytail gave me a bland expression. "You told the CHiP that you'd been assaulted and kidnapped, and he asked you about your work here. He was aware of a missing persons case, too." She held out her notepad with a case number written on it. When she cocked her head, I realized she was listening to something on her earpiece. The radio on her hip no longer blurted intermittent messages.

I asked, "Missing person?"

"Sort of."

"Sort of?" I cleared my throat.

"Missing person 'til the body's found. The fact is, there's a man named Sabino Arriaga who comes around asking about a missing person case and where it's leading. You're the first new witness or info in over a year, and you dug up a dead man!"

Assuming that it was Vicente Arriaga I'd unburied, I didn't envy the police going to talk to the nephew of the dead man. I shook my head. "I'm no witness to something that happened here a year ago."

"More than."

"Okay, more than a year ago. I got here Saturday morning."

"And what are you going to do now?" Ponytail asked. "Where will you be when we need to contact you?"

"I'd like to go home as soon as . . ." The sound of a four-wheeler and at least one vehicle coming and going distracted me. "Soon as I do a couple-three shoeings."

"Shoeings?"

"Horseshoeing. Ivy's been more than kind to me. I offered to get her horses caught up on shoeing before I hit the road."

"Our detective will need to talk to you. He'll have some preliminary autopsy results by tomorrow. And our polygrapher will be working then. This isn't like the old days when cops would tell you not to leave town, but with you being from out of state, you can see how inconvenient it will be to reinterview you if you're on the road or up in Oregon. And it's a little incredible, this digging up a body where your dog lays down."

"He used to be Vicente Arriaga's dog."

"So you said." She made a friendly, accommodating face, like we were buddies and surely I'd understand the pickle the law was in.

I did understand.

She concluded our interview with nothing much settled, and we went to the front door of the bunkhouse together, the three of us, Charley panting in anticipation of what might come next as we stood on the porch and pulled the door shut after us.

"Can we count on you?" Ponytail asked, handing me a card. "I'm Deputy Steinhammer. This is my cell number. And I wrote Detective Orvell's number on it, too. He's the homicide investigator. If it comes to it, can we count on you?"

Her quiet question shook me. "What do you mean?"

"I think you know." Ponytail cocked her head and studied my dog, then looked me square in the eye. "And by the way, Ms. Dale, I understand about the mourning."

"About this morning?" I said.

She eyed me, steady and solemn as a wolf. "There was a guy from Black Bluff who was killed in Afghanistan. And the last one at his funeral, the picture they carried in the paper, was his German Shepherd downed, alone, in front of that flag-draped coffin."

There were other kinds of shepherds, I reflected, than the little herders I love.

And I realized one thing I'd missed before. Billowing in my brain was the memory of yesterday's traffic cop and his pointy-eared, black-faced dog hesitating in Ol' Blue's cab. I remembered how the police dog paused right where a package from this ranch had been set in my cab.

Chapter 15

DRUGS ON THE RANCH WERE NOT my business, but getting cross-threaded with the police isn't my thing, either. If I allowed myself to speculate, I'd wonder who really ran things on the Beaumont ranch and how the real money was made. When Ivy had wanted a package delivered, Gabe had said something about Eliana doing it, then Ivy had set the package in my truck. Ivy owned the place, but was she in charge?

A couple of shoeings, I said to myself. And then I'm clearing out.

Outside, the unmarked police car, now unoccupied, was still there, along with two marked police cars—one with Pudgy sitting behind the wheel, writing away—the crime scene van, and the marked SUV that had towed the little trailer. Where was Ponytail? I went up to the big house. Stuckey let me in just as Gabe and Ivy were facing off, both flushed beetroot-red.

She paced within a stride, energy seething out her pert body, cell phone in one hand, cordless house phone in the other. One phone rang. She lifted the cordless to her ear. "It's about time."

Gabe looked away. With his face safely turned so Ivy couldn't see, he rolled his eyes.

"No!" Ivy snapped into the phone. "You've got to come. They

119

have a warrant now. A search warrant. What?" She paused and listened for two or ten seconds. "No. They said up on the hill. Right.
Not in any buildings. Not at this time, they said."

I kind of hate standing around while someone has a loud phone
conversation. From Gabe and Stuckey's foot shifting, I reckoned I
wasn't the only one who was not at their favorite pastime.

"Okay. Okay," Ivy said. "That's what I'll do. But you get up here
right away." She slammed the cordless phone down, pocketed the
cell, and looked around her great room.

There was no sign of Oscar or Eliana, but I could see shut bedroom doors down that hallway. There was no scent of breakfast. I
bet on a regular Sunday without police crawling around outside,
bacon would have been sizzling. I could have eaten a plateful.

"Stay," Ivy said. "You've all got to stay with me."

Stuckey looked at Gabe, who looked at the ceiling.

"And you could hang out and heal," Ivy said to me. "You're
concussed, after all."

Stuckey shifted away, his head bowed. I figured he'd have been
fine with sleeping in or leading a pig hunt or counting sheep while
awake, but this day was too much for the likes of him. And me.

"Look," Gabe said, "it's my day off. I already did the feeding.
The delivery guys will stack the hay. Duffy's coming out. There's
no hunt. It's Sunday. Everything's taken care of."

"I have to go up the hill," Ivy said. "We'll take one of the
four-wheelers. I don't want to go up there alone."

Gabe faced her, calm and stillness in his face, but determination, too. "Then make Stuckey go."

"Gabe," Stuckey protested, his whine almost desperate.

Before, I'd reckoned they wanted the cops gone so that Eliana
and Oscar didn't get deported, but now I wondered a lot of things.
Still, it wasn't my place to make their situations worse.

"I don't know how long I'll stay," I said, "but I did promise you
a couple of shoeings—"

"Yes!" Ivy seized on this. "Stuckey, you want to shoe. Stick around here today, okay?"

He looked at Gabe, who pulled out car keys from a front jeans pocket.

I told Ivy, "The police want me to stick around for a bit anyway—"

"I want you to do something for me," she said. "I want you to come up there with me. My attorney told me to take pictures of everything. I want to see what you saw up on top of the big hill."

Going back up to the body did not sound like fun to me. I didn't want to be there.

Ivy read my reluctance. "Come on. After all I've done for you, I thought you'd help me. Please? Come with me. I'm kind of scared. This is upsetting, and I don't quite understand what's going on. I don't know who I can trust. I can trust you, can't I?"

She could. I'm as trustworthy as a shepherd. I wasn't sure I had an iron in this fire, so to speak, but I felt a loyalty to Ivy that I couldn't explain. When she grabbed a camera, I thought I understood a little bit. Anyone would feel intimidated standing up to a bunch of cops with a creepy crime scene on her own property. Taking pictures made sense. So did having some company, and I could give that much to Ivy.

"I'll go," I agreed, hating it.

***

Ivy drove a four-wheeler like she hated the ground she pointed the tires at. She sat bolt upright to prevent the huge long-lensed camera hanging from her neck from smacking the four-wheeler's gas tank. My right arm was wrapped around Charley, who was hugging my lap, and I'd scooted back from the long seat onto the cargo rack so we wouldn't be crowding Ivy. My left fist ached from clutching the rack so tight, but it was necessary to keep Charley and me aboard given Ivy's speed and the way she hit bumps. The tires regularly went airborne.

***

Oh, the police had done a lot more excavating than me. They'd been busy.

Yellow crime scene tape was strung up in a giant square. The police four-wheeler was there, along with Ponytail, three jumpsuited specialists and the man in the plaid shirt. There was a tarp on the ground with various objects laid out, numbered with little cards, but I couldn't see those things well, because they were behind Ponytail and I was looking over Ivy's speeding shoulder.

Ponytail raised both hands at Ivy as we approached, blocking our way.

Ivy didn't slow down.

Ponytail didn't move.

Behind that uniformed deputy, Plaid Shirt and one of the jumpsuits looked up.

At the last second, Ivy veered and braked hard, raising an instant dust storm. Charley squirmed in my arms, wanting off the blasted machine before it fully stopped. As the dust settled, I released him.

"Keep the dog away," one of the jumpsuited men ordered me.

"No problem." As I dismounted the four-wheeler, Charley glued himself to my leg.

"Is that *the* dog?" one of the jumpsuits asked Plaid Shirt.

Ponytail said, "Yeah, it is."

I stared all around as the jumpsuit gave Charley a second look.

There was a body bag, empty, but rolled out. I had to avert my eyes from looking at the exposed corpse. I'd never be able to un-see it if I caught a glimpse, and I didn't want the memory.

The cops' metal detector and the portable X-ray unit had been worked, judging from the dust on the units.

It seemed like forever since I'd ridden up here on Decker, but it was still the same morning.

Ivy leaned into me and whispered, "Stay with me. Don't talk to these people."

I didn't respond loudly, but it wasn't a whisper, either. "Ivy, I've got nothing to hide."

She was already stepping forward, raising her camera.

Right away, the cops didn't like it when Ivy marched to the edge of the yellow crime scene tape with her big fancy long lens. She held it in front of her impressive chest with both hands and started shooting, rapid-fire, twisting the zoom feature.

One of the jumpsuits reached for a light blanket and covered the dead man's body, saying as he did so, "No next of kin wants civilians to photograph their dead loved ones."

I was glad that Vicente—assuming that was Vicente Arriaga—was covered up. It was hard to keep my eyes averted.

Ivy said, "It's my ranch. I have every right in the world to take pictures. You can't stop me. I checked with my attorney." She clicked away while she spoke, working two-handed, her left twisting the zoom lens, the right trigger finger zapping countless volleys of shots with each click.

The plainclothes cop in the plaid shirt waved to the jumpsuited men, and they began to ignore her photo-taking.

This was so not my world. I wanted to be home, I wanted to talk to Guy about all this weirdness. He has a terrific mind and all kinds of college learning on why people do the things they do. I didn't warm a chair four years at a university or senior year of high school. Guy is the jelly to my peanut butter.

And on this summit, there should be cell reception. I could talk to Guy on my phone. I palmed the cell phone in my jeans pocket. Like anyone else with a decent set of manners, I paused. Yakking to my fella did not seem like a respectful way to stand around in front of a dead man. I shot a guilty look all around and pulled my hand out of that pocket, empty. As much as I wanted to talk to Guy, it would have to wait. I stepped back to the four-wheeler and stood beside Charley, who planted on his butt.

The tarp between Ivy and Plaid Shirt held the coke shovel I'd tied to Decker's saddle first thing this morning. I pointed at it. "That's what I brought up here. It's what I used to dig."

"So I gathered," Plaid Shirt said. "You and I are going to have a follow-up conversation about what you said to Deputy Steinhammer."

"Who?" I'd remember names if they had anything to do with horses.

He pointed to Ponytail. I nodded. Some kind of look passed between me and her, then her and him. She straightened her green clip-on tie.

Ivy clicked away, photographing everything. I stared at the other items on the tarp. There was another shovel, this one an Army-green folding fire shovel. There was a small widemouthed thermos with a weathered red plaid exterior. And they'd opened the dead man's wallet, carefully spreading out the contents.

He'd had seventeen dollars—a ten, a five, and two singles—and a few wallet-sized cards that I couldn't see well enough to know if they were credit cards or what.

"How long," Ivy asked, her voice subdued, "are you guys going to be here?"

"We don't rush things," one of the jumpsuits said.

Ivy covered her eyes with one hand and turned away, taking in one or two shuddering breaths. "I'm sorry about the way I reacted when you first got here. I was really shocked, that's all."

"That's understandable," Plaid Shirt said, his voice so even, so modulated that I wondered what else he meant to convey.

***

The post-photo-session four-wheeler ride down from the scene was a lot less aggressive than the drive up the hill had been. Seeing a real dead man on the ranch seemed to have changed something in Ivy. She turned and glanced at me now and again, her blonde hair blowing in my face. No, she didn't risk getting helmet-head, went for the wind-tousled look instead. There'd been something gutsy in her when she rode up. Maybe now she understood that the cops weren't the bad guys in this thing.

Halfway down the big hill, she slowed enough on a switchback that we could hear each other over the engine without all-out shouting.

"There's Jack and Joe with the flock." Her observation sounded as natural as could be, but her face was stiff, tight and lined.

I was holding Charley fast on my lap, and felt his muscles tighten as he spied the sheep. The ewes and lambs—one wearing a bell, the others with unencumbered throats—were spreading out in that bottomland far to the east. If Ivy had cut the engine, we might have heard the copper bell hanging on one big sheep. A good-sized donkey stood chewing on brush along the high side of the flock. A dark mule with a few white hip spots grazed among the sheep. Beyond her animals, we could see a few cattle in the haze over a rise on the property bordering the east.

The roar of another four-wheeler came from below us. Not the cops' machine, but I remembered that Ivy had at least a couple of those machines. Too many ranches use four-wheelers instead of horses these days.

"I met that rancher next to your place," I began, searching in my mind for something I hadn't put my finger on. "Does he have a pup from—"

Ivy waved a dismissive hand. "Oh, he's a meanie." And she laughed as though her assessment was comic-worthy. "I have no clue what his problem is, but he's got it in for me. Don't pay any attention to him or anything he says."

"He did say something kind of odd."

"He always does. He thinks I can't run this place because I'm a woman, because we bought the place instead of inheriting it like a fifth-generation ranch family. Well, you know what he can do with that attitude." She looked away from the neighbor ranch, giving it the back of her scalp while she narrowed her gaze at the road to her ranch's front entry.

Was that white vehicle we could barely make out by the gate another cop car of some sort? The air to the west looked smoky, but it was a mix of exhaust and the nitrous fertilizer that gets in the air over agricultural areas.

Ivy peeled out, adding some pollution to the world. As we were about off the hill, a slick black Lexus SUV pulled in at the flagstone.

"That's my attorney." Ivy goosed the throttle enough to whip my head and shove Charley harder against my chest.

The space between Ol' Blue and the bunkhouse that had been occupied by the beater green Bronco was empty. The other four-wheeler zoomed up, the burly rider spinning a brody then roaring back east, where he repeated the maneuver. It was Stuckey, I realized, riding for fun.

Ivy frowned. "Gabe's gone. And Robbie Duffman isn't here yet. He's supposed to be coming for shoeing, too. You're going to shoe with Stuckey, right? Come on, Rainy."

A thought occurred, as I considered the absent Bronco. "Is it Stuckey's day off?"

She emitted a quick little giggle-snort. "Every day is Stuckey's day off." I looked at her. She gave a half shrug. "It's just a joke. It's what Gabe says."

I wondered if her shoer Robbie Duffman was avoiding the ranch and me, maybe because he'd been the one to hit me in the head and steal my dog, my tools, and Ol' Blue.

Chapter 16

A GIANT TRUCK WITH TANKS OF propane and oil backed up to the cinder-block section on the far side of the barn, and a bearded man, clean-shaven in the mustache area, began unloading sacks of coal coke. I imagined Ivy had paid extra to motivate a Sunday delivery. After she let me off the four-wheeler and headed for the house, I went for the barn and saw Stuckey. Charley pushed himself hard into the back of my leg. Stuckey dusted himself from the dirt four-wheeling had coated him in, then paid the delivery-man in cash. Delivery Man didn't tarry, just got in his truck and roared out.

Stuckey and I dumped plenty of coke in the forge and lit her up. We'd need to wait for the heat to build, but Charley pushed himself into the far corner of the room while Stuckey fetched Ivy's big Appaloosa mare.

In order to shoe as close to the forge as possible, I had Stuckey bring the horse down the barn aisle, at the end that opened into the cinder-block add-on. Logistically, it was a shorter carry to bring my gear in from Ol' Blue through what they called the smoke-house, rather than carry it all the way down the long barn aisle, so

I went through the anteroom where the slaughtered pig had been hanging the day before and wondered who had dealt with the carcass and when. It was gone. The dark room had the scent of damp concrete. It had been hosed clean. I brought my anvil stand, hoof stand, and chaps in, placing the stand between the forge and the doorway to the barn aisle.

The barn wall by the doorway to the forge room had a tie ring, plus there were cross-ties hanging on each side of the aisle, but Stuckey just dropped the Appy's thick cotton lead rope. The mare was the kind who would reliably ground tie. She had wise eyes, full of kindness and reserve. I stroked her neck respectfully and enjoyed her good scent. While I put my chaps on, I considered her hoof angles and wear.

My work chaps—some call it an apron but the rest of us call them chaps, because who wants their work clothes to sound like a cook's?—are homemade, Utah-style. Each leg is shaped like the state of Utah, then stitched together at the flap. According to the road map behind Ol' Blue's seat back, the flap covers everything north of Salt Lake City when talking the state and everything east, west, and over the jeans' zipper when talking my shoeing chaps. And I'd stitched them right onto a good back support, with my four-dollar awl.

Stuckey hadn't put any leg protection on. Apparently, he just shod in his jeans. And he had no propane forge, yet they'd never used this wonderful old coke-burning forge.

"Horseshoers can make good money," he said.

"Stuckey, this job isn't going to please your folks, and it isn't going to get you a lot of prestige with a whole lot of people. And you won't get any better at anything they ever tried to teach you in regular school."

"Like what?"

"You know, like when they taught you the three Rs."

"If I could spell and use grammar, I might not become a shoer,"

Stuckey admitted, "but then I wouldn't get to learn horseshoeing neither."

A fella with logic like that has potential. As a shoer.

I pointed at the microscope on the counter by the big sink in the forge room's corner. "Where'd that come from?"

Stuckey scratched his head. "Something to do with worming horses."

I nodded, happy, realizing I liked it when one person confirmed something someone else said. Then I frowned. Nobody goes around confirming what one person said with another unless there's a basic lack of trust.

"Is Ivy good to work for?" I asked, trying to make my voice sound conversational.

Stuckey's head bobbed up and down immediately. "She's real good to us. On my vacation, she paid the tuition for me to go to shoeing school."

That information made my eyebrows take a quick hike up my forehead. My shoeing school had taken two years. Just how long a vacation did ranch hands get around here?

I knocked the Appy's left front shoe off in a few seconds of work with the cheapie rasp and third-class pull-offs Stuckey produced from the plastic bucket where he kept his tool collection. Then I waited and waited while Stuckey worked on removing the right front while he talked to me about both weeks of his shoeing school.

A two-week wonder, Stuckey was.

Two weeks of training does not a horseshoer make. I stepped through to the forge room, fetched my good hand tools and four fresh shoes, leaving a pair at the edge of the fire on my way to depositing my toolbox by the horse. I was away again in an instant for my last trip, hefting my 112-pound anvil from Ol' Blue through the back of the smokehouse to my anvil stand, when a one-ton truck pulled up at the open end of the barn aisle.

The Appaloosa tilted her head to look but didn't so much as

shift a hoof while she checked behind herself. However, the distraction proved more than my shoeing mentee could resist while I jumped in and removed both hind shoes, which are a little more dangerous than the fronts.

"I'll go see," Stuckey strode down the barn aisle with interest while I got to work like a shoeing demon, trimming the mare as I shed her old shoes, slipping a shoe back into the fire in between balancing the fronts, banging on hot metal and even getting the left fore nailed on.

I was burning on the second hot shoe when Stuckey returned from his visiting with the male voices mumbling down at the open end of the barn in between grunting and hefting bales of hay, pausing only long enough to pass some smokes between them. Didn't they know the taboo about smoking in a barn?

"It's the hay delivery," Stuckey reported, now wearing a cigarette behind one ear. "They'll stack it. Hey, you're almost half-done."

"Yessir," I said, releasing the hoof between my knees.

"The last person I called 'sir,'" Stuckey said, with an enormous grin, "was that big gal bucking hay. And it made her mad when I did it."

At my water bucket, I gave the shoe a good dunking. After I set the first two nails on the last shoe, Stuckey tapped the final nails in. I looked and considered the burly woman at the other end of the barn, slamming her hay hooks into big bales along with the man working beside her. She paid me no never mind, neither of the hay stackers did, but it looked like they had quite a bit of work in front of them. Ivy had ordered tons of sweet-smelling alfalfa-mix.

Stuckey and I finished the mare together. It was clear he'd never done hot shoeing, and certainly never worked fast enough to earn any money at this. After he led the Appy away, Stuckey fetched Decker, the bay I'd ridden that morning and the day before.

"Decker's not due," I said. I'd checked the horse's feet as a matter of course before I ever mounted up yesterday. "What about that chromey colt in the end stall on the other side of the aisle?"

Stuckey fetched another halter and brought back the flashy chestnut with a flaxen mane and tail, and long, chipped hooves. He whoa'd it where the Appy had been, within a stride of my toolbox. I left the forge and considered the straight legs in front of me, the strong, but untended hooves.

"Good-looking horse," I said. The colt was nicely proportioned, perfect angles in the geometry that creates a good hip and shoulder, with straight legs, but it was his white face and four white stockings that stretched up well above his knees that most people would have noticed. I thought of the fourth horse I'd seen on this ranch. "Does that buckskin belong to Gabe?"

Stuckey gave a vigorous shake of his head. "It's Ivy's. Everything is."

Ivy liked flash. That bright blood bay Decker was the plainest horse on the property. It had taken me too long to notice.

"Who put those last shoes on the buckskin?" It was a good job, those clipped shoes, egg bars on the front, making me think someone thought the horse had a little navicular.

"He came that way. He's new." Then Stuckey asked, real bright-like, "You got horses?"

It would have taken me four heats to get that buckskin's shoes shaped, then forge welded. Jeez, I've got to get a new forge. Sometimes, I'm embarrassed by my beater hotbox, especially now that I'm a much better established shoer than when I first became a real journeyman. Now I buy better rasps that last a good forty horses and have Cadillac-quality nippers. But, oh, my forge. Slow to heat, slow to cool, inconsistent, and clumsy to boot. I'd relined it with new fire brick, but it didn't help enough. I'd bought it used, and it's plainly been used hard and was never that great a forge to begin with. For next-level work like building egg bars and heart bars and needing to pull clips, my forge does an only okay job. I long for an ass-kicking—oops, fanny-frying, is what I mean—super good, fast-heating, efficient, larger-capacity professional forge. Doesn't everybody?

Horse folk can understand a conversation drawn out over a forge, and I answered about my horses after working metal. "A good Quarter Horse. A young Quarab. Plus, we're letting a Belgian rehab at our place."

"What was that middle one you said?"

"Quarab. Half Quarter Horse, half Arab."

"An Arab?" Stuckey pronounced the breed "AY-rab," like a dirty word, the way some folks say EYE-talian.

"Truth is, he's not my horse anyways, he's my fiancé's."

A burly male voice hollered down the barn aisle, making several horses snort and whirl in their stalls and the run-out paddocks. "Yo, Stuckey? Yo!"

"Smokehouse," Stuckey hollered back, his voice echoing a bit in the cinder-block cell encasing us.

A black cowboy hat poked through the top of the doorway, followed by a young man's friendly, unshaven face. He looked barely able to legally buy alcohol. "Hey Stuckey, when'd you get out of jail?"

Stuckey shot me a look. "He's joshing. I ain't been in jail. Not really. Just the weekend."

Black Hat grinned, eyed the fire in the open forge, and tipped his hat at me. "Robbie Duffman. Folks call me Duffy."

I offered my right paw. "Rainy Dale." I made myself act all casual as I waited to see his tools. If he'd been the one to attack me at the bull sale, and if he'd seen Ol' Blue when he pulled up to Ivy's barn, he might be smart enough to not pull out my stolen track nippers, crease nail pullers, or nail cutters. Rasps are more generic, but mine are a top-of-the-line brand. I'd wait this out.

Duffy said, "Gabe called. Said you guys were going to light up the forge."

Hard to describe the scent a good coke fire makes, and maybe only a horseshoer would understand that heat can have a scent, but all of us who like to move metal and outfit a hoof just exactly right are drawn to lighting up an open forge.

Stuckey poked the fire with my tongs. "Duffy went to the same shoeing school as me."

"At the same time?" I pulled the tongs out of the coals. Tongs are meant for grabbing a horseshoe. No tool should just cook in a coke fire. I can't cotton to tools being mistreated or misused.

Duffy waved the idea away like a buzzing fly. "I went last year. Been working on my own ever since. Me and Stuckey were going to be partners."

When he said "partners" I wondered for a split second if he meant, well, like wink-wink partners. Good for them. I didn't need to be distracted and yet something else he said drug my mind from what I ought to have been paying attention to. "You got out of school last year?"

With a nod, this Duffy character owned up to my accusation.

"Got good tools?" I asked.

"Some."

With a good metallic clunk, he dropped the foot-and-a-half chunk of railroad track he'd had tucked under his left arm. I realized it was what he used for an anvil. I'd been precious low on tools myself when I first started. This new punk was a lot like me a scant few years back, but maybe nicer. Not that I'm so mean, but managing not to say anything smart-alecky about Duffy's worldly experience took some effort. For sure, I'd need to bide my time to get a glimpse of his hardware. I cleared my throat and dealt with the other problem.

"I don't want to step on your toes," I said. "I owed Ivy a favor 'cause she let me stay here last night and fed me, too. If my shoeing for her means taking food off your table, then I'll step aside."

Duffy's head shake made it plain he took no offense to another shoer being there. "Nah, it's not like that. We can all pitch in."

Chromey threw a fit about having his feet handled. Not kicking, but dancing away, shuffling, and yanking his hooves from our hands no matter who tried which hoof.

The colt was spoiled, not standing politely when vehicles came and went beyond the barn aisle, taking little nips like no one had ever taught him enough manners to stand with patience while his feet were worked on. The second time he made to put his teeth on me, I growled like a truly put-out demon and popped him with my hand cupped against his shoulder to make a good loud clap. We had no more of that nipping business, but still had a dancing horse. It was bad enough for me leave the barn to get my secret weapon from Ol' Blue. When I brought my roll of duct tape back through the smokehouse, I made a ten-inch strip mostly doubled up and pressed the short sticky end to Chromey's nose, letting the long chunk of tape dangle over his muzzle. He found his manners and stood like a champ. After I cleaned Chromey's left front, Stuckey set to cleaning out the other hooves. I'd have rather trimmed that first foot as long as I had it between my knees.

"What the hell's that all about?" Duffy pointed at the duct tape strip dangling off the now-placid Chromey's velvet nose.

"No one knows," I admitted. "But sometimes it just works."

Duffy moved to the colt's hind end, waiting for a turn.

This was going to take a while.

I'd about decided that Chromey was bored, too, as the employees here seemed to use four-wheelers a lot more than horses for their ranch work. Duffy didn't have crease nail pullers or nail cutters handy to remove a shoe, but then, we weren't pulling old shoes off Chromey. The rasp he used was second rate, though.

"You have to get it flat," Duffy reminded Stuckey while he took uneven chunks out of Chromey's toe with a pair of Diamond nippers he brought from his truck.

"You're young enough to know everything," I told him. The old-timey ranch shoer I had worked with for a year had said it to me, and I'd been itching to use it on someone ever since. So, I dished it out. But I was supposed to be mentoring, so I talked aloud about medial-lateral balance and bringing the heels back and debriding the seat of the corn. Though these boys were smarter and more experienced than a box of nails, it took some work to notice the fact.

"Saw the cop cars," Duffy said. "Gabe said someone like found a body or something out on the ranch somewhere."

"Yeah," Stuckey said.

"That's kind of cool." Duffy's judgment came with another grin. "They figure out who it is?"

Stuckey wiped his forehead as his words burst out. "Man, this morning when I heard a body got dug up, I thought . . ." He stopped himself and frowned. "Gabe said they think it's a guy who used to work here. Vincent."

I paused in trimming and balancing Chromey's left front hoof. "Wasn't his name Vicen—"

"I know," Stuckey said. "I ain't stupid."

Duffy honked a laugh. "We putting that to a vote?" He dropped the horse's leg when he was done with it, nothing gentle to the motion, and Chromey threw his head up in response.

"I'm not dumb," Stuckey said, defensiveness rising in his voice. "It's just a joke, calling him Vincent." He lifted his chin to Duffy and pointed at me. "She's marrying a guy who's got an Ay-rab."

"Bah, Arabs," Duffy said. "They're so narrow-chested, both front legs come out the same hole up."

"What you got for horses?" I figured he'd say he owned Quarter Horses, but the answer surprised me.

"None. They're hay burners."

I've heard this weird thing in some people's voices before, that they don't like horses. I heard it now.

"Why're you a shoer?" I'd wanted to ask why he was *trying* to be a shoer, but a little diplomacy might make the middle of my day smooth out.

"Why're *you*?" Duffy asked.

"I get a kick out of it." Getting quizzed on why I'm a shoer is pretty common, but it's a bit weird from a baby-shoer who doesn't like horses. And wit like mine is mighty sad to waste, but I fear it was unrecognized in the present circumstances. I turned and asked Stuckey, "You got a Shod Wand we could bonk this Chromey colt on the head with?"

He frowned and answered slowly, "I don't think we have one of those."

Speedy on the uptake, Stuckey wasn't.

Duffy laughed. "Stuckey's so green he hardly knows which end of a hammer to hold."

I tried again. "Fellas, the shoe fairy ain't going to show up and finish this horse for us. You want to gab or shoe something?"

"Oh, um, shoe something." Stuckey gave a game smile that showed he knew he'd been ribbed hard and was used to taking it. "Yeah, let's shoe."

And I felt like a bully, probably 'cause I'd been acting like one. I got nicer, talked about getting efficient with motion to go faster, when to put a shoe in the fire, when to get it out and fit it.

Now and again, we could hear someone—Gabe, I figured—pushing a wheelbarrow from one paddock to another, apparently picking up manure, but we stayed on task.

"The anvil is a heat sucker," I told Stuckey. "Keep that shoe off it 'til you're ready to shape it."

I gave them all the time we needed to get Chromey shod. It was good for the horse and the humans.

"I'll finish him," Duffy said when the second shoe was needing just one more nail to be ready to finish the clinches.

Duffy's clinching was ugly—too long and unevenly folded.

He noticed the difference, too, eyeing the foot I'd finished. "Maybe yours come out better because of how you squint or bite your lip or something."

"That's probably it," I agreed.

There was no way Robbie Duffman was making a living as a shoer.

***

By the time we finished Chromey, Duffy said he was going to blow off. That wasn't a speedy process—male voices did a good deal of loud jaw-jacking and revved engine sounds at the open end of the barn aisle while I hauled my gear out to Ol' Blue through the cinder-block end of the barn.

The police vehicles were mostly gone, and the beater green Ford Bronco was back, pulled up beside Ol' Blue. When I brought my anvil to my tailgate, I paid enough attention to hear the Bronco's engine crackling with the sound of cooling metal. It hadn't been there long. I looked around after I pushed the anvil in.

Gabe was striding across the bunkhouse porch. I hurried after him. The back of his shirt and jeans were dirty, like he'd been rolling around in the barn aisle or some such. Maybe he'd been around a while and he'd helped unload the hay delivery. Or maybe not.

"You and Stuckey go at it again?" I asked, just loud enough, right behind his dirty back and butt.

"Beg pardon?" Gabe turned, took in how I'd been looking at the dirt on the back of his clothes, and brushed at it with one leather-gloved hand.

I stood a good ten feet from him and didn't come any closer. "I know you hit Stuckey this morning."

And I knew the police were watching this place for drugs and someone had put Vicente Arriaga in the ground and Stuckey didn't seem like the brains of whatever underhanded business was going on at this outfit.

Gabe looked me square in the eye without flinching. "And I know he hit you the morning before."

My jaw dropped. "You think Stuckey's the one who went after me at the Black Bluff bull sale yesterday?"

"Yes, ma'am." Gabe tugged on the front of his hat and gave me a nod. "I'm sure of it. Stuckey jumped you."

Chapter 17

As I'd heard my Texan ranch-hand daddy say a number of times, timing has a lot to do with the successful outcome of a rain dance. Confirming a few things would sure help clarity. I gawked at Gabe on the bunkhouse porch, then all around us. Quiet up at the big house. Lawyer's fancy car still there. Fewer cop cars around, no cops in sight. A truck powered up over near the barn behind us, which made me pretty sure Duffy was finally, truly heading out.

"Charley, come," I ordered my good dog, who'd gone back to Ol' Blue when I'd gone to chat with Gabe. Couldn't blame him. I was more than ready to head for home myself, but I joined Gabe on the porch, wondering where exactly Stuckey was. "You got proof?"

Gabe spread his hands wide as though the truth was obvious enough to read on a billboard. "He admitted it."

"He admitted to you that he'd hit me, dumped me, took my truck, all that?"

"Near enough." Gabe nodded and looked for all the world like he'd been satisfied with whatever mini-investigation he'd conducted.

139

I wasn't near satisfied. "Please tell."

He pointed behind me and I turned to look. There was only the ranch road leading past the barn, running toward the east end of the property. It was the road he'd guided me in on when I'd been following his four-wheeler in Ol' Blue just the morning before.

"I figured when he disappeared for too long yesterday morning," Gabe said, "that he was playing hooky. He'd wanted to go to the sale. His license got suspended, and he's got no car anyway. He's got no way to get to town unless I take him or Ivy takes him. Turns out, he got a ride from Robbie Duffman."

"He got a ride from Duffy . . ." I considered this.

"And Duffy said Stuckey didn't need a ride back. That's because Stuckey drove your truck back. Like an idiot. That moron saw your dog and freaked."

"Why would he have hit me?"

"He overreacted. I'm telling you, he saw Flame, got grabby. He swings before he thinks sometimes. It's been a problem. He must have been scared shitless after he hurt you. And he probably didn't mean to hurt you, but after he did, he didn't know what to do. He panicked. Drove onto the ranch a ways to get clear of your truck, went back to checking the flock and all that. What an idiot."

And he had to go hide the tools he stole from Ol' Blue, I thought. Stuckey being the one to truck-jack me would sure explain why he'd acted uncomfortable around me the day before, I thought. He'd created an awkward situation. I said as much to Gabe now.

He nodded. "What are you going to do? You told the police about it, right? Man, that's why I thought they were here this morning. That one cop was talking about you being jumped at the bull sale. I'd just woken up and saw all that. I was so pissed at Stuckey, for being so stupid. Are you going to press charges on him?"

"I . . ." I didn't know what I was going to do. I needed to think. I needed to get out of here, get home where I felt good and grounded. Things were mighty muddy here in this desert.

"Gabe?" I stepped close and looked right into his eyes for the truth.

"What?"

"Would Stuckey tell me the same thing you're telling me?"

"Ask him. And ask Robbie Duffman. He picked Stuckey up at the east gate yesterday early morning. Gave him a ride to the stupid bull sale."

I twisted my ponytail hard enough to turn my hair into a stick. "And you hit him this morning because . . ?"

"He had it coming. I knocked some sense into him. Discipline, it's called. You follow?"

***

The fancy Lexus SUV that Ivy had said was her lawyer's car was still parked right close to the flagstone. Standing there knocking on the big house's double doors, Charley and I waited a good while. Gave me time to note the remaining police cars better. A hearse-like vehicle was parked behind the remaining marked SUV from the sheriff's department. Their four-wheeler had apparently been ridden back down the hill, loaded up in its trailer, and hauled away. The unmarked sedan, the other marked police cars, and even the crime scene van were gone.

The cops just about had the mess I'd uncovered cleaned up.

Eliana let me in, a dish towel in her hands, her smile missing.

I'd figured Oscar was keeping quiet inside the spare bedroom where I'd slept Saturday night, or maybe in Milt's office, but no, there he sat in a white leather chair in Ivy's living room, as silent and out of place as a bucket.

Ivy and a short, round bald fellow in a sport coat, dress shirt, and slacks stood at one of the dining tables, a platter of sandwiches before them. Bread in multiple shades, screaming red tomatoes dangling out, thick with roast beef and ham, bright yellow cheese and lettuce of the deepest green. I could have stuffed it all in my face with both hands. It was past noon, and I'd skipped breakfast and been shoeing, which makes a girl hungrified. The other two empty tables had again been arranged into a nice spacing of diamond shapes across that end of the great room.

They looked up at me. Baldy asked Ivy, "Is that her?"

Ivy gave a sideways smile that quickly fell off her face and was replaced by a stony expression. "That's her."

He slid his palms into his slacks' pockets. "That's the dog?"

"That's him," Ivy said. A hint of her smile came back as she eyed Charley.

Baldy merely gave Charley a hairy eyeball and turned sideways as though discouraging any approach lest the dog hair factory that my good boy is got too close and risked contaminating the city-man slacks. Ivy pointed at Baldy and performed introductions in a way that sticks to my brain cells like air.

After she'd said his name and mine, she told me, "He'll go with you if the police interview you again tomorrow."

"And we'll be talking privately beforehand. Soon." Baldy the Lawyer offered me a brief nod, looking with some measure of distaste at my dirty jeans and mussed ponytail.

Yeah, I don't look or smell awesome after shoeing.

"Um, Ivy—" I began, but got cut off.

"Because they will," Baldy said.

"Who will what?" I needed clarification because he was not discussing horses and that's when I kind of quit paying attention.

"The police will want to talk to you again. I'll be there with you." He said it like a man in charge, a man who knows plenty about what the police do and how he can smooth things over.

"And with everybody," Ivy announced. "The police are going to interview everybody tomorrow. Lie detector tests and stuff. Even Oscar and Eliana. It's all arranged. Cooperation looks best, is best. And they're not going to go after Oscar and Eliana right now for being undocumented. We can get their paperwork started, and it will probably all be okay, their status here. Oscar was able to go out and clean the stalls and all. I had him lock the east gate, too."

"Um, that's good," I said. I wanted to tell her what Gabe had told me. She should know that Stuckey was enough of a loose cannon that he'd just haul off and conk a stranger in the head when he saw Flame—I mean, Charley. And they should all know that he gets sticky-fingered. Ivy had been the one to say we women have to look out for each other, lift each other up. But I didn't want to belittle the discovery of Vicente Arriaga on her land with my comparatively minor assault yesterday. I'd tell her, privately, within the hour, right before I drove out, I decided, clinging to the ponytailed cop's words about how the police couldn't order me not to leave town, yet it seemed wise to keep my exit plan unspoken.

Ivy nodded, and I realized I'd lost the thread of whatever she'd been saying. I was still thinking about Gabe saying it was Stuckey who'd jumped me Saturday morning at the bull sale. I remembered writing down Robbie Duffman's phone number at the bulletin board. Maybe I could call him and have a private chat. I cleared my throat. "I was thinking maybe I could take a quick shower. Can I use the bunkhouse?" I wanted to hit the road and figured the police wouldn't be thrilled with my heading back for Oregon this afternoon. I had shoeing clients scheduled for Monday afternoon, and my own wedding to attend on Wednesday. Guy and I had picked the date for the number, before we consulted a calendar and found it was midweek. And then we stuck to our guns. I wanted to talk to Guy and was about to ask Ivy for the favor of her phone again.

"They understand now," Ivy said, a bit of a blush slipping across her high cheekbones. Her skin glowed with perfection, the rosiness of whatever embarrassment she was explaining just made her look healthier. "The police understand why I reacted the way I did. I'm all about my peeps, you see. I was protecting Eliana and Oscar, and now that Leonard is here and handling things—oh,

I wish Milt would get here already—it's going to be a lot better. Leonard's looking after our rights. He's talked to the detectives, and it's all out in the open."

"Excuse me," I said. "I shod—that is, Stuckey and Duffy and me—we shod your Appy mare and that chestnut colt. Decker and the buckskin weren't due. They're looking good. Everybody's looking good now."

"You put shoes on Flyer? Wow. That's great. Was he good? He's never been shod before."

Would have been nice if Stuckey had told me that. "He's a real nice horse."

"Maybe you'll shoe Joe, then. He's ready for his first set. And he needs to be ridden. Do you want some lunch?" She pointed at the platter and I slinked up like a stray dog offered a full bowl of kibble.

The sandwiches looked fantastic but tasted even better. I stuffed my face.

Baldy cleared his throat and spoke to Ivy in a voice loud enough for me to understand, "If it is who we think it is, the police will be asking about his personal property. Do you have any retained? Anything stored? That could give them grounds for an additional search warrant."

"Just because someone's died, the police get to look through their stuff?" Ivy sounded outraged on behalf of dead people everywhere.

A coldness clutched my chest, my throat, and I couldn't speak, couldn't breathe. I'd sized things up wrong, which is not unusual for me, but the risk is not usually such a deal-breaker. I closed my eyes, trying to think.

"Commonly," Baldy replied.

"Well, he didn't have anything anyway. Vicente lived with the flock, like a real shepherd. I know the police find that unusual. It is unusual, except for with those herders. They stay with the sheep. It's their way."

"He never stayed in the house?" Baldy asked.

"Certainly not in here. But the bunkhouse, well yes, sometimes.

He came down about once a week. Took a shower, ate. Sometimes I'd take him to town for a day off."

Baldy seemed to be getting tired of Ivy not getting to the fine point, but asked again with the practiced patience of a man who gets big checks from his client, "Would Arriaga have personal property in the bunkhouse?"

"Oh!" Ivy leaned back in her chair. "I wouldn't think so. It's been so long. I don't know. We should check."

Baldy folded his arms across his wide frame and appeared to be considering things. If this had been my fire to poke, I'd have wanted to run things by my buddy Melinda, who could give me a solid police perspective on pre-searching things for the police and whatnot.

But this was not my fire to tend. I could exit and leave things smoking.

Ivy leaned forward, her voice different enough to indicate a whole new angle as she talked to Baldy. "About the shop."

He pushed back from her, flicked a glance at me.

"Close it?" she suggested, waving the cordless phone at him. "I can call Solar now and we'll just close it up."

Baldy puffed a lot of air when he muttered something I didn't hear. Ivy called to the kitchen. "Eliana?"

Eliana appeared in an instant and Ivy told her, "Please see if Rainy would like something to drink."

"I don't drink." I said. Or get waited on, in a natural setting. I don't get having servants.

"Everybody drinks," Baldy chuckled.

The phone rang and Ivy looked at it, announcing, "My doctor, finally," before she answered it and started in about what she wanted and when she wanted it.

"Right away." Ivy told the person on the phone to hang on then called out, "Eliana, would you bring me my meds?"

Eliana swept out of the kitchen down the left hallway past Ivy's office and was back in a minute carrying a two-tiered purple wooden tray full of enough prescription bottles to tranq a herd of fit horses.

"Xanax, fine," Ivy said into the phone. "No, I think I'm out of Halcion. I need something good or I'll never sleep tonight."

I needed to take my leave, that was all. The police weren't going to make me stay; they'd as good as said so.

Across the room, Oscar seemed to catch motion behind him. The blinds were only half open, but he was right close to the big windows. Realizing he might have a partial view of the driveway and watching him rise, I moseyed my way to the fireplace side of the room as well.

Charley thumped his stub tail at Oscar, who obligingly rubbed my good dog's head but did not look down, just stared out the window. Made me look out, too.

A couple of hundred feet away out there sat the hearse and the last deputy's SUV. Above those cars was the hill. Ponytail and one of the jumpsuits were working a single-wheeled stretcher down the hill. The knobby wheel, the size of a small bicycle tire, was centered under the stretcher. It was a backcountry evacuation device that enabled the load to be balanced at each end by the jumpsuited man and Ponytail, her uniform now all dirty.

The stretcher's load was in a zipped-shut orange body bag.

Oscar raised his right hand and pinched at the air near his forehead. Then he shook himself with some sort of realization and I guessed he'd been about to remove his hat out of respect for the cargo on the police stretcher. We stood in silence as they loaded it into the hearse, which apparently had a driver waiting inside. Then Ponytail and that last jumpsuit climbed into her patrol SUV, and both vehicles drove out toward the main ranch gate. I thought about that white Jeep Compass and wondered whether it was still holding vigil near the front gate and would see the hearse. Had that Sabino Arriaga character been listening to a police scanner? Had he known hours ago when I first made the nine-one-one call from the hilltop and the dispatcher sent Ponytail and the others to handle my announcement about a body at the summit?

When I left, I decided, I would take the long way, go out the far east gate where I'd first entered the ranch. I wanted no more contact with any Arriaga.

"*Los muertos no hablan,*" Oscar said, his voice so soft, he might not have meant for me to hear, and certainly not Ivy and her attorney way over at the dining tables, or Eliana, clattering in the kitchen.

My Spanish is weak, real weak. But I heard enough growing up, both in Texas and in Southern California, to have learned a few stock phrases such as the one Oscar had just proclaimed.

The dead don't talk.

Chapter 18

A WEIRD HISSING SOUND OUTSIDE OF Ivy's double front doors gave me pause. I turned the knob slowly. Stuckey was spraying Roundup. One edge of the flagstone was wet with the chemical, and the stink soaked the air. As I stepped out, I closed the door quick to keep the smell from drafting into the house and leaned down to put a hand of caution on Charley's neck.

"Is Duffy gone?" I asked.

"Yeah, he left." Stuckey looked at the way I was crouching to keep a hand on my dog. "Don't worry. They don't eat it."

Probably true enough—I'd never touched my tongue to glyphosate, but I've learned from my vet that many herbicides have a salty flavor that leads some horses to lick weed-killers that people spray on unwanted plants. Even if Charley didn't lick or sniff the stink Stuckey was spraying, my dog didn't need to get poison on his fur.

"Charley, heel."

I needn't have worried. Charley was properly glued to my left leg, perfectly on the side of the flagstone where Stuckey wasn't working. I avoided looking where the hearse had been, and headed for my truck, where I grabbed a fresh shirt from the plastic bag in Ol' Blue's cab and headed for the bunkhouse.

Through the bunkhouse's front window, I saw Gabe plunked down in a recliner in front of the television, watching a basketball game. He noticed me and tipped his straw cowboy hat, his smile polite, maybe with a touch of sadness or something else resigned.

"Can I come in?" I called through the glass.

Gabe came to the door, tipping his hat again in an automatic reflex as he waved me inside. He stepped back like a gentleman, shut the door behind me, turned the TV off, and said, "Stuckey's an idiot, sometimes. He doesn't mean to hurt anyone. Doesn't mean any harm, he's just a big clumsy dolt who doesn't . . ."

As Gabe's repeated speech trailed off, he removed his hat, ran a hand through his thick wavy hair, and kept the hat off this time. He gestured for me to sit in the well-used brown corduroy recliner and placed his hat on the floor upside down next to the worn cloth couch where he took a seat. "You decide what you're going to do about Stuckey?"

"Oh, I . . . haven't, I reckon." I recalled how Gabe had protected Oscar this morning, gotten him out of the bunkhouse and into Ivy's house, out from under the cops' noses when it seemed to matter. He was trying to protect Stuckey now. He was a good guy.

I missed my Guy something fierce. Probably I could get a cell signal not too many miles from the ranch and give him a call before I started driving home in earnest. I said, "I asked Ivy if it'd be all right for me to take a shower." That she hadn't actually given me permission seemed a mere oversight. She had plenty on her plate.

"Oh," Gabe said. "You leaving?"

"Pretty quick."

He looked as pleased as if everyone else had forgotten his birthday and I'd just brought in a big cake. He rose again, taking his hat. "I'll give you some privacy. Forgot to grab a few brewskis when I was out earlier anyway."

He left, good as his word. I told Charley to wait for me in the living room and saw the Bronco pull away before I even made it to the bathroom.

***

The old farmhouse offered five doors, two to the right of the eat-in kitchen across from the living room, and three to the left. Between the two on the right was an alcove with a washer and dryer. One of the righthand doors was open, revealing a bedroom. I imagined Oscar scampering through it this morning, out the window, making an intermediate hiding stop in Ol' Blue, and then a break for Ivy's big house. I figured the closed door next to it was a bedroom, too.

All three doors to the left were closed. I opened and shut them all in quick succession, not being nosy, just having an unclear memory from my morning glimpse of the layout and now searching for the correct door. I'd have won the prize if I'd started on the right, but working from the left I found bedroom, bedroom, and then the bathroom on my third try.

The bunkhouse had a simple sort of bathroom, a small sink in a yard-long counter next to a commode next to a tub shower with a plastic curtain. It smelled like Irish Spring and had just a bit of black mold in the white corners where the shower wall rose from the tub.

The little sink counter held three shaving razors spread out: an electric, a plastic disposable, and a heavy, reusable model next to a pack of razor blades. I put the toilet lid down and stacked my clothes on it so I wouldn't be moving the men's stuff around. I made my shower fast, using the manly soap and two good pumps from the giant discount bottle of shampoo in the tub corner. Fresh water streaming over my body was a blessing. I hadn't been soap-cleaned since Thursday night, when Guy and I had last taken a shower before bed. I dried off with the dirty T-shirt I'd been wearing since Friday and stopped dead when I thought I heard a door creak.

"Out in a minute," I called, just in case it was one of the other fellows who might not expect a girl to be in the bunkhouse bath-room. "It's Rainy. I'm in here."

There was no response. I listened hard, heard nothing, tried to wipe the heebie-jeebies off my body as well as the water.

"Charley?" I pulled my underwear, jeans, and sports bra on quick as I could, the clothes pulling on my damp skin. Hearing him pad around outside the bathroom and slump against the door, a bit of yellow fur sticking under the threshold, let my shoulders sag with relief. I didn't need to creep myself out.

But I opened the door as soon as I pulled the clean cotton T-shirt over my head, and knelt to hug my good dog, happy to have him climbing in my lap as I pulled dirty socks and boots back on.

"Anyone here?" I called out as Charley and I edged into the narrow hall.

Nope.

I opened the bedroom door beside me.

Bed made with a thick, navy blue comforter, single pillow on top. At the end of the bed was a blue plastic footlocker with a pair of work boots on top. I lifted the boots with one hand and the trunk lid with the other. Empty. I put the boots back. On top of the dresser was a Bible, in Spanish, and a receipt from *La Tienda* for wiring two hundred dollars to someone in Jalisco. Oscar's room, I decided.

The next bedroom bore not a hint of personality. A neatly made bed, dust on the locker at the foot of the bed, dust on the little dresser. I lifted the locker's lid and blinked at the contents, a set of colored pencils, charcoal drawing sticks, and a sketch pad. I opened the pad and looked at a drawing of my Charley, younger, eyeing sheep from a good vantage point, awaiting the next word from his shepherd.

I was in a dead man's sometimes-bedroom. Most nights, he'd slept under the stars, Charley at his side. Shepherds like Vicente

Arriaga, well, they were a dying breed. Had Charley ever slept in this room? I looked at my dog for a hint of understanding. He looked back without blinking.

Sometimes, dogs are too stoic. I bowed my head, tapped my thigh for Charley to come, and left the room, closing the door behind us.

On the other side of the house, I stared into the open bedroom with the unmade bed. Two big pairs of worn shoes—plain, brown cowboy boots and a set of white high-top athletic shoes—poked out from underneath the dangling corner of the sheet. A denim jacket rested on the bed. The footlocker was secured with a small suitcase-type lock.

Was this Stuckey's room or Gabe's?

I considered the padlocked trunk at the foot of the bed, then opened the dresser's top drawer. T-shirt, socks, underwear. Was I really going to search this whole room? Any second now, someone was going to come in here.

I stepped out and opened the last door to a messier version of the bedroom I'd just been in. The trunk at the foot of this bed bore no padlock.

I knelt and opened the trunk's lid. Western shirts, jeans, socks. Hunting magazines, without a mailing label sticker on them. A big shiny revolver. I pushed it aside without touching it, shielding my fingertips with a blue yoked shirt. The pistol rested on underwear. Beneath the underwear lay something hard, long, and metal on top of a large, crinkled paper sack. I lifted the pile of tighty-whities and stared at the shoer's tools resting on the brown paper. Nail cutters, two rasps, a crease nail puller, and a new pair of very nice track nippers—exactly what had been stolen from Ol' Blue. Bingo.

***

When I grabbed the tools, wrapping them in the crackly old paper sack they were laying on, I was doing what came natural. Charley and I walked our sweet selves out of the bunkhouse, looking every direction as I carried my reclaimed tools out.

Right, no more police at all.

When it comes to police cars and hearses, gone is usually a good thing. Now, it was starting to feel a little lonely. Would I have run straight to Ponytail if she'd still been here?

If what Gabe said was true, it explained one or two things—the way Stuckey avoided me at first, heck, how even Charley avoided Stuckey, now that I thought about it.

But it wouldn't explain everything, not by a long shot.

Stuckey wasn't the sharpest knife in the drawer. Anyone could have planted the tools in Stuckey's locker. And then told me whatever story he wanted me to believe. And maybe that wasn't Stuckey's locker.

The Lexus fired up, and I glimpsed Ivy's long blonde hair in the front passenger seat. They sped for the front gate without noticing me trying to flag them down.

I stowed my tools in Ol' Blue, reflecting on how I couldn't lock the topper since I only had the spare ignition key.

If Gabe was right, and it was Stuckey who'd jumped me and taken my truck and tools, what had Stuckey done with my keys?

The Bronco was at the end of the barn, not in its usual spot between Ol' Blue and the bunkhouse.

Had Gabe driven away at all? Or was he just back that fast from his beer run?

Charley didn't want to come down the barn aisle with me to face off against the voices I heard at the far, dark end, maybe in the forge room.

I went alone. I heard Stuckey's voice first.

"Maybe we should tell the truth."

That froze me, until I got the smarts to turn myself around. The police weren't handy anymore. Ivy wasn't here, either. Maybe Oscar and Eliana were up at the house, or maybe they were down there with Stuckey, trying to decide whether to come clean with someone about something.

Charley was right. I was in over my head. Quiet as we could, Charley and I piled into Ol' Blue, got the key in the ignition, and glanced around like thieves while we waited for the glow plugs to tell me it was okay to start the truck.

But Ol' Blue was dead. I wasn't going anywhere.

Chapter 19

A BRIDLE WAS ALL I TOOK as I slipped into the paddock attached to Decker's stall. He took the bit easily, and I brought him out through his paddock gate rather than through his stall and into the barn aisle. Gates don't want to be stood on. It's bad for the hinges. But in my haste, I used that paddock gate for a mounting block and landed lightly on the bare red back, felt his warmth beneath me. And I only hand waved to Charley that he should come along, because I wasn't going to make more noise by calling to him or even slapping my thigh as we escaped.

In minutes, we were away, bareback in the last hour of the afternoon.

If anyone spied us or called out when we trotted off, I didn't notice. I eased Decker down the ranch road eastward before striking up the hill, less in view of the house and the barn. In time, the route brought me to rustling sounds beyond the brush and of course it was Charley's intensity that communicated the presence. Wild pigs? No, Charley wouldn't have any interest in pigs, but sheep drew his fancy, sure enough.

Paying attention to my dog gets the best answers. A clearing in another hundred yards showed the flock. The donkey jack rested

157

in the middle of the ewes, a king with his minions. The mule john some distance from them was much taller, darker, and slenderer than his sire, and interested in us as well. Too interested. It started following us, wanting to join up. I wheeled Decker away to discourage the mule. In another five minutes of riding east, I was in view of the neighboring ranch and the old cowboy who'd stopped his horse there.

He swung his hat in a big arc from one side of his horse to the other. I waved and rode on, trotting Decker up the hill with occasional walk breaks, but when I looked back, the horseman was flailing a yellow kerchief back and forth, the gloved hand reaching as high into the air as he could. That steady horse under him swiveled its ears with the commotion but didn't dance or shift around a speck.

So, the rider was flagging me. I considered ignoring him but thought better of it. There's a code. He needed to make talk. Maybe he was having trouble. I turned Decker and made for the fence between us, trotting to get the deed done while the rider waited on his side of the fence.

"Oh, it's you," the old rancher said as I got closer. "I thought from the distance it was one of the boys."

"It's me," I said.

He racked one knee on his saddle's near swell and I knew we were going to parlay if I'd take the time. His brown gelding cocked a hip and looked like it would wait all day. I wondered if this old cowboy before me had a herd of bays, browns, and chestnuts. He sure hadn't given in to Ivy's predilection of choosing flashy-colored horses.

The good old boy ahorseback pointed at shrubby manzanita on his side of the fence. A trench had been dug along the edge of the brush.

"Saw one of you slip through the fence this morning. When I come down, he . . . or she . . . was gone and this was there."

The earth was scooped away under that manzanita, shoveled into a mound six or seven feet long. Too linear to blame it on wild pigs rooting.

"I got no problem defending my property." His tone offered a challenge.

And that's when I noticed the butt of a pistol on his right hip, the side farthest away from me.

Apparently, silence wasn't the right response to his veiled threat, because his grew harsher. "Did you do that? Come digging around on my ranch?"

"No, sir. I just now saw you flagging me and rode over. Did you see what the person was wearing this morning?"

"Just saw the dark hat. I was pretty far away."

"A black cowboy hat?"

"Baseball cap." He spat and studied me some. "You lose your saddle?"

"I just . . . went for a quick ride." I put a hand on Decker's rump and looked back toward the Beaumont buildings, but we couldn't see them from this part of the property. I was glad. It meant no one back at the barn or houses could see me. "You said something a bit odd to me yesterday, sir."

"Did I?"

"Yessir. You were talking about the hands on the Beaumont place, I reckon, and you called them by names I've never heard."

"You've never heard of Laurel and Hardy?"

"Well, I have heard of them, but you used some other names."

"Reese Trenton."

I sat on Decker, blinking, lost. "Huh?"

"Howdy. I'm Reese Trenton."

"Oh. Rainy Dale. Pleased to meet you. Mr. Trenton. About what you said yesterday . . ."

He looked at the western horizon for some time and finally came back with, "It doesn't do to talk."

Well, that was the end of that conversational branch.

Today, Trenton rode alone, without his dog, and he gazed at my Charley.

I cleared my throat. "That dog with you the other day, you said Fire was supposed to have been the sire. Is that what you were talking about, the thing that someone should have told Ivy Beaumont?"

He adjusted his horse to study Charley from the side then adapted to a new notion, calm as could be. "Damn, that is him. Excuse me, Miss Dale, but that's the old herder's dog, isn't it?"

I felt the defensive possessiveness rise like a volcano through my core, ready to boil out my mouth. *He's mine now. He's been mine the last two years.* I didn't want to argue for ownership with anyone ever again. I tried on Trenton's nonchalance, looking at the sky as I said, "That's my Charley dog."

The truth was before me, this one slice of it anyways. When Trenton and I first met, I'd been looking at my dog's son. If his dog were there now, sire and son would be face-to-face.

Imagine seeing your son. Oh, Charley, I thought. It's a story for another day, but my, what I wouldn't give. And how odd that the way it worked out, Trenton and I had met up along this fence line and our two dogs had come face-to-face. The rancher's voice was still droning while I stared at my sainted old dog.

"Nah, what I was talking about the other day was the stuff in Nevada. Wildlife Services."

"'Scuse me?"

"I've got friends who ranch in Nevada. One of them has a Basque herder who takes care of five thousand sheep for five-day stretches. They send out a tender to him. That herder's got it all figured out."

"Nevada." I considered that information, setting aside the way the classic Basque herders of the west had long minded sheep. "You've heard some things about Oscar or Stuckey or Gabe?

Vicente? I mean, the other day you'd said someone should have told her . . ."

He blew out enough breath to accidentally whistle. "Word was, one of those jokers was a Wildlife Services agent. Set an M-44 that killed a good dog."

They're all good dogs, I figured, and this was a bad story that we've all heard a version of, those of us who work in the ranching life.

But I wondered if Ivy knew her hands' history.

"There are quite a few stories like that," I finally allowed. It's an ugly fact of life that Wildlife Services sets those cyanide traps on Federal grazes and ranch land to kill coyotes, but pets sometimes trigger the M-44s and get bombed in the face with a lethal dose of poison. It's not new or news. I remember it happening in Texas when I was a kid.

"We run cattle," Trenton said. "Our herd's in four digits. I don't reckon taxpayers ought to have to pay for a man to work his own land, but I don't reckon they ought to interfere with me or any other rancher protecting what's his. City people don't understand predator problems and fencing or disease and feed costs. They don't know a thing about this way of life." He pointed at the land where Decker stood, waiting under me.

"This little hilly piece was cut out of my grandfather's land. My daddy owned it all. We never should have sold but needed the cash at the time."

The Beaumont ranch was new money. That had always been clear. But the fence between Reese Trenton and me was a fairly new property line.

Trenton went on. "She's got a few dozen sheep. Maybe fifty?"

When all those ewes lambed out every year, of course, Ivy's flock nearly doubled, but there didn't seem any point in arguing. Ivy wasn't entirely my kind of people, but I still felt a loyalty to her and said, "Ms. Beaumont's applied herself, I think, in learning how to run the place. She was new at it, starting from scratch, but she means well enough."

It felt odd, defending Ivy to him.

He spat tobacco juice. "How old are you?"

I sat up straight on Decker. "I'll be twenty-five next birthday."

"I got underwear older than that."

He might ought to think about acquiring some new underwear but before I could decide on whether to make the suggestion, Trenton took up more grumbling. "A hundred sheep on a couple hundred acres. Do the math."

Cattlemen hate sheep men, say that virgin wool comes from ugly ewes, but we didn't need to get into that old feud. I kept my manners on and said, "Sir?"

"Costs and income."

Chewing on his prompt, I considered things I'd missed. Pretty quick, I saw he was right. What might Gabe and Stuckey and Oscar and Eliana be paid? What did the feed and electric bills run and what could the Beaumont ranch produce in income, even adding in the pig-hunting or her dog supplement business?

The balance sheet didn't add up. Ivy's outfit was strictly a hobby farm, not a moneymaking operation. The ranch was her pastime.

But I had an idea of where some real money was made. I'd been ignoring that poison and it was time to quit. I gathered my reins. Decker lifted his head, ready. Charley rose to his feet and took his position flanking Decker. But I turned to ask one more question.

"Was it Gabe who worked for Wildlife Services?"

"I don't know the names on your ranch. It was the big one,"

My gaze fell on the trench again.

"That's a grave-to-be," Reese Trenton said. "And it wasn't there yesterday. I don't know what the hell's going on over the fence, but I don't want it spreading to my outfit. Maybe you'll pass the word."

He was right, and I was, well not wrong, but definitely in the wrong place.

"I'm Rainy Dale," I said, again, trying to check the stress pitching my voice. It was late afternoon by now, and I'd have to drive all night to get home for my Monday-afternoon shoeing clients. "Having truck trouble now. I live in Cowdry, Oregon. It's a tiny town you've never heard of, in Butte County. I'm about to marry Guy Kittredge. That's supposed to happen this Wednesday. And if you hear sometime soon that someone else has gone missing from this ranch, it was me, and it would be great if you'd get in touch with Guy and let him know."

"Young lady, er, Rainy Dale, was it? If you think you're not safe, maybe you'd better come with me now. Unbridle that horse, turn him loose, and come through the fence."

"No, I'm going up the hill to call my Intended." And I squeezed my calves to make Decker take us there.

***

At the summit, I had a couple bars indicating a connection, but was short on battery life. I should have charged it today. I tried home, then Guy's cell. When I didn't get through, I hung up to check my messages. Texts and voice mails were waiting for me. I steadied Decker and stared all around while listening to the first voice mail from Guy.

"Rainy? Sweetie? Where are you? Melinda said that you got ripped off and . . ."

The police had turned up quite a bit of dirt on the hilltop. Charley gave their tilling a cursory sniff, peed on the rock cairn—what was the weird name Ivy had for the stack of stones?—and walked to the edge of the hill. I stepped Decker closer to the west edge of the hill and heard Interstate-5 traffic noise in one ear, Guy's worried messages in the other.

As Guy talked about me coming home, I looked north, where the neighbor's cattle ranch wrapped around the Beaumont property. A mixed herd of Herefords and Angus dotted the faraway sloping ground all the way to the heavy fence that buffered the interstate. Immediately to the west, where I got the most bars of cell reception, the descent was treacherously steep, straight down to the interstate. The scent of exhaust lifted with the sound. I couldn't help thinking about finding Charley down there two years ago.

Working a great dog at the Black Bluff bull sale had been on my bucket list for a mighty long time. When I found Charley, I'd been trying to restart my life. In short order, I not only found my childhood horse who'd been sold off ten years before, but the night I bought Red back, I met Guy. Things went on from there to my building a better-than-good life up in Cowdry. Me and Guy are for keeps.

Mercy, hearing Guy's voice was good for me. But I missed more than his voice. He's got a way of thinking things through that's good for me, too.

Guy's next message screeched. "I didn't get so much as a Post-it telling me you were leaving."

I blinked, thought, figured it out. Spooky, Guy's useless, chocolate-colored feline.

That stupid cat who thinks Post-its are playthings to be batted off wherever I or Guy, or in this case, Melinda, put them.

Guy hadn't calmed down any on his next voice mail. "Your mother's all upset about you being at Milt Beaumont's place. Your father's hauling up empty, and I don't know where he's going to park an eighteen-wheeler . . ."

Daddy left ranching years ago to be a long-haul driver, usually doing the I-10 route across the bottom of the country, trading for a run on I-5 whenever he wants to visit his only child, such as to come give me away at the wedding in two days.

Guy's message got louder. "I want you to come home. I don't like any of this. And please stay away from that bull sale. Hollis said you shouldn't be there. Your tools are just stuff. There's no reason for you to put yourself in jeopardy and—"

Guy looks out for me. It's kind of sweet. He recently bought me earplugs and safety goggles and knee pads. Imagine that. The man picked up my horseshoeing magazines—I have two subscriptions—and read about shoers damaging their ears from the ring of a hammer striking a shoe on the anvil. And he read about a half-blind shoer who didn't used to be. A chunk of hot slag kicked off a red-hot shoe the man was forming, and it caught him in an unlucky landing place—his eye. And he read plenty about shoers getting their kneecaps adjusted by one quick move from a horse they were working on. Then Guy went shopping, bought me all that protective gear. He's like my mama in ways, only without the Southern California wannabe actress silliness and without having slept with my daddy at least once. And he's a way better cook.

Like I was writing a vacation postcard, I thought, *wish you were here, Guy*. I tried hard to tune back into his fussing.

". . . you have no idea if those people are trustworthy, and you stayed overnight, and that makes me even more worried about you and—"

My, but he does go on. Guy sounded fit to be tied, like a groom on his wedding night, even though that wasn't to be for two whole more days. And my battery would not last forever. What if I could only get in one call?

"For crying out loud, Rainy," Guy ended at last. "Call me and tell me what's going on."

Yeah, I'm signing up for a lifetime of this fussing, and Wednesday won't come soon enough.

But I didn't call Guy again. His mention of Hollis made me call the Buckeye ranch first.

One time when Charley and I were at the Buckeye spread for some herding and hollering, Hollis had petted my dog and looked at me real strange. I remember it like anything. He'd quit admiring my dog and he'd looked like he'd touched an electric fence somewhere in Charley's thick fur. It was around the time of Hollis and Donna's actual nuptials. And Hollis had discouraged me from ever exhibiting Charley at big herding events.

Heck with him. We were going to get to the bottom of this. I was thrilled when Donna Chevigny answered.

"It's Rainy, I'm so glad you're back, I—"

"My goodness, girl. I want to thank you again for recommending that Manuel Smith. It was such a pleasure to be able to go back-country. We had the best honeymoon, riding and camping. Isn't that what you're going to do? And I want to thank you for taking Dragoon to the sale when Manuel had truck trouble, although Hollis had some things to say about—"

"Would you pass the phone to Hollis," I asked. "It's kind of urgent."

There was the sound of them talking in the background and then Hollis's grizzled voice came up. "Well, hello there, Miss Rainy."

"Hollis," I hollered into the phone, "what do you know about my dog?"

"His ears are trimmed."

Charley's ear fringe grows shaggy, but of course I never trim those feathers. They help hide the fact that his ears are actually a little funky, shorter than they should be. While I tried to move my mind, Hollis went on.

"I'm not talking about the hair, I'm talking about his ear flaps. They're short."

"I don't mind that his ears are short," I muttered, wasting a shrug that Hollis couldn't see. But the notion that Hollis had seen something I'd missed, and that he'd seen it long ago, caused a sick dread to descend on my shoulders like a wet cape. Maybe I hadn't wanted to see.

"When it's both ears," Hollis said, "you know it was done on purpose."

"What do you mean? Are you saying someone meant to cut Charley's ears?"

"That's what I mean."

"Someone cut off the ends of his ears? What kind of a sick . . ."

I sucked in my lower lip because I was ready to cry or kill at the thought of someone hurting my little old dog. With a long, stop-the-sniffles breath, I asked. "Why would someone do that?"

"To take off his tattoos."

Crying didn't help a thing, and didn't help me hold up my end of the conversation either. The now-obvious truth of what Hollis Nunn had guessed from the get-go made me sick. I pictured one of Ivy's or Eliana's or Gabe's or Stuckey's or Oscar's hands coming at Charley with garden shears, peeling back the hair and slicing off a part of my dog's body, blood pouring, doing it again on the other side. I wiped my wet cheeks while Hollis made it plain.

"At some point," he said, "someone thought your dog was valuable enough to need to be identifiable. Ear tattoos proved the dog was who they said it was. But later, someone cut his ear flaps off to get rid of the tattoos. That's why I always thought you should stay away from herding events. Didn't want whatever happened in that dog's past to come bite you."

I lost the connection to Hollis, hadn't even realized I'd pointed Decker down the hill, picking up speed with every stride. I was ready to fight whoever on this ranch had hurt Charley.

Chapter 20

RIDING BAREBACK PRETTY WELL RUINED MY shower. The bunk-house, barn, and big house looked to be abandoned in the low light of dusk. I put Decker away without brushing him down. The other horses were munching hay, and someone had thrown a few flakes in Decker's stall as well. He got busy without minding the wet mark the bridle left on his poll when I pulled it from his head.

The Bronco was gone. I called out toward the forge room, "Anyone here?"

No one answered.

I dug out my key, unlocked Ol' Blue, and tried to start it again. No deal. My gaze fell on the big paper bag wadded around my recovered shoeing tools, all resting on the center floor hump. I pulled the hood release, hupped Charley into the cab, and brought the track nippers with me as I raised the hood.

The feeling of wanting a weapon was an odd one, and track nippers weren't the world's best choice, but they had some heft and added reach. I pushed the head into my hip pocket. The nippers' long, hard reins rubbed high along my ribs as I poked at Ol' Blue's dual batteries.

All the battery connections were secure.

The sight of a car pulling up beside me was a shock. The approach had been soundless.

The ninety-pound waif who worked in Ivy's dog specialty store and looked like a younger version of Ivy got out of the electric car, in electric clothes. Striped orange and green leggings and some kind of stretchy yoga top that turned into butterfly wings when she waved her arms. I dropped Ol' Blue's hood and we locked eyes. Her expression of distaste was not lost on me.

She started first, her little nose wrinkled. "Is Ivy here? I've got to talk to her. You, you're, like, a mechanic or something?"

"Or something." I tried to remember her name. She cheated, reading mine off Ol' Blue's door.

"Dale's Horseshoeing."

"That's right."

"And *you're* Dale?"

"Yep."

The Lexus pulled up between the electric car and the big house. Ivy got out of the passenger's seat. The driver's window was rolled down, allowing Baldy to hold his e-cigarette by the side mirror. Their parting words poured out for Waif and Charley and me.

"I thought you'd still feel that way," Baldy said from the driver's seat. "We just needed to respond to the request."

"No," Ivy said. "N-O. Just, no."

He gave a raspy chuckle and stroked his chins. "What about keep your friends close and your enemies closer?"

Ivy slammed the car door and waved him off. The attorney pulled away in his fancy car, leaving in the direction he came from, the front gate. The waif stood on one leg and stretched a foot behind herself while holding the toes with her fingertips. She told Ivy that they should stop shipping special supplements but keep the shop open and they needed to talk about the last delivery. I made my announcement loud enough to be heard by anyone within shouting distance.

"They cut my dog. They hurt him."

"Flame? Who hurt him?" Ivy's nostrils flared, and she swiveled on her feet, checking all directions. It was still just us girls. "What are you talking about? Where is everybody?"

"I rode off, and no one was here when I got back. But while I was out, I figured out some stuff, and I want to know who hurt him."

"Who hurt Flame?"

"Charley," I insisted. "He's Charley. And someone cut his ears. Before he became my dog. Back when he was Flame."

"Cut his ears?" Ivy eyed Charley, her Botox brow barely wrinkled.

"Took the flap ends off to remove his tattoos."

Ivy's eyes widened. She reached for my dog. He wiggled at her in acknowledgment and took the petting he understood in her fondling his ears. "Oh, my God."

For fashion, some people cut some dog breeds' ears. Charley is a bobtail, too. Tail docking, illegal in England since the 1940s, may have happened to Charley's little litter when he was still a milk sucker, or he might have been born a natural bobtail. This ear-cutting was different, and worse.

"It's a safe bet," I said, "that Vicente wouldn't have been any happier about someone hurting Charley than I am."

***

Inside the big house, Eliana had pushed the tall square dining tables together, and set many places with chargers, cloth napkins, and all the extra glasses and silverware for fancy eating. The house smelled like dinner would soon be served. Solar—I'd heard Ivy say her name—danced around wanting to talk to Ivy about the last delivery but turned down Ivy's offer to stay, then drove away in her silent little car.

Ivy paced the great room and shook a manicured fist. "Oscar lied."

I stood like a stone. Wondering which one of her yahoos had clipped Charley's ears hadn't gotten me anywhere close to know-ing which employee it was. I was ready for answers and liked the realization that Ivy had been searching too.

She snatched a folder of papers from the coffee table by her fire-place. "I track and deduct everything I can for the ranch. I went back through the travel records, different receipts. I checked my notes about the last breeding. But yesterday, I asked Oscar if he remembered Flame, and he said that was before his time. But my records show I hired Oscar to work here a couple of months before that. It was before Vicente left. And of course, Vicente didn't leave. Someone killed him!"

Her final shout made Charley duck his head. He hates shouting. I do, too.

"So, Oscar was hired and Vicente disappeared all around the time of . . ." I folded my arms across my belly, but didn't state the likely truth, "um, Fire's last breeding?"

Artificial insemination is common enough in horses, but not in dogs. Someone had pulled a fast one on this ranch and gotten away with it, even though one of the victims—Reese Trenton, the neighbor who'd lost part of his family's ranch to the Hollywood hobby-ranching woman—had a pretty good inkling. And now I'd figured it out, too.

Ivy shook her head and gestured for understanding. "What are you talking about?"

"All around the same time," I said. "And you weren't around much? Oscar hired on? Vicente disappeared. And your stud dog Fire had his last breeding. Was supposed to anyways."

"What does one have to do with anoth—"

I cut Ivy off with a sharp wave. "Reese Trenton has a small dog."

Ivy's eyes widened in exasperation and her voice pitched. "What does *that* have to do with—"

I stopped her with both hands raised, shifting eye contact from her to my loyal, fluffy gold wonder of a little old dog. Should have checked with Reese Trenton about who sired his dog, should have made him say it, but I ventured the truth aloud now. "Fire didn't sire that last litter. Charley did."

Ivy closed her eyes and got it a split second after me but voiced the long-hidden truth. "Because something happened to Fire. That's why Flame was used to sire that last litter."

I nodded. "And someone removed Charley's ear flaps in case someone else was going to check the tattoos to verify who the dog was."

Ivy strode across the great room, covered her eyes with both hands and doubled over on the couch. "That's so sick."

"So who managed that deception? I want to know who hurt my Charley." Top guesses would include someone who worked for Ivy. I took a breath and walked her through Gabe's smacking Stuckey this morning, his assertion that it had been Stuckey who hit me.

"Oh, this is awful." Ivy thrust her hands on her hips. "Gabe and Stuckey ran the show when I wasn't around here much. Well, mostly Gabe. Oscar does whatever they tell him to, feeding, cleaning. Everything with the flock. The hunts. Taking care of the horses and the machinery. There's a lot to a ranch."

Even a hobby ranch, I thought. I told her about finding my tools in the bunkhouse, and I pulled the track nippers from my hip pocket as I explained.

She planted her elbows on her knees and took it all in, gaze darting about. No slouch, Ivy. She made her mind move to the new information and came up with a new notion.

"Whoever hurt you and Flame is the one who hurt Vicente."

My mouth gaped like a door blown open by a sudden stiff wind. No words came out as I took half a lap around the room. I considered the folder on her table, saw a calendar she'd marked with: LA, ranch, breeding, hay purchases, and all sorts of dates that she'd been piecing together since this morning when I'd exploded her world and she'd had to call in her attorney.

"I can come pretty close to figuring out the exact night I found Charley." I pointed at her calendar. "I know the date I found my horse, up near Cowdry. I found Charley just before I drove into Oregon."

That had been a dark night. I was on the interstate, pulled over, alone. And then I wasn't, thanks to Charley befriending me.

The cuts to his ears had to have been a good month old by then, and I bet Vicente hadn't been much more than a week or two dead when Charley had to come down the hill for food, where I found him.

Because Charley would not go to the ranch houses or barn for help by then. He understood the people at those places as dangerous.

Ivy was struggling with this as much as me. I thought about what she and her attorney had been struggling with half an hour before.

I asked, "Where'd you go? I saw you drive away with your attorney and saw you come back when I came back from . . . riding." I thought about Ol' Blue being dead. Needing to get my truck running should have been at the top of my list.

"The police made another request," Ivy said, "and my attorney said we should go out to the gate and talk to them. Actually, it was a request from a civilian that the police were passing on to us. They've made a preliminary identification of the body. They do think it's Vicente. And they've talked to the next of kin, his nephew, who was requesting to come to the site where the body was found. But we don't want him on the ranch."

Thinking about the dead man's nephew made me picture him standing over me as I'd awoken the morning before, outside the ranch gate after getting pasted in the head, probably by Stuckey. And thinking about the younger Arriaga made me feel bad, though I avoided pondering on it too much. Feeling bad made me want to talk to Guy. I paused and sent him a text about how I loved him and missed him, even if it might not go through until

I had better cell service. I couldn't believe how long it had been since I'd heard his voice in real time. And how long since we'd been face-to-face, or better, lip to lip. Two years ago, I hadn't loved anyone, not even myself. Now I'm clean, clear, and crazy in love with Guy Kittredge.

Friday. Friday morning, he'd made me coffee before he headed for work at the Cascade Kitchen, before I went out to shoe. I'd known I'd be ending the day at the Buckeye ranch, figured I'd shoe a couple of Donna Chevigny's geldings. Sure hadn't figured on making for the Black Bluff bull sale and running my dog on the stock in their famous arena the next morning. I frowned.

"My truck's dead. Maybe I just need a jump. Can I use your house phone?"

She rose and accompanied me to Milt's office, where the phone rang.

***

"Wow, Leonard, say that again." Ivy punched the speakerphone button as she spoke. The attorney's voice crackled into the room.

"As I said, my source is not at your local sheriff's department, but up at the medical examiner's office. We were wondering what the deceased died of? Well, I'm hearing that the X-rays don't show any foreign bodies."

"Foreign bodies." Ivy repeated the term without comprehension.

The attorney's voice blared over the speakerphone. "Bullets."

Ivy picked up the phone, killing the speakerphone, and told her lawyer, "Then he wasn't shot."

That was too much of a deduction, I reckoned. No bullets inside a man might just mean the lead had passed through. The sight of the pistol on Reese Trenton's hip came back to me. So did his stern words.

Ivy listened, interspersing the pauses with, "Right . . . right . . . okay, tomorrow."

When she hung up, Ivy pushed the phone across the desk and gave it a grand wave. "All yours."

Every punch of a number on the phone felt closer to a bend in the road.

"It's me," I told Guy, flushing with relief and apprehension to not get his danged voice mail. Now I'd have to talk in front of Ivy, who stood there looking right at me.

"Are you okay?" His voice rose unnaturally as he talked fast and loud, like someone was turning up his urgency knob. "Why haven't you called? Where are you?"

"I'm with Ivy Beaumont, on her ranch outside of Black Bluff—"

"Please explain this to me," Guy screeched. "Why is your mother so flipped out about you being at Milt Beaumont's place? Melinda remembered the names you said, and I've been telling people that's where you are. Who is Milt Beaumont?"

Jeez Louise, Ivy was going to overhear him. I cradled the phone tight to my ear. "I love you, too, Guy. Yep, miss you bad. Oh, tonight, huh? How about that." Then I slipped my finger on the disconnect before Ivy could hear him scream the Beaumont name again. I talked away to the dead line, flicking Ivy occasional smiles. "Sure, Guy. No problem. Yeah."

Ivy stood sideways to me, looking at Milt's bookshelf as I made a show of hanging up the phone.

I gave my best sheepish smile. "He wants me to call my mom."

"Oh, sure. Go ahead. I'm looking for a book."

While Ivy dealt with her sudden urge for literary entertainment, or not, I thought about what to say and how to say it when I called my mama. It's a shocker that she was excited about my exact location.

Calling my mama is something I don't do often enough to have memorized her number. I used the directory in my cell to find her number before dialing.

"This is Dara Dale." My mother's voice was reserved, full of a snootiness I know she can fake, though I've never understood why she does it.

"It's me. Rainy."

"And you're calling from Milt Beaumont's! Honey I don't want you anywhere near that man! Everybody in the industry knows what Milt Beaumont's all about, and—"

As I hung up on my mama, Ivy sat down on the leather chair, pulled a drawer open, and fished through the USB cables and recording equipment stored inside. Had Ivy heard my mama or heard Guy?

Ivy snapped her fingers in my direction. "Now, everything's out in the open."

Chapter 21

IVY PLUGGED HER CAMERA INTO A laptop, then plugged the computer into Milt's big wide-screen monitor. She powered up the camera, rousted the computer, and, with a few swipes and taps of her fingers on the computer, we were looking at her photographs of the hilltop crime scene. I hadn't moved a muscle. Charley lay on my boot toes, making my feet, like him, fall asleep. The pins and needles started shooting up my legs. My breath hadn't returned to normal.

"What, does your husband, uh," I tried to make my voice sound super casual, like Ivy and I were just having a friendly, get-to-know-one-another conversation, and I hadn't just hung up on Guy then my mama as they screamed about Milt Beaumont. "What does he do for a living?"

She flipped through her pictures on the giant computer monitor. "Milt? He's an attorney."

I chewed on that answer, imagining the bald man with the Lexus she'd been consulting all afternoon and who'd phoned with the inside scoop from the medical examiner's officer minutes earlier. "If you're married to an attorney, why'd you need that other fellow?"

179

"Leonard? Different kind of law practice. Milt handles financing and contracts in the industry." Ivy waved at the red carpet photos on the office wall.

"The movies?"

"Right. Milt's not a criminal attorney. Leonard is. It's completely different work."

Ivy had a criminal attorney on retainer. I chewed on that, wiggling my toes to stop the pins and needles. Charley rolled over and stretched, then tucked himself into a little fur ball for a snooze.

Ivy pinched her fingers together on the laptop and swiped them out, over and over, zooming in on one of her crime scene photos displayed hugely on Milt's wide screen. "Oh, oh. Look at this."

I didn't want to see a picture of a corpse. I'd averted my eyes that morning when I'd dug him up, and again when she'd taken me up there on the four-wheeler.

But it was pictures of the evidence on the police tarp she'd enlarged. The coke shovel. A folding camp shovel. Was that second shovel what someone had used to bury Vicente? Next to the shovels was the dirty thermos the cops had found somewhere up there. I wondered when the coke shovel would be returned. It had nothing to do with the crime. Should I buy Ivy a new coke shovel for her forge if the police wouldn't give back the one that I'd left up there?

I asked, "What do you think's the deal with that thermos?"

Ivy cocked her head and swiped on with a shrug. "Sometimes, we sent hot meals up to Vicente. But look at this."

The computer screen filled with a close-up of Vicente Arriaga's state identification, library card, and a business card for a massage parlor called Pleasures in downtown Black Bluff. The card showed a silhouette caricature of a long-haired, high-heeled woman reaching out, which led me to believe it was not the kind of massage place where an athlete like Guy would go to get his leg muscles worked on.

"Pleasures massage parlor," Ivy said, copying the phone number down on a piece of paper she grabbed from Milt's desk. "Sounds sketchy. Let's go."

When Charley and I followed her out of Milt's office, it was with the intention of getting my truck running, not playing junior detective in the poky little town of Black Bluff.

Eliana met us in the dining area. "Dinner ready."

Ivy waved with a flourish. "Take some out to the men, if you don't mind."

"They not here."

"Oh," Ivy said, looking a tad miffed and jiggling her keys. "Well, it's, um Oscar's day off anyway. Gabe must have taken him to town. I need to talk to them, to everyone, when they get back."

"You not eat now?" Eliana asked.

Ivy shook her head and said, "You go ahead and eat. Rainy and I are going to take a ride."

It wasn't my kind of ride. But I bet if I went to town with Ivy, got off this ranch where I was stranded, then I could get cell reception and perhaps the privacy to talk to Guy about everything.

***

Pleasures was a house. An old one, with dark blue siding, wrought iron security doors and windows, and a vague light inside.

"Come on, Rainy." Ivy swung out of her Benz SUV, which she'd chosen over the Hummer and the sports car in her immaculate triple garage.

"Right behind you." I turned to tell Charley, on the back seat, to wait.

From the car, I watched Ivy walk up the front yard's stepping-stones to knock. I fished out my cell.

My dead cell.

I twisted my ponytail into a stick, muttered something unlady-like, and got my sweet self out of the Benz.

Ivy was already storming back. "I bet someone's in there. I left a note, promised money for answers. I wonder if the police have already been here."

This was all too much for me. What I needed was to be back at the ranch, jump-starting Ol' Blue with this giant Benz. "If the guys are back when we get back, I'm going to confront them about Charley, 'cause it was probably one of them who hurt him a couple years ago."

And then, I thought privately, I was out of there.

"I'm going to be all over them," Ivy said. "And I've already caught Oscar lying."

"About what?" I asked. "And Gabe says it was Stuckey who jumped me at the bull sale."

Ivy exploded. "How could he do that? What was Stuckey thinking?" She was already driving, but we didn't seem to be going straight home. We went deeper into Black Bluff, past gas stations and a grocery store that sat kitty-corner from a smaller, dumpier *tienda* that advertised a whole lot of peppers and money transfer services for its clientele. There was even an actual pay phone on the outside wall of *La Tienda*. I didn't have enough punch in me to dial the thirty-seven digits that would be required to use the public phone for free, but I wanted to jump out of Ivy's car, hit the zero, and tell an operator to get my almost-husband on the phone.

The library was down the main street, where cute stores like an ice cream parlor, a quilt shop and, oh yeah, Great Dogs specialty shop had frontage in between a couple of coffee shops.

"Good," Ivy said, nodding with satisfaction. "Solar put a notice up."

There was a handwritten sign on Great Dogs' door that announced the store was temporarily closed. I took that to mean more than the fact that it was Sunday evening. The store was not going to open in the morning.

"Can I charge my phone?"

Ivy pulled out a mini-USB cable for me. So I had power, and

a signal, but the same person sitting beside me who had made me uncomfortable earlier when Guy and my mama screamed the name Milt Beaumont.

I didn't call. I texted my mama: *Still in Black Bluff. On your way to OR, can you come get me if I can't get my truck started?*

Approaching the ranch gate though, it was a reunion. Gabe's beater Bronco blared his horn at the white Jeep Compass. Sabino Arriaga moved to the middle of the road, trying to flag us down after Gabe went around him. Ivy floored it, and we left Sabino behind as we roared through the ranch gate.

***

This was going to be my first time going toe-to-toe with Stuckey since I'd learned from Gabe that he was the one who knocked me out at the sale grounds. I'd sort of let that crime go when I realized that, long before he was my dog, someone had hurt Charley, but maybe that Saturday-morning crime mattered, too. Maybe Ivy was right—solving one thing solved everything. She figured the same person who hurt Charley had hurt Vicente. It kind of made sense. But as the Bronco pulled up between Ol' Blue and the bunkhouse while Ivy cut sharper to the right to go into the giant garage attached to her giant house, I realized something else.

They'd deny it.

Whether all three of those men were in on it, or just one of them, all three would deny it. If only one of them did it and the other two didn't even know, then all three would deny it and one would be lying. I explained it to Ivy as we pulled into her garage.

She shut the Benz off and looked at me as the garage door closed behind us.

"We have to be subtle," she said. "And we have to stay on point."

"I want to get my truck started."

And I wanted to leave, but I chose not to say that part aloud.

"I'm sure the men will help you. Oscar's staying in the bunkhouse tonight, like usual, now that the police thing has cooled off."

She meant the immigration angle, not the, well, the murder problem.

Ivy added, "Please ask everybody to come up to the house after you do whatever with your truck. Don't take too long."

***

Standing out there in the dark with my truck was more than a little creepy, but I hupped Charley into the cab and popped Ol' Blue's hood like it was no big deal.

Then I screamed like a girl when someone touched my shoulder. Someone big.

"Stuckey, you scared me. My truck's dead."

His voice came out jokey. "Then you can't leave."

Gabe, behind him in the dark, spoke up. "I've got jumper cables."

It was the most helpful thing anyone had said to me all day.

But the batteries weren't Ol' Blue's problem. We gave them time to charge, I cranked. Ol' Blue stayed dead. When Gabe and I gave up, I dropped the hood and the news. "Ivy wants everyone to come up to her house. I think she wants to talk."

"Beautiful," Gabe said, rolling his eyes. "When's she going back to LA?"

I gave a wide-eyed shrug. Inside Ol' Blue's cab, Charley eyed me from the safety of the passenger side. I could almost hear his thoughts as he watched me.

Let's go home.

Gabe coiled his jumper cables, stuffed them in the Bronco, and told Stuckey, "Go get Oscar."

We watched Stuckey head off on his errand, watched different lights switch on and off inside the bunkhouse. I asked, "Is that first room on the right in there yours?"

"Yeah," Gabe said. "Why?"

Studying him with all my attention, I said, "I found my shoeing tools—the ones that were stolen when I got hit at the bull sale—in Stuckey's locker."

"Jesus. You did? What an idiot."

I blinked a few times and waited.

The light was dim, so it was hard to tell, but Gabe might have reddened a shade or two with his comment. He patched things up with, "I meant Stuckey, not you. You seem like a real smart girl."

No, I don't. I seem like a girl in the wrong place, and for way too long, and way too slow to put things together.

***

Stuckey was the first to report to Ivy's house. I waved him to the window by the fireplace for a little one-on-one time. Instinct told me to get him to come clean before Gabe and Oscar walked in. Across the great room, Ivy organized her calendar and papers at the head of the table while Eliana cleared away the many unused dinner dishes with plenty of clatter.

"Did you hit me Saturday morning at the bull sale? Move my truck? Take some of my tools?" I asked Stuckey, not interested in Ivy's plan for going subtle.

"No!" His gaze darted around, resting longest at the front door.

Waiting for Gabe to come and save him, I decided. "People clapped after I worked my dog in the arena, they made an announcement. You saw Charley. You recognized him and freaked."

"No!"

Air whistled out my pursed lips. It was sort of like dealing with a four-year-old who'd taken a cookie but was still married to the hope that no one had seen the naughtiness. I glanced across the room and could tell Ivy was keeping tabs on us. I liked the backup but doubted she could hear much of what Stuckey and I said, if anything. I remembered standing here with Oscar hours earlier, looking out the window that now showed only a black square of night. We'd been looking at a body bag. I started from scratch, again.

"Did you ride a four-wheeler out to the east gate of the ranch, get a ride to the bull sale from Robbie Duffman?"

Stuckey's lips parted into a soundless oval and he nodded.

"Then at the sale, you saw my dog."

Another nod. He did better with statements than questions.

"And you recognized him. You knew he was Flame."

The nods came full and hard. Then he folded his arms across his chest. "You looked in my room? Went through my stuff?"

What could I say to that? That I had been putting laundry away for Eliana? I remembered the washer and dryer in the bunkhouse alcove. They did their own laundry. They had a real sweet setup on Ivy Beaumont's ranch. It would be a lot to lose.

"Yeah, Stuckey, I snooped." I pulled my track nippers out of my hip pocket. The reins had been up in my shirt. "These are mine, aren't they?"

"I guess."

I wanted to bonk him between the eyeballs with the nippers and recalled how I'd picked them up from my pile of reclaimed tools when I felt the urge to have a weapon handy. Stuckey was the kind of fella who had to be talked into the truth. I needed to make it easy for him to admit his wrongs. And there were bigger hooves to trim, so to speak. I thought of Charley, alone and happier in Ol' Blue's locked cab. I'd vented the windows to keep him comfortable, since he'd been clear he wanted to stay in the truck. I promised to deal with whoever had hurt him. I tried to make my voice steady as I said to Stuckey in a matter-of-fact way, "It was you. You hit me on the head at the sale grounds, and a couple years ago you—"

"No, ma'am."

"Gabe said it was you."

"He told?"

"You took my truck. You dumped me and my truck, and you stole my tools. Charley ran from you, and that's why he was wandering the ranch."

Stuckey's face turned dark and hard, his eyes shiny. "'Bout what happened Saturday, what are you going to do now?"

"I've already done it. I took my tools back."

A coat of anxiety fell off Stuckey's shoulders and a better invisible garment, this one made of relief, settled over him. "Is that all?"

"Why'd you do it, Stuckey?"

"I ain't sure."

I smacked my hands on my hips. Mommed him a bit. "C'mon. You can do better."

He tried harder. "I don't know. Just because. Maybe you can't understand, 'cause you've never done something that seemed like you might ought but might shouldn't and you didn't think it through or know why you done it at the time."

Well, he'd just described a lot of my life.

"Did you ever hurt Charley?"

Stuckey looked at the door. Men's voices muffled on the other side of it, stomping on the flagstone as they kicked dirt off their boots. We were out of time. Stuckey wasn't going to offer more than he was forced to admit.

He grabbed me. I gasped. Voice hoarse, he asked, "You found the other thing?"

I wasn't playing dumb, though I'm pretty skilled at it. "Other thing?"

Eliana opened the front door.

"Don't tell. You have to hide it." Stuckey's whisper was sullen, a bit angry, but urgent.

"What?" I asked, leaning an ear close to his mouth as Gabe and Oscar came in.

"I'm not telling." Stuckey's eyes dilated, dark and flared. "That could get you killed."

Chapter 22

Tick tock. I looked around Ivy's dining table. We were where we'd been twenty-four hours earlier, but without the food and friendliness. Eliana had put the chicken dinner away while Ivy and I were in town. The slightest scent of roast fowl lingered, and the bare table made the atmosphere worse. Tense. I hadn't heard the clock before, a big antique in the living room end, on the mantel above the fireplace, but now it filled my ears. Tick, tock, tick, tock.

Eliana and Oscar sat on one long side, as far from each other as possible, which put Eliana close to Ivy at the far head of the table. Stuckey wouldn't look at me, wouldn't look at anybody. I wanted to pull Ivy aside and compare notes, so to speak, but she commanded everybody to sit down and listen up. I wasn't about to sit between Gabe and Stuckey now, so there I was at the other head of the table, in the always-absent Milt's spot.

Ivy asked, "Who here knows anything about Pleasures massage parlor?"

That was her idea of subtle? Or getting to the point? I should have told her the details about confronting Stuckey minutes before.

189

Eliana looked at Ivy and said nothing. Oscar, Gabe, and Stuckey looked at each other in a way that made me think *all* the boys knew about Pleasures.

"I've got some questions," Ivy said. "I want to understand what happened here a couple of years ago. We are going to reconstruct the timeline. We're going to figure this out."

I nodded. The police wouldn't care about my dog getting mutilated two years ago. I cared. Ivy cared.

"You were gone, right?" I suggested. "You used to spend less time here."

Ivy patted the folder of receipts with the calendar on top. "I narrowed it down to the weeks I wasn't here. I used to come to the ranch about once or twice a month, and I missed some long weekends."

I thought about what Ivy had already deduced from her records. *Oscar lied to me.*

I said one word to Ivy as we eyed each other down the long table. "Fire."

She nodded. "Fire."

Calling my dog by his old name was hard, but I managed to say, "You thought Vicente took him and Flame."

She looked down at Oscar.

He sat frozen, not volunteering a word.

Ivy pointed to her tally of purchases and her calendar. "I hired you in February two years ago. Fire had a breeding scheduled in March. And you were here then. I made a big hay buy. I paid all five of you, counting Vicente. And I deducted the mileage when I took you and Eliana and Vicente to town. You two went to that little Mexican market and Vicente went to the library."

Gabe started to make a face but straightened it out and waited. Stuckey still studied the table. Eliana watched Ivy, who watched Oscar.

Oscar shifted on his chair and folded his hands on the table where a plate should have been. "Perhaps I make a mistake on when I began work for you."

Ivy rolled her eyes and thrust her chin at me. "Of course, yesterday, I didn't know Vicente was dead. I guess I thought that wherever Vicente was, he still had Fire and Flame." Now she rapped her calendar like a lawyer making a closing argument in front of the jury, or in this case, a whole bunch of suspects. "But as soon as we realized that your dog is Flame, we should have wondered where Fire was. Two years ago, Fire's breeding was for Reese Trenton's bitch. It was spring lambing time."

"What happened to Fire?" I asked the table. As soon as we got Ivy's old dog squared away, we were going to deal with what happened to mine.

Stuckey's shoulders hunched and shook. Shame and stress came off him in waves as he cried. Eliana wrinkled her face with discomfort and looked at Gabe and Oscar, their impassive faces giving nothing.

"I didn't mean to," Stuckey mumbled.

Ivy started to rise. Her neck stretching tall and tight. I caught her eye and shook my head with the barest movement.

That won't work.

She reconsidered, stayed quiet. I made my voice understanding, sympathetic. "You didn't mean to."

"I didn't!" Stuckey's voice grew fierce.

Ivy sat back down and spoke like a sweet big sister. "You didn't mean to what?"

"Shoot him. I was trying to save him."

"Aw, Stuckey." I said it like a gentle admonishment, resigned, rubbing my forehead with both hands. Yeah, a shot dog trumps one with cut ears.

"I didn't mean to." Stuckey's repetition bordered on a whine. "I'm sorry. I was trying to save him. You can do whatever you want to me. I'm sorry."

Ivy was floored. "You . . . shot . . . Fire?"

Stuckey's voice spiked with stress. "I didn't mean to shoot him. I was trying for a coyote. It would have got him. I was trying to save Fire."

"You shot Fire." Ivy's voice was quiet now, hurt and resolute. "You killed him?"

Stuckey nodded and shot a grateful look at Gabe. "Gabe stood up for me, buried him."

"Where?" Ivy asked.

Gabe cleared his throat. "Down where the flock is now. East. Between some oaks. It's a nice spot."

Stuckey shot his guilty look all around and clasped his hands over his head.

Ivy rose and stood with her back to us. Was she crying?

Ti-i-ick to-ock. Was the clock really in slow motion while the near silence stretched, or was that just the situation torturing us? I watched Ivy but felt one or two people at the table glance at me.

Finally, Ivy turned and faced us. "Tomorrow, you guys are going to dig up my dog and take him to be cremated and . . . I'll spread his ashes, I don't know, in the sea, or . . . that's not the point. You should have told me the truth. You should have been more careful. Poor Fire."

"Stuckey screwed up," Gabe said, "real bad. And we should have told you. He was just real scared. Asked me to cover for him. I'm sorry, Ivy. I really am."

"I was scared," Stuckey said.

Ivy glared at Gabe and Stuckey, ignoring the other side of the table. "Tell me, did he die immediately, or did he suffer?"

"It was a clean kill," Gabe said, his voice quiet and respectful.

Ivy seethed. "A clean kill. You guys shot my dog, and you kept that from me, let me think Vicente had just taken off with him."

Gabe started to bristle at her accusation. I could tell he wanted to point out that he hadn't shot the dog, but to his credit, he kept his trap shut.

"What did Vicente say when Fire died?" I asked.

Stuckey looked at Gabe, then the table. Gabe looked right back at me and said, "He never knew."

Ivy thrust her hands on her hips, her face as flushed. "I get that this has nothing to do with Vicente, but you guys have to tell the police if they ask about this part. I've told them that I thought Vicente had taken off with Fire and Flame, because that's what I thought had happened."

"I'm scared," Stuckey said. "I don't want to be in trouble with the police."

"It had to be just some vagrant or something," Gabe said. "I mean, that got Vicente. You know how people sneak onto the ranch, dump garbage. We had those homeless people who came in from Trenton's north section off the interstate that one time. People have dumped stuff over near the east gate."

I remembered mention of trespassers before. It's a problem for ranchers all over the west, people traipsing across the private land, camping illegally, dumping garbage. It's come to blows, and worse.

Ivy paused and pulled a photo from her folder. She'd been busy while I was out there trying to get Ol' Blue started.

She'd printed a full-size picture of the thermos.

"Spring lambing," Ivy said again. "Eliana says she was sending meals up to Vicente. One of you would have brought them up to him."

My mouth opened as I got it, and I wondered when Ivy had put it together.

If Vicente wasn't shot or stabbed, he might have been poisoned.

I remembered Ivy's huge tray of meds. Plenty to kill with an overdose.

Gabe's nostrils flared as he eyed Oscar, Eliana, and Stuckey. "Well, I sure as hell didn't fetch meals for him."

Stuckey ducked his head down like a scolded dog.

What had been inside the thermos the police found near the body and tagged as evidence?

"I know nothing," Oscar said.

Ivy and I looked at each other down the length of the tables. I figured we were reading each other's minds.

Someone's lying. Who is it?

I watched Ivy study her employees one by one. Didn't she get it? It was certainly occurring to me that if whoever hurt Charley had been the one to kill Vicente, then that person had a whole lot to lose and this was not a safe table to sit at. But then, I'd gone to sleep the night before thinking that someone around this table knew, like Charley and I did, where the body was buried.

I'd proved the body was there, but that was all I'd proved.

Maybe I was wrong the night before. Maybe the other person who knew where Vicente Arriaga lay dead and buried hadn't been around Ivy's dining table but was one of those other people in Ivy's orbit. I tried to think it through.

What about her little waif Solar, who was involved in something hinky at the *Great Dogs* shop? What about that fellow who delivered the coal coke? He passed cash with Stuckey. And something had passed between Stuckey and the hay deliverers, a woman and a man. Maybe someone else who came onto the ranch regularly had a whole side business that involved money and contraband. What about Duffy, who sure wasn't a good enough shoer to earn real money at it? What about Ivy's lawyer, who had way too much influence with the medical examiner's office and was a criminal defense attorney to boot? What about her doctor, so free and easy with major meds? And what about Ivy's too-absent husband, Milt?

What about Reese Trenton, the rancher who'd lost land with Ivy's purchase of her hobby ranch? He was packing a pistol and a grudge. A grave was waiting for someone on his land.

I wanted to go home.

Whatever was going on here likely involved more than one person. Which meant more than one person was lying.

Chapter 23

THE THREE MEN FILED OUT FOR the bunkhouse. Eliana went for her bedroom down the hallway and shut her door with a click. I drummed my finger on the table near Ivy's folder of receipts, her calendar, and the enlarged photo of the thermos.

"Can I use your phone?" I asked. "I need to tell Guy I'm having truck trouble and may have to stay another night."

Ivy flipped one delicate wrist in half a wave. "Sure." But then she motioned me to join her at the other end of the great room as she sank onto a white leather couch. "I've got to figure this out."

I nodded and sat beside her. "Okay. What did Vicente do in his time off?"

"Other than go to a massage parlor?" Ivy smirked. "I'd drop him off in town on my way to the store, pick him up on the way back."

"Did he go to bars, friends, the bank?"

"He didn't use a bank. He usually wanted to go to the library. He liked to read in there."

That surprised me. I don't know why. I should figure that people are way more interesting and confusing than they seem at first.

"Wait a minute," I said, harking back to the sight of the dead

195

man's wallet contents spread out on the tarp in front of the cops. I snapped my fingers. "Let's go look at your photos again."

We went back to Milt's office. With a few clicks on the computer, countless thumbnails filled the screen.

Ivy asked, "What are you looking for?"

I paged through her shots until I spotted one that showed Pleasures massage parlor as one of the three cards from Vicente's wallet.

"Can you blow this up?" I asked.

Ivy frowned, clicked and tapped, making her computer show a full-screen version of the cards extricated from the wallet, laid out one by one. There was the California State Identification for Vicente Arriaga, there was the business card for Pleasures massage parlor, there was the library card.

"Can you zoom in more, so we can read the library card?" I asked.

Ivy swooped two fingers apart on her computer monitor repeatedly then we inspected the cards one by one.

"Do you know if your local library has online access?"

Ivy pointed at the Pleasures business card. "I think the massage parlor is more important." Then she frowned. "But I suppose the police noticed the card and are checking on that angle."

"Get us into the library," I said.

Ivy opened a search tab on the Internet and soon was in the library's website.

Clicking back to the blown-up photo, we were able to enter the correct identification number and be given access, signed in as Vicente Arriaga. The library portal offered the borrower's history right there on the screen. Ms. Computer I am not, but I can sure click a thingy.

"DNA," I said. "And clinical parasitology. Huh. Your herder had some serious tastes in reading material."

Ivy peered over my shoulder. "Wow."

We gaped at the screen, then at each other.

"Okay," I said. "Parasitology. You said he'd asked you for the microscope."

Ivy drummed her fingers on Milt's desk. "We missed something. I missed something."

"Let's go look at that microscope," I suggested.

***

Halfway to the barn, I stopped at Ol' Blue, unlocked it, and made Charley come give us company in the dark.

Chromey and the buckskin nickered at us from one side of the barn aisle, Decker and the Appy mare from the other.

"Indigo Eyes," Ivy said.

I'd never known her name. As we paused in the dark, I asked, "She's the dam of that mule?"

A hulking shape came at us in the end of the dead dark barn aisle and a male voice boomed. "What's going on?"

I jumped. Charley was already gone, skittering out in a flash.

Ivy assumed her boss voice. "We're looking at the forge."

"I lost her coke shovel," I said. "I'll need to replace it for her, and I'm showing her what I mean."

"It's the little flat spade that goes with the forge," Stuckey said.

"Go to bed, Stuckey," Ivy said. "Go back to the bunkhouse and call it a night. Things are going to be okay tomorrow."

"Thanks, Miz Beaumont. I was just doing a night check on the horses."

***

We found what we were looking for in a space between cinder blocks under the forge. The dust was so thick on the two baggies of white powder, they looked brown and blended into the cobwebbed crevices.

"Oh, my God, Vicente was . . ." Ivy stared hard. "I never suspected him. Never."

"The police would probably like to know about that stuff." I wasn't going to get my fingerprints on the baggies. I was in enough trouble for digging up a body on the ranch and didn't need to add possession of the white powder—cocaine or heroin?—to my rap sheet. During the few dozen days of high school that I managed to attend, baggies of white powder were something I stayed away from. Those dope users were some of the hardest-to-figure kids I'd ever known, or never come to know.

"It doesn't look right." Ivy opened both baggies and sniffed the white powder. She *tasted* them. And then she asked, "Why would he have salt and sugar in baggies?"

"Huh?"

"This isn't coke," Ivy said.

Smacking my forehead helped me think. I did it twice. "I get it."

"I don't," Ivy said.

"You have to make a special saline solution, a salt solution. With sugar in it, too, to do a flotation test at home."

"Flotation test?" Ivy asked.

"To do a fecal," I said, "To examine manure for worm eggs and count them. You know, flotation. You said Vicente was learning to do flotation tests. That's just another name for the fecal counts."

I tried to remember the Internet tutorials I'd read and watched on making the sugar-saline flotation solution and doing the fecal tests. How I've coveted a microscope like the one Vicente had talked Ivy into buying.

"Look at this," Ivy said, kneeling below the forge where the baggies of salt and sugar had been stored. She pulled out a folded wad of papers, blew the dust off them.

Just a dozen sheets of beat-up paper. Maybe he'd printed them out at the library. A complete set of directions on how to make the saline-sugar solution for a fecal float test, set up the slides, and do the count.

Ivy nodded. "He was learning to do fecals for the ranch."

I considered that. So, Vicente had printed off material at the library on how to do fecals. He'd ordered a book on veterinary parasitology. He'd asked Ivy for a microscope and slides.

But that wasn't all. I shook my head and looked at Ivy. And thought about white powder, and a police drug dog showing interest in Ol' Blue. And being where I should not be.

Missing something.

I frowned, fingering the knobs that change which eyepiece was centered under the microscope's viewer, and considered the strength of the optics, the textbooks Vicente had requested on his library account. DNA? We couldn't look at something as small as an intracellular double helix with this hundred-dollar machine. What else had Vicente been doing?

"The sequence of events," I said, deciding as I spoke, "is Stuckey kills Fire not long before the breeding to Reese Trenton's female, they cut Charley's ears and use him to breed, Vicente tries to prove it, someone kills Vicente. Vicente wanted to study DNA. I think that's what he really wanted to do with the microscope, but he didn't know it wasn't powerful enough."

He'd been trying, I decided. Vicente had been trying to honor Charley, or rather, Flame.

***

To cover a counterfeit dog breeding didn't seem like a good enough reason to murder someone.

"What did Vicente spend his money on?" I asked Ivy when we were back under the stars, out of the dark barn and forge room.

"I have no clue." Ivy tossed the baggies of salt and sugar in the air beside me, her other hand holding the sheaf of papers Vicente had printed off on how to do a fecal exam.

"But you paid him in cash?"

"Right."

"So, he didn't have to use a bank." I stopped at Ol' Blue and told Charley to come with me though a part of me thought about climbing in the cab with him and sleeping there, locked inside. It was late at night, and my truck wasn't going anywhere. But maybe Ivy would give me some space to talk to Guy in privacy. I grabbed the big paper bag on the floor's center hump, wrapping the rest of my recovered tools in it as I followed Ivy back to the big house. Charley followed me. When we went inside, it was the first time I'd seen her lock the front door.

And it became the first time Ivy told me to use the kitchen phone if I wanted to make a call. I showed her my tools. She wasn't impressed but still shook her head over what Stuckey had done to me. As I handled the rasps and crease nail pullers and nail cutters one by one, I felt something small and squishy inside the paper bag. I'd assumed it was an empty bag wrapping my tools, but when I looked inside for the first time, I knew what Stuckey had been warning me about earlier.

Though I still didn't know who'd done it, or why, I now knew how Vicente Arriaga was killed. I was holding the murder weapon.

Chapter 24

THE LIVESTOCK PROTECTION COLLAR INSIDE THE paper bag had one rubber bladder still packing its poison. The other had been slit long ago, now empty and dry. Right there in the foyer, I held the paper bag wide open and showed it to Ivy, explaining as she looked inside. "That's what was in the thermos, salting some Zuni stew or some such."

Ivy shook her head as she peered into the bag. Her brow didn't wrinkle, so I couldn't tell if she was thinking hard.

"Who prepared Vicente's food, and who delivered it?" I asked. "Who's lying? Oscar? Gabe? Stuckey? Eliana?"

"What are you saying, Rainy?"

I squeezed the intact bladder through the paper bag, bulging the black rubber before her eyes. "This stuff's poison. And your lawyer told you that the cops think Vicente didn't have a bullet in him, right?"

Ivy shook her long blonde hair. The roots were dark, the tresses clumping with a day's worth of worry.

"I don't have a clue," Ivy said. "I wish Milt would get here."

Her comment gave me pause. "How often does he come to the ranch?"

201

She waved a hand. "Almost never. This ranch was supposed to be our retreat. But I'm the one who really wanted it. It's my escape from that other world. I wish I could call someone."

Those last words sunk like a stone in my chest. I couldn't help blurting, "Me, too."

But I could, if she'd let me. I had people to call. Guy. I so wanted to talk to him, not just read texts or listen to messages we left for each other, but really talk.

Actually, I wanted to be with him, face-to-face, touching while we talked. Or while we didn't say a word. That's what it's like with me and him. We are happy together. We just want to spend time together. All our mornings, our evenings, our free time, our lives. I'm going to marry that boy. Maybe he was asleep now. Should I wake him?

"What?" Ivy asked. "You are or aren't?"

"Huh?"

"I asked if you're hungry."

"Oh. Yeah, sure." I'm always hungry. The part of my mind that flickered a warning about poisoned food had to be shut down for the sake of my stomach. In Eliana's absence—she was earlier to bed than us night owls—Ivy pulled out two neatly wrapped plates full of the sandwich fixings that had been on the table at lunch-time—cheese, tomatoes, onion, lettuce leaves, and much meat. The fridge also held a plate of roasted chicken—the good-smelling, uneaten dinner. I could have cleaned up all three plates.

Without Eliana to get things cuted up, we'd have plain sandwiches. Ivy pulled out a loaf of artisan-type bread, definitely not Wonder-white. Oatmeal bubbled the top edges of the brown crust. The slices were thick, meant for open-faced sammies. Ivy picked at a lettuce leaf, toying with it, nibbling. I pushed my hands deep into my front jeans pockets and sealed my lips, trying not to think, thinking. Trying.

"You wanted to call somebody," Ivy said, her voice whisper-soft. "I'd like to call a friend."

She was lonely, I realized. She had no one to call. I felt myself go soft with sympathy. She shook herself, like a horse getting up from rolling in dirt, and put the lettuce down. "Help yourself. I'm going to bed."

And I'd be going to bed next to the cook.

I used Ivy's kitchen phone and dialed. Felt like a thousand hours ago that the woman cop with the ponytail had given me her card.

Can we count on you?

She'd posed the question mid-morning. Now it was midnight. I took a breath and dialed, thought I heard a click on the line, and wondered if someone else had picked up Ivy's house phone. For the first time, I wondered what Eliana's bedroom was like. Did she have a phone extension in there?

Did she—like Stuckey—have something hidden in her room that didn't belong to her?

"Steinhammer." Her way of answering the phone seemed intended to let me know she was someone who stayed on top of things and slept a lot less than me.

"This is Rainy Dale," I said. "The horseshoer from—"

"I know who you are. Didn't recognize the phone number on my cell. Are you still at the ranch?"

"Yeah. I wanted to tell you, well I mean, there's that rifle in the bunkhouse over the mantel—"

"We saw the .22—"

"And one of the men has a pistol in his locker—"

"Which one?"

"I'm not a hundred percent sure, but I heard your dead man might not have been shot anyways."

There was a good long pause, as maybe she weighed what I was asking against my right to know, what she and I might share. She said, "They're hoping for good results from the toxicology screen."

Making myself give this information was hard, but it was the right thing to do. I glanced around the empty kitchen, cupped my palm to the phone, and said in lowest decibels, barely moving my lips. "Sodium fluoroacetate."

"What's that?"

"A poison you should tell them to look for in your dead guy. I found a cut livestock collar. One pouch is intact, but the other has been sliced open and it would have had plenty of power to kill a man. Or six."

"Sodium . . . spell it."

"Can't." But I said the name for her again and added, "It's also called Compound 1080."

I heard the clatter of typing on her end. "Google says this 1080 stuff is almost impossible to acquire."

"Except for sheep sometimes walk around wearing rubber pouches of it."

"The hell you say."

"Wear it around their necks. It's called a livestock protection collar. They're still legal in lots of places. Nevada, Texas."

Her breath came out in an exhale that probably used up thirty seconds and both lungs. Then she said we'd talk later, 'cause she had to make another call.

***

My next call, to home, went straight to voice mail.

The outgoing message on our home machine had been changed. It used to be my voice, saying, "You've reached Guy and Rainy's. If you have a message about a horseshoeing appointment, please be sure to leave complete information about your horse and how I can reach you."

Now it was Guy's voice. "We're out of town. Leave a message."

As I left him a solid message about how much I missed him and I'd be home as soon as I could get Ol' Blue running, I wondered why he'd done changed our home message, and I wondered what my cell's voice mails would say, if I could play them. I wanted to call my friend Melinda, but I have just enough decency to not do that after midnight. I called my mama. She shouldn't be too busy, should be heading north for my wedding. I told her voice mail that I was having truck trouble and I was stuck in Northern California. Maybe she could come get me.

***

The knocking on my bedroom door made Eliana stir in the next room. Maybe even whimper. I opened it to Ivy, who was not happy.

"The police are here for you." She folded her arms across her chest. "I don't want them here. If you're going to talk to them, if you're taking sides against me, you have to leave my place."

"Ivy, I haven't hurt you or the ranch in any way. I've no bad intentions, please believe me. I haven't done anything to bring trouble to your place."

She gave a twisted smile. "Except for that little part about digging up a dead body on my ranch?"

"Yes, ma'am, except for that."

***

A uniformed deputy with hair so short I couldn't tell what color it was stood waiting outside on Ivy's flagstone doorway. Younger than me, twice my size, with all the goodies on his hip belt, including a nice big gun opposite the radio. Snaking from that radio was a coiled black wire that ran to a combination speaker and mic on his shoulder. He pushed the button when I came out and agreed that I was Rainy Dale.

"Ten-four," he announced. "I've made contact." Then he nodded at me. "Ms. Dale, I'm here to collect a collar of some sort."

Ivy snapped at both of us. "This couldn't wait until morning?"

They went at it until he calmed her down, staying on the flag-stone side of her open front door, and I agreed to tell the police to call if they had more questions. They were not to come to the house. Ivy said I could give them the house phone number, but I knew they already had it

Charley pressed his head against my knee. He hates tension, people having any kind of argument. I'm with him.

The cop said, "You told an off-duty day-shifter you found something."

"Day-shifter?"

"Deputy Steinhammer."

Like Ivy, I'd assumed handing over the livestock collar could wait 'til morning. "I didn't expect them to send someone out in the middle of the night."

He gave me a bland, lip-locked smile. "Yeah, we're funny like that. Like to secure evidence immediately."

When I went to the spare bedroom for the paper bag and my tools, I didn't hear a sound from Eliana's room.

But I didn't think that was because she was asleep.

I looked back and noticed Ivy standing there watching me.

She didn't look pleased.

My rasps, nail cutter, crease nail puller, and track nippers were laid out on the paper bag which still held the squishy little bladder of death and the Velcro straps that form a protection collar.

I brought the works to the cop at the door. "You should be care-ful with what's in this bag. You should put on rubber gloves before you touch it."

He looked me in the eye, cocked his head, and, from his left front pocket, pulled out a pair of yellow latex gloves and donned them with the stretchy snap sound.

This man was a Boy Scout, I thought, prepared. I could practi-cally feel the rubbery tug to the backs of my own hands as I watched his knuckles bulge under the Latex second skin.

"And what do we have here?" He was staring without

comprehension at the contraption of black rubber pouches—one full, one dry—that he'd pulled out of the paper sack.

"It's called a livestock protection collar. It looks old. And you see, one of those bladders has been cut."

"Did you wear gloves?"

I shook my head. I do have rubber gloves in Ol' Blue, wear 'em with some of the glues I use in specialty shoeing jobs. "I was real careful. Well, not at first. I didn't know what it was. I thought the paper bag was just wrapped around my tools."

"And you say these were your stolen tools that you've recovered?"

I nodded.

He inspected them one by one. I could have fallen asleep on my feet in the time it took the uniform to finally announce, "How could you be sure these are your tools? They bear no engraving, no identification marks."

"They're mine. I'm sure enough to have liberated them."

Unfortunately, he liberated them from me, said he was taking them for evidence. He even wanted the track nippers I'd been packing around in my hip pocket half the afternoon. This was not working out well. He stepped farther from the front door, maybe being respectful of the hour as he got loud on his portable radio, asking advice. Charley was at my side as I pulled the door shut and followed the cop out onto the flagstone.

The night was cooling off fast. I rubbed my arms.

"Ten-four," he said into this radio. "Yeah. Copy that. No, from another building. Does he want me to wake 'em up?"

I waited.

He listened to his radio, said, "Ten-four," again, then turned to me. "Ms. Dale, we'd need your cooperation to charge Mister Stuckey with the assault and theft from you. We'll take a statement from him in the morning and refer it to the prosecutor."

I rubbed my head. "I'm kind of over it."

He shook his head. "Would you rethink cooperating fully? Charging that man for assaulting you at the bull sale needs to

happen. You're not the judge here, and there are diversion pro-
grams down the road anyway, but you victims who give passes for
that kind of behavior are not helping."

I nodded. "I guess I take your point." But I felt bad.

He headed for his vehicle with all I'd given up.

"Will I get those tools back?" I called.

"Eventually, probably."

"That's it?"

"You have the case number. That's good enough for a receipt.
I'll be doing a supplemental report and the detective is working
now. Talk to him in the morning." And he fired up his patrol car,
driving off for the main gate in the dark.

I turned to go back inside but found the front door had been
dead bolted.

***

She got it, I suppose. Ivy understood why I'd called the police to
report the collar with the slit pouch. Maybe she hadn't meant to
lock me out. Or maybe Eliana had bolted the door without realizing I was still outside.

Or maybe someone was playing games with me.

I hate games. And I didn't want to play knock-knock.

Ol' Blue is where I went, me and my dog piling into the cab,
locking the doors, which I almost never do. We'd slept in the truck
Friday night, we could do the same for what was left of Sunday.
I tried the ignition. No go. I tugged on the leather jacket that
I'd slept in Friday night. There's a reason shoers like leather and
cotton and wool and silk. We need clothes that don't melt when
hot sparks fly. A hole burned in a natural fabric is fine, but syn-
thetic clothes that runners wear melt like plastic, stick to your skin
and keep burning. I don't want to get burnt. I snapped my jacket's
metal buttons, turned the collar up, and pulled Charley close.

"We'll get Ol' Blue towed to a shop tomorrow," I told him. "If it can't get fixed quick, we'll meet up with my mama and ride with her back home." I hated to leave my truck, but I wasn't going to miss my own wedding.

And that's where I slept until Charley's low growl awoke me, along with the sound of someone rapping on the driver's window.

A silhouette in the sunrise asked if I'd seen anyone coming or going. Gabe's voice was muffled through the glass, which was blurry from the condensation of Charley and me breathing inside the cab for the few hours' sleep we'd grabbed.

I twisted the ignition key halfway so I could power down the window, remembering only after I got no juice that my truck was dead. I unlocked and opened the door.

"You slept here?" Gabe asked. His glance went behind me, to the house. "Ivy kick you out? We had an extra bedroom in the bunkhouse."

"It was real late," I said. "Didn't want to disturb anyone." I wasn't going to add that I didn't know if it was Ivy or Eliana who'd locked me out, and I'd been too unsure of my prospects to try knocking or ringing the bell at the big house, and the bunkhouse might have been hosting whichever fellow had a hand in doing in my dog's last person.

Gabe adjusted his cowboy hat. "Anyone else up and about? I can't find Oscar." He turned and hollered at the bunkhouse. "Stuckey, check the barn again."

Oscar making himself more than scarce made me think a good couple of times. I rubbed my eyes and redid my ponytail.

Ivy came out of the big house via the garage, driving her Hummer, Eliana in the front seat with her. Ivy shut the giant SUV down and flung her door open when Gabe gave her the news.

"You guys can't find Oscar?" she asked.

Stuckey shuffled up. "Ain't he up at the house?"

Ivy's face offered her version of a frown, her mouth forced down at the corners for part of a split second. "Did he take off last night?"

Gabe and Stuckey looked at each other. Everybody seemed to be pointing a finger at Oscar having lit out for good.

"I could ride around and look for him." My offer was sincere. Riding always sounds to me like the best thing to do. If I rode to the summit, I could call my mama again or try my daddy. Either of my folks were my best chance for getting out of here today, given the stubbornness Ol' Blue was displaying.

"Not for long," Ivy said. "You're going in to see my lawyer before the police this morning, just like everybody else."

Everybody but Oscar, I thought, unless we find him quick. Apparently, we weren't going to be discussing that I'd slept in my truck last night. I figured that she could have been sleepy and kind of accidentally turned her lock while I was outside with the cop in the wee hours, or it could have been what Guy calls a passive-aggressive move. He'd probably call not talking about it passive-aggressive, too.

Gabe made his report while swiveling in place, looking in every direction. "Both four-wheelers are here. All the horses are here. He's not in the smokehouse. We've looked everywhere twice. No one fed the horses yet. He didn't come out to do chores."

"Look again," Ivy ordered. "Split up. Everybody check something, everything."

She pointed down the ranch road to the east then west toward the main gate. That's the direction I chose, waving Charley along with me. I hadn't gone far when Ivy zipped out of the garage in her Hummer, heading east for the ranch's back gate, while Gabe and Stuckey fired up the four-wheelers.

The solo stroll out toward the header at the ranch gate should have been the nicest little walk Charley and I had had in a while, but I pondered on Oscar hightailing it.

Either that, or someone had done something to him, making him the next Vicente.

Then I saw the white Jeep Compass just beyond the open ranch gate.

Sabino Arriaga looked better than I imagine I did. His hair was wet and his face clean-shaven. He hadn't been there long this time, I reckoned.

I'd been avoiding him, and I didn't even want to face the reason why.

He got out of the car, raised a hand, and stood waiting. I turned on my heel and walked back to the ranch house, slapping my thigh.

"Charley, come. Heel."

I put my dog away in Ol' Blue, the one-ton kennel good for nothing else at the time, then went to the barn and saddled up. Decker and I made a speedy loop out to the flock, calling for Oscar, stopping just shy of spooking the sheep. The donkey jack brayed once, and I was sure he'd betray any person hanging out down there. His son, the mule, started to follow Decker again, so I wheeled off and loped back to the barn though I'd have liked to ride for the summit and certain cell service. The others had made no progress. Gabe reported in from a four-wheel ride down to a pig wallow and back. Stuckey had tried up and down the ranch land near Reese Trenton's place. Eliana checked the house, though it didn't seem necessary and we all searched the barn and smoke-house and bunkhouse.

It was time to face facts. Oscar was gone.

Chapter 25

Eliana didn't want to be taken to the police interview. Ivy laughed it off with a shake of her head. "I could not get that girl to stop with the food this morning."

She had pulled the Hummer back into the garage, waving me to come along inside the bay. As we entered the house, she explained that Eliana had been the first one up. The tables were piled with a spread of cinnamon French toast, pancakes, and sausages, plus all sorts of little bowls of goodies on the side to add—maple syrup, whipped cream, pecans, blueberries, strawberries, and chocolate chips.

There wasn't enough chocolate in the world that could be slathered on this situation to make it appealing.

Hustling around looking for Oscar had used up the time that was supposed to be spent in consultation with the attorney. While Ivy got on the horn with her lawyer and arranged to meet at the police station, Eliana put away all the untouched food she'd assembled. Ivy hung up the phone and waved us to the garage, rolling her eyes as she did.

Back in the Hummer, Ivy explained how she was to drive Eliana and me direct to the police station. Gabe was going to take himself and Stuckey in for the second round of appointments with the cops. Ivy promised everybody her attorney would make sure everything was on the up-and-up, too.

Maybe there wasn't enough time to fix the possible monkey wrench that had been thrown into whatever agreement the police and the lawyer had come to on interviewing and polygraphing everybody, yet not take action on Eliana and Oscar. Probably Oscar would get less leniency now, but perhaps Eliana, who hadn't made a run for it, would still be okay. I told Ivy about the trench dug on the neighbor's ranch, how he'd seen a man in a dark baseball cap slipping onto his land.

"It was Oscar," Ivy said.

But we both knew proof was hard to come by.

***

"In Southern California, everyone has a Maria," Ivy told me, looking in her rearview mirror at me as she drove us to Black Bluff. I'd slipped into the back seat naturally when she said I could bring Charley, but then Eliana joined me there, so here we sat on each side of Charley like a row of children behind Ivy.

"Ma'am?" I glanced at her, then at Eliana. She was looking younger by the minute, her frightened face childlike this morning.

"Everybody has a domestic," Ivy said. "A Mexican. No one cleans their own house. And those girls, those beautiful Latina girls I've hired and all of my fake friends have hired to clean our houses, and cook and take care of kids, those girls don't drive or have a car. You have to go pick them up and bring them to your house for the day and everything ends up spotless and no one even bothers to learn their girl's name. Everybody just calls their girl Maria. Everyone has a Maria."

Their girls. Probably in Ivy's class of friends, yeah, people are that far off base. But other people live in Southern California and know their help's name, or don't have someone else to do their chores. My mama, for one. I frowned, thinking of what my mama had been trying to tell me, and managed an "I dunno" for Ivy.

"You're adorable, Rainy. You're so naive in some ways."

But I am just barely smart enough to shut my mouth some-times. Because undocumented workers weren't the only reason Ivy Beaumont didn't want the police on her ranch.

My mama had known about the Beaumont reputation in Hollywood.

"I want to call my mom," I felt like I was six years old. "Even with your husband in the movie business, you probably never heard of my mother, but she does a little acting. Her name's Dara Dale."

"Your mother is Dara Dale? A horse rancher type woman?"

My mama?

Oh.

My.

"Uh, no, that's the wrong one," I said. I'd never known there were two people packing that name. My mama thinks horses smell bad.

Ivy started in again as she parked at the government building's visitors' section.

"You live up north," she said. "Things are different there. Down here, it's important to provide a safe space for these people. They're good workers, and they're not bothering anybody."

These people. Did she have to provide her workers with a safe working space for six or seven days a week, instead of five? For once, I kept my mouth in check, taking time before I finally allowed, "I'm from Texas, ma'am. I've bucked hay beside many a Mexican. And men from farther south, while we're at it. I do understand those hard workers and the fix they're up against."

Ivy rolled her eyes toward a Lexus in the lot. "At least Leonard's here. About time he earned his retainer." She slammed the tranny into park, flung open her door and then mine.

Eliana looked at me with tears in her eyes as she got out on the passenger's side and whispered, "It was Oscar."

She was fast pulled away from the Hummer by Ivy. I double-checked to make sure the windows were all left a bit open for Charley then dawdled to try my cell phone as they entered the government building.

***

Between my mama and my daddy, she'd be the one with the more maneuverable vehicle. My phone had three bars of connection and I'd gotten enough charge in Ivy's car on our foray into Black Bluff.

I hung up on both Guy's unanswered cell and our home message machine. I told my mama's cell phone, "I think I need a tow truck. I'm at the Black Bluff police station right now."

For good measure, I texted her, asking, *Are you nearby? Can you come get me at the Black Bluff police station?* Both my folks were driving north for the wedding right about then, and I wondered which was closer to Black Bluff. My wedding was going to mark the first time my mama and daddy had been in shouting distance of each other since I was thirteen years old. That friction was one good reason Guy and I had planned an outdoor wedding. In Oregon. In the springtime.

We're not made of brain cells.

Here in California, the weather's always perfect. Shirtsleeve weather, which made Ivy's attorney, in sport coat and tie, look pretty out of place to me. But, inside the climate-controlled lobby of the Black Bluff town hall, sheriff's station, courthouse, and licensing department, it was downright chilly. A sign in the lobby said no cell phone use. There was a crowd waiting for us. One tie-wearing fellow said he was a special agent with the state's Bureau of Investigation. Another was a local officer with the town of Black Bluff. Others wore Tehama County deputies' uniforms. Ivy and her lawyer frog-walked the terrified Eliana down a hall. Hanging near Mr. Special Agent was the remaining plainclothes detective, with collar-length hair, in dress Wranglers and a plaid shirt, with no tie, sleeves rolled up. I think he was the one who'd been in the unmarked police car on the day before.

"Rainy Dale," Plaid Shirt said, waving me down the opposite hallway from where they'd marched Eliana.

I nodded, cell phone still in hand. "I'm trying to reach my fellow." I kept thinking about Guy having changed our home phone machine's outgoing message. I wanted to keep hitting send 'til I got an answer from him. I was just about to call the Cascade Kitchen to see if he was at work. I'd try Melinda next, just so she could tell me things were all right in the home pasture.

Plaid Shirt knocked once, and someone opened a heavy door from the inside. We were in another hall, just outside what looked like a little interview room.

He said, "How about you put the cell phone down for a couple of minutes so we can talk?"

I pocketed the phone and gritted my teeth. "Okey doke."

"Great. We'd like to talk to you about what happened this weekend."

"About me getting thumped and my stuff getting stolen?"

"No, this is about the other matter, Ms. Dale. We'd like you to sit down with me and Agent Mattingly for an interview."

"About what?"

"Murder." Mister Special Agent stepped forward as Plaid Shirt faded out of the room. "I'd like to talk about whether or not you killed Vicente Arriaga."

"I didn't kill anyone. I never knew Vicente. He was probably a good fellow, though, I can tell you that."

"And you know that because?"

"Because I have his dog." I explained the proof that Charley was a good dog, so it was reasonable to figure he'd had a good person. I squinted at this tie-wearer and wondered whether he was playing bad cop or not playing at all. Po-lice are an odd herd. My buddy Melinda has a weird sense of humor. And it mushroomed when

she went to deputy-sheriff-school last fall. By the time she got
back this winter, she made the squirrelliest small talk ever heard.
So maybe this tie-wearing super special agent had the same afflic-
tion of canted humor that Melinda Kellan achieved after going to
police school. I tried to allow for it.

The agent looked a lot like the easygoing plainclothes detective
in that general cop way—same build and a white guy and all—but
was somehow on a whole 'nother level. This piece of work had a
file under his arm and failed to make himself clear in any form. He
was six feet stupid in a five-nine body. Asked me why I thought I
was there.

"Someone hitting me on the head, stealing my shoeing tools,
and my dog finding a dead body." My hand went to the back of my
skull and rubbed. It still hurt to touch, like the bruise was spreading. Maybe it was a little mushy there, too.

"Did the deputy or the Black Bluff officer or the sheriff's investigator tell you that?"

"No, I told them that." I spoke slow enough for him to catch up
and tried a little not to roll my eyes.

Then we sighed at each other, and he looked at me while I
looked around the tiny room.

It had a mirror on the far side, honest to goodness. Like, someone could be eyeballing us from the other side of the glass. I stared
at the goggle-eyed gal in the mirror. My frayed ponytail needed the
use of a comb. Brown eyes looked black from being dilated in the
bright light, lids a little wider open than usual, spooked-like. And
I saw his reflection, too. Maybe younger than I'd thought at first
glance, thirty-five or so. Folks in that range that used to look like
they had some real age on me, but shoeing's an in-the-weather job.
Makes my face older than my years. High mileage, I am. His sport
coat was a real dark navy that had looked black in the hallway,
and his pants were dark gray. For no good reason, my brain went
to thinking about how gray horses change shades over their lives,
and then of course I thought about how two grays might not make

a gray and how a little Arab I've trimmed since it was a baby was born looking chestnut and is now a light gray and—

"Tell me everything you know about Vicente Arriaga."

"Okay." I paused a second, quit thinking about horse colors and their heritability, then told him, "I'm done."

"You're done? You think you're leaving? You in charge here?"

"Huh?"

"Do you have a hearing problem or is it something else?" He gave one sharp downward tip of his head that was meant to be a reprimand.

Hate that. Especially from guys do I hate it. Oh, the face I put on could resemble a stiff, close-lipped smile but was all about telling him what a jackass he was. And I wouldn't excuse my potty mouth and mind for thinking of him as a jackass. Which got me thinking about how a decent donkey jack is what I needed to find, one that had been bred to the right mare. The resulting mule baby would be earmarked for Melinda. I had Charley back. Once I got Ol' Blue going, I could pick up the stock trailer and be home tonight and these last couple days would be just a bad daydream. And I have been known to daydream. But I can control it and I proved it right then with, "I hear pretty good still, though I'll surely lose my hearing early."

"Wilson!" Mr. Special Agent called out as he lurched to his feet and the door opened.

Plaid Shirt man entered the interview room with a photo of the livestock protection collar I'd handed over to the deputy fellow in the wee hours. Super Special Agent and Plaid Shirt looked at me then stepped out together and muttered to each other long enough to get over themselves about whether or not I'd killed Vicente. I reckon people who had a hand in doing someone in are a mite more skittish in a police interview than I was, even if it wasn't my favorite indoor place to be.

Plaid Shirt came back in and shut the door. No more special agent for us. "You know, Miss Dale, Deputy Steinhammer—"

"She's the one with the ponytail?" I twisted my ponytail into a tight stick then set it free, trying to picture him in yesterday's plaid shirt, trying to keep all these police people sorted out in my mind.

"Yeah, she's the one who did the preliminary interview with you after you called nine-one-one. Said you hadn't known the Beaumonts before Saturday morning. She sold me on your digging up a body where your dog lay down. Quite a story." He clicked his pen and poked the photo of the livestock protection collar. "Where exactly did you find this thing?"

"In a locker in the bunkhouse. I was looking for my stuff. See, some tools were stolen from my truck Saturday morning—"

"At that bull sale? And you were assaulted there."

"Right. So yesterday, after I did some shoeings for them, I grabbed a shower and sort of took it upon myself to peek into all those lockers at the foot of the beds. Found my track nippers, crease nail pullers, cutters and rasps."

He shook his head. "You're speaking Greek to me. I'm not sufficiently familiar with horseshoeing to know the difference between these things."

"You've heard of horses, haven't you?"

He glared at me. "You got this out of Herbert Stuckey's locker?"

Well, no wonder he went by Stuckey. I nodded. "Stuckey can get baffled by a water glass, but I think he might have a good heart after all."

Plaid Shirt blinked a few more times. "When did you go into his locker?"

"Yesterday. Afternoon. Maybe I shouldn't have taken the stuff, but I wanted my track nippers back. They're new." While he studied the photo, I wondered again, did Oscar or Gabe plant the stuff in Stuckey's locker? Poor Stuckey didn't seem much smarter than a nail. "We heard through Ivy's lawyer that the dead man didn't have a bullet inside himself."

His face darkened, like he hated that we knew something. After a hesitation, he said, "Clothes have no puncture wounds.

X-rays show no fragments or bullets. No broken bones. No signs of trauma. Those livestock protection collars carry enough poison to kill five men. And there's no antidote to the poison."

I nodded. "That's the way I heard it, too." I thought about the neighbor rancher's story about one of the hands killing a dog with an M-44 in Nevada, and Stuckey admitting he'd shot and killed Fire. And Stuckey or someone cutting Charley's ears. I didn't have to make these guys understand me, but I gave it a quick whirl. "Someone on that ranch hurt my dog a couple of years ago. Nobody's going to care about that but me."

He frowned and waved me down, tried to soothe me but I was getting madder than a gut-shot cat. "I'm talking to you about another case. But let's think about this for a minute. These tools that were stolen—"

"But really, it was my dog that I—" I stopped as he shook his head. Took one big breath and let it out with, "Gabe's sure that Stuckey was the one who jumped me at the sale grounds. And that was over the same dog."

Plaid Shirt sighed. "This dog of yours sure seems to get some undue attention."

"I've been thinking that myself."

"How long are you going to be a guest on the Beaumont ranch, Miss Dale?"

"I'm out of there today. One way or the other. I'm calling a tow truck if I can't get my truck started and hoping to get my mom to pick me up."

"That's great."

I thought of my buddy Melinda pontificating after she went to police school about the proper ways they had of doing things. I made a mental note to ask her when I got a chance. "Going into those lockers in the bunkhouse like I did, is that what you police people call a bad search?"

Plaid Shirt gave a flat smile. "Not when a civilian does it."

Chapter 26

THE GOOD COP DETECTIVE WITHOUT A tie leaned back in his chair, riding its back legs, rearing the fronts, and pushed another photo at me. It showed scrubby oak on Ivy's hilltop—the rock cairn was clear in the background. Someone had carved letters and a scene on the oak.

"What's that?" he asked.

I'm for honest observation. "Looks like someone carved something on a tree."

He folded his arms behind his head. "Eliana Gomez has her own bedroom in the house, but Oscar De La Rosa stays in the bunkhouse?"

"That's the way I understand it." I wondered why we were discussing the sleeping arrangements.

"They're not a couple?"

If Oscar and Vicente and Eliana had been in one of those three-way stories where a bunny gets boiled, so to speak, it could explain a few things. I shook my head.

"I guess I don't rightly know. Reckon it'd be easy for everyone to assume that, I suppose because they're the two who work in and

223

around the house, but I think they met here. Hey, aren't you the one interviewing Eliana?"

"A specialist does polygraphs. Takes a while to prepare for—there's a preinterview and the attorney is sitting in on that—then the actual test is run a few times."

I opened my big yap some more. "Ivy wanted her attorney to be here when you talked to me."

"What do you want?" he asked. "I'd like to talk to you. Do you want to talk to me? Can we talk about mules?"

This, I could do. I leaned forward, nodding eagerly. "I saw a real good-looking john—"

"A john? They're into prostitution, too?" He looked at his notes, frowned and leaned out the interview room door. "Hey, Mattingly, you know anything about Beaumont managing prostitution?"

A man's voice came back with, "First I've heard."

He took his time sitting down, then reared his chair again. "Miss Dale, what have you seen or heard?"

"About mules, right?"

"Right." He nodded encouragement at me. "Drug mules."

"Drug mules? Oh, you're . . . not talking about the sixty-three-chromosome hybrid between a horse and a donkey."

He frowned. "A donkey?"

Air escaped my sails, my lungs. This conversation was not going my way at all. "You're not talking about the pig-mules either."

"Pig-mules?"

"Wild pigs running around these hills," I said. "From European boars and feral domestics."

The door opened and the super special agent leaned in to wave Plaid Shirt out of the room. Just outside the heavy door, Super Special asked a question.

"Is she retarded or something?"

There are times when my excellent hearing is not a good thing.

A couple of people laughed out there, but then I was rewarded with a comment from a voice I recognized as Ponytail's.

"The second one."

"Yeah," Plaid Shirt agreed, "or something. I've seen this before. My sister is one of them."

"One of what?" Mr. Special Agent asked.

"A horse person. They're just . . . different."

"As in stupid?" Special, My Not-Fan said. "Johns? Prostitution? Beaumonts are cocaine incorporated."

"That they are. That they are." Plaid Shirt laughed as he came back in the interview room and gave me a sideways glance.

Thinking about the baggies of salt and sugar in the forge room, I replayed Ivy's reaction to the find.

I'm such a big, fat hairy idiot that sometimes even a big, fat hairy idiot like me can see it.

What and all with the Beaumonts maybe being busy, big deal drug dealers, no, I guess they didn't have time to check all their land for disappeared employees. I whistled. Ivy's hired help did some very odd jobs for her. Had Vicente the herder had another job beyond tending sheep?

My mental note to ask Melinda about a few things kicked in as I stepped into the sunshine outside the building where the local police had their offices. Across the street was a Starbucks, and there was Ivy in the plate glass window, phone in one hand, five-dollar coffee in the other. I whispered to Charley through the few inches of open window on Ivy's Hummer, "Hang in there." I texted my mama that I'd be in the coffee shop across the street, then walked over to make it true. Ivy didn't notice me enter the coffee-soaked air, and I caught her end of the call.

"Well, that is quite concerning. Thank you. You'll keep on top of this with the others?" Ivy hung up. As I sat down across from her, she gave me a look of triumph.

I asked, "How old would Fire have been now?"

She looked startled by my question and flipped her long hair from the sultry pose it held seconds before, half-draped across her face. "Let me think." Her nose wrinkled and her lips moved as she counted up the memories. "Thirteen. He was eleven, just bred his last litter when . . . I thought Vicente took off with him."

Sick to my stomach is what I felt. Charley, Fire's littermate, was thirteen now. That was years older than I'd guessed my dog's age. I felt like some of my future years with him had just been stolen.

This weekend had whipped me in every way.

Ivy folded her arms and pushed back in her chair, looking like she was about to take on the world. "Eliana is showing deception in her interview."

"Deception?"

"That's what they called it. Leonard heard one of the policemen talking to another. They think she's being deceptive."

I thought about how Ivy had four employees on her ranch, three in the bunkhouse and one in the big house. I'd only searched three of those four bedrooms. What would have been found in the fourth? I asked, "What would Eliana be lying about?"

"Obviously," Ivy said, "about Vicente. That's what they're interviewing her about."

I thought about the other things the cops had asked me. No one in this mess ever showed all their cards. I was no different. It didn't make sense for me to talk to Ivy about the cocaine business. Instead, I asked, "Can you picture Eliana up on that hilltop, burying Vicente?"

Ivy shook her head "She's not really outdoorsy, likes the indoor work." Then she gawked out the window. "Oh, my God! What is *she* doing here?"

Solar walked right in and sat herself down at our table. She wore an ultralight windbreaker like the one Guy wears to run in the rain, over all the stretchy, bright yoga clothes. She plunked down a little brown package that could have been the one Ivy set down in Ol' Blue Saturday morning.

Ivy's gawk morphed into a glare. "Do you have any idea what you're doing? The police are right across the road."

Looking from Solar to Ivy and back again didn't clear things up for me. A two-door convertible pulled up in the parking slot straight at our table and flashed its headlights. The woman driver wore sunglasses, but I was pretty sure—

Ivy gave the orders. "Solar, get out of here. And take that with you."

My mama flashed her headlights again. I was safe. I relaxed enough to think and smiled at Ivy who peered at the convertible and pointedly ignored Solar.

After a good long minute or three, Solar took her package and flounced out.

I said, "Eliana made the meals for Vicente."

Ivy smacked her coffee cup down. "Oh, my God, Rainy, you're a genius."

It was a sentence I'd never heard. But Eliana had made break-fast, lunch, and dinner since I'd been in Black Bluff.

Ivy said, "Eliana poisoned Vicente. She put poison in the stew and had someone else bring it up to Vicente."

I considered the accusation. "Do you figure the person deliver-ing the thermos had no idea or was in on the murder?"

Ivy snapped her fingers. "Oh. Oscar. That explains why he took off. Maybe it wasn't Eliana who poisoned Vicente. It was Oscar. Oscar put the stuff in the thermos. But, no, Eliana must have been in on it, since she's failing her polygraph."

"Where's Vicente's money?" I asked.

"What?" Ivy sounded like she was snapping at me, but the espresso machine whirred suddenly, making enough noise that we had to raise our voices to hear each other.

Inklings of ideas that made more sense than at first blush were creeping in on my mind. I sounded them off for Ivy. "You said Vicente didn't use a bank. You didn't take him to *La Tienda* to wire money home to family, like Eliana and Oscar do. So where's Vicente's money? What did he spend it on? Where did he keep it?"

Instead of answering me, Ivy answered her phone's chime. She listened for a piece then said, "Right. Right. Then, get the key back from her. Right. No, my house key. Yes, she has one, she lives there, Leonard. So, get the key back." When Ivy hung up, she gave me a look like goodbye. "Can you get a ride? Gabe will be in town with Stuckey in another hour or so. I'm swamped. And I have to meet with my attorney, like, immediately."

I blinked, as dumped as Eliana. But I'd never wanted to be dependent on Ivy. I kept my voice even. "My mama's here for me. Just let me get Charley out of your car."

***

These days, my pretty mama was driving a sea-green Mercedes two-door, ragtop lowered. Her fake blonde bob fluffed in the breeze as she peered over her sunglasses at Ivy and me crossing the street. When I got Charley out of the Hummer, my mama watched us in her rearview mirror. Charley was barely at my side when Ivy drove off with careful determination that did not include attracting any attention through aggressive driving. She never chanced a glance toward my mama. It was like two panthers thought about fighting but went back to their own territory.

"Hey, horseshoer."

I turned. Ponytail's head poked up from the other side of a row of parked cars beyond hedges at the back of the police building.

"Who's in the car at Starbucks?" she asked.

"My mom."

"Good. Take care."

From the Starbucks lot, Charley and my mama and I watched Ivy's attorney drive away from the police station. I figured Eliana was still inside, with no one in her corner. It stunk.

Mama managed to not look thrilled when Charley and I both piled into her car. She wanted to tell me all about the new part she'd gotten in a modern western where she'd play the plucky ranching woman—she'd sold them on her massive familiarity with horses.

"You haven't been near a horse since I was five."

"Practically yesterday. Now tell me what you're wearing—"

I cut off her questions by raising my cell, and waved her toward the Beaumont ranch while I got Melinda on the line, and my mama went on about how my Daddy was pulled over near Black Bluff, waiting to see if we needed him to come into town. Only because my folks were heading up north for my wedding was I able to have them handy when I needed them.

Mel had to listen for a while to get caught up to speed. Not enough time. I hit the high points, including having just been interviewed by the local police. "She sent her attorney in with the gal, Eliana, was going to send him in with me, but I guess the cops were talking to both of us at the same time and the lawyer couldn't be in two places at once."

"Why'd she send her attorney?"

"I suppose because she's got a snootful of cash."

"Shit fire," Melinda said. "If it's her attorney, then the man is working for Ivy Beaumont, not the interviewee."

"Can he do that?"

"I think he did do that," Melinda said. "Might not hold up in court or church."

"Farting in a rain suit don't make you a balloon," I explained. I saw my mama wince. Then I told Melinda all about the detective and his buddy, Mister Special. It was a great way to fill my mama in at the same time.

Wow, the looks she shot me while I gave Melinda the scoop about all I told the cops and all they asked me while I was behind those heavy doors. And my arm got slapped when I twisted my ponytail into a stick with my left hand, holding the phone in my right.

Melinda asked, "So, you thought you weren't free to leave the police interview?"

"Guess not."

"Then it was custodial interrogation without Miranda and nothing you said can be . . . wait a minute. Have you done anything?"

"Nope."

"Do you know that Guy is . . ." The connection crackled but I finally caught Melinda saying something about mules and then, "You ought to get out of there."

"We're either getting Ol' Blue started or towed in the next hour."

The connection kept cutting in and out as my mama got us nearer and nearer the Beaumont ranch. But I heard enough to get the gist. Melinda's theory was that the police had turned Solar, figured the girl was wearing a wire, and was supposed to have made Ivy incriminate herself on the drug business. Mercy.

"I'm losing you, Mel."

There was no answer, just silence. Mama filled the air with recriminations of how I should have never set foot on Milt Beaumont's property.

She asked, "Now which one of all these people you mentioned is it who did in the poor man you found on the hilltop? The young woman they have down at the police station?"

I wondered if there could be another explanation for Eliana failing a lie detector test. What if she felt guilty about something else? I thought about the store where Oscar wired money home to Jalisco. Did Eliana wire someone else's money? Vicente only had seventeen dollars in his wallet. He had no expenses and had earned a steady wage for a long time.

A big pickup with dually exhaust roared by us, raising a dust cloud as it charged the Beaumont ranch. Robbie Duffman. My mama peered at the white rental car at the side of the road. The ranch's open front gate loomed ahead.

"I should talk to the dude in that car," I said. "His uncle is the one who worked on the ranch and died here. Been avoiding it."

"How did he die?"

"Pretty sure he was poisoned," I told her.

"Accidentally?" she asked. "People do that. Maybe someone buried him at his home, a peaceful thing. But now that you discovered it, it looks bad, so they're afraid to say anything."

The notion of accidental poisoning started me to thinking about the bracken fern and horsetail back home in Butte County, johnsongrass and locoweed where I'd grown up. There's worse things, for horses and people, like oleander and castor. There were plenty of natural poisons growing in the dirt. I could be all wrong about the Compound 1080 answer. A natural death?

Maybe no one had any ill intentions, and someone buried a shepherd where he was happiest.

Suppose Vicente's burial had been an act of kindness.

"Pull over, Mama."

She probably thought I was going to be sick. She braked hard enough for me to open the door and step out. The soil crunched under my feet, bitterly dry on the road edge.

If my heebie-jeebies were to be believed, someone was watching over me, like the song says, but not in a good way. I figured the time for a talk with Sabino Arriaga was way overdue. We needed to settle up.

I hadn't been honorable.

Chapter 27

SABINO ARRIAGA SENT A HARD STARE my way. "You. I found you. And you found my uncle."

"Rainy Dale," I extended my right hand, not recalling if we'd actually introduced ourselves outside the east end of the Beaumont spread on Saturday morning.

He was past the point of polite introductions. "Did you see him? You saw my uncle's body?"

"The police covered him up. It was respectful." His face changed, softened. I tried not to cry as I pointed at Charley in the front passenger window of my mama's coupe and told Sabino Arriaga, "I found this dog two years ago, along the interstate. Piecing things together over the last couple of days, I think what happened is someone here killed your uncle. After a time, the dog came down the hill, and I found him. But he was your uncle's dog, there's no doubt about that."

"Why?" Sabino spread his hands wide as he demanded understanding. "Why did someone kill him? For what grudge?"

I exhaled several seconds. Fair enough. "I don't rightly know but, your uncle, did he know plants? Like, dangerous plants and things?"

233

He cocked an eyebrow at me and gave a quick shrug. "Sure, he knew plants. My uncle would have treated animals with them. He knew comfrey and willow and others."

I nodded. Nice try, Mama, but no way had Vicente accidentally killed himself with a bad plant and then been buried by a caring fellow employee trying to do the right thing and now scared to say so. "It seems they used Flame—the dog I call Charley," I pointed at my old fellow, met his eye when his face studied mine from Mama's front seat. "They used him as a stud dog in place of Fire, the big champion. They cheated on the last breeding and that was to the neighbor's female."

"My uncle had nothing to do with such a deception."

"No, I don't reckon he did. Beforehand, they cut the dog's ears to stop identification. The way I figure it, he didn't like them messing with his dog."

It was the last two words that were going to finish ruining my day. I'd gotten Ivy's blessing to keep Charley, but it didn't add up. Charley had belonged to Vicente, a gift from Ivy. But the dog wasn't Ivy's to give away now. You don't get your gift back when the person you gave it to dies. Having gotten used to the fact that Charley had belonged to Vicente Arriaga, I'd come to realize that I was every kind of a moron to not have seen this plain.

The heir owned him. Sabino had a claim on my dog, on Vicente's dog.

And now that I thought I knew all of Vicente's secrets, I was afraid Sabino would want to keep Charley. I realized that this was why I'd been avoiding him.

"They gave your uncle this dog and a donkey. Pretty standard stuff for a herder."

Sabino waved a hand with impatience. "I have no use for a donkey."

"It sired a mule there, too, though maybe she'll lay claim to that as it was her mare that carried the baby. Maybe not. They're not doing anything with that mule john."

Sabino's face clouded some more. "A mule?"

Dancing around the subject on my heart was only making things worse. I cleared my throat and pointed at Charley again. "Your uncle got himself stirred up over that dog. My dog. What do you want to—"

"I want my uncle back." He paused long enough for us to both acknowledge, without saying it, that he wasn't ever going to get what he wanted.

"His sketchbook is in his old bedroom. That might have some meaning for you."

"I want to see where he lay." He cocked his head. "Even the police say I cannot go and see where my uncle lay in the ground all this time."

Pursing my lips, I considered the problem now before me, then nodded up the solution. "There's a place on the interstate, the northbound side, with a little pull-off. It's not an official rest stop, not marked, not even a milepost. But you'll see it next to a really steep slope on the private land."

"And?" The clouding sky reflected in Sabino's dark eyes, and the air smelled like rain was coming.

"And it's exactly down the hill from where I found your uncle. They'd never see you on the ranch if you took that route. Climb up that really steep hill from the pull-off on the interstate. You'll know you're at the right spot when you see the rock cairn."

"*Harrimutilak*," Sabino said. "The rock cairn. It is also called a stone boy."

I'd heard that phrase somewhere, and recently, but all I came up with at the moment was, "Huh?"

Sabino said, "A *harrimutilak* is a marker made of a pile of rocks. It is a Basque thing."

"Climb the hill from the interstate. It will be very, very steep, but it's doable. Your uncle was buried next to the *harrimutilak*."

***

Gabe drove out, holding up one index finger in a quiet salute over the navy blue baseball cap in the middle of his dashboard. My daddy does the same thing in his truck—the cap covers the radar detector.

Stuckey wasn't with Gabe, unless he was ducking down avoiding Sabino in shame.

So, Gabe was going to his appointment with the police, but Stuckey was skipping out. I wondered if Ivy knew. And if she'd abandoned Eliana completely.

Duffy's truck sat alone between the barn and the bunkhouse. Was he picking Stuckey up?

My mama parked next to Ol' Blue. At the big house, I tried the front door, expecting nothing but getting a knob that turned. I wondered if the stone boy up on the hilltop was built before or after Vicente disappeared, and what Ivy would say if I asked.

***

Eliana's room smelled like candles. Burned stubs lined her dresser under a picture of Jesus. In the top right drawer, I found receipts for money transfers, just like Oscar had. A steady stream of Eliana's little income that probably meant the world to someone in Guanajuato. But one of those deposits was in five digits, made a month after I'd found Charley and made him mine.

Outside, hoofbeats and hollers were followed by more shouts and a four-wheeler revving.

I went to the kitchen and dialed fast.

"Steinhammer."

"Rainy Dale again," I said. "Look, I just searched Eliana's bedroom. She made a big transfer of money, twenty thousand bucks, to Guanajuato in May, just under two years ago."

There was a silence on the line.

I kept going. "I already had my dog by then. I was living in Oregon. So, it was after Vicente died. I'll bet it was Vicente

Arriaga's money that she wired. That's what she's hiding from you guys. She always kept Vicente's money for him, whatever he didn't hide up on the summit. And after he was gone for a while, she wired his money off to her family. But she feels bad about stealing his money, so she's failing your polygraph. Ask her. Ask her about Vicente's money. She wired it out of *La Tienda*."

A police radio crackled in the background. Steinhammer said, "Ten-four," then spoke to me again. "The Mexican store in town?"

"Right."

"I'll let them know. Are you leaving the ranch?"

"Soon as I can."

But I couldn't. Outside, my mama stood with her hands on her hips in a cloud of dust. "What on earth is going on? A man on a horse took your dog and rode off. That big lad got a *rifle* and zoomed after him on a four-wheeler."

"With Charley? A man rode off?"

Duffy ran up. "Where's the other four-wheeler? I'll back Stuckey."

"Which way?"

My mama pointed east.

"The neighbor," Duffy snarled. "Trenton? Is that his name?"

Reese Trenton had ridden in and grabbed Charley? Stuckey had peeled out after him? How wrong had I been about everybody?

"Charley!" I lunged past Ol' Blue, ignoring Duffy and the bunkhouse, charging the barn.

Duffy caught me, grabbed my arm. I smelled the booze on him. By now, he should have discovered that whiskey did not improve his talent at getting along, fighting, or shoeing. I yanked free, bolted and grabbed the halter and lead rope hanging on the first stall door but scared the hooey out of Decker as I flung myself into his stall.

"Easy, easy." I tried to slow my movements enough to not further spook the horse. Quick as I could, I haltered Decker, tied the lead rope end to make a loop rein, and took him out bareback. We galloped east, leaving my mama and Duffy in the dust.

***

Reese Trenton's mind must have jumped a fence. He stole my dog. Stuckey had gone after Trenton and Charley with a rifle. But Oscar, what about Oscar? Where had he gone? I remembered Trenton saying he'd seen a black baseball cap on the fellow who'd come onto his ranch, probably the fellow who'd prepared a fresh grave under the manzanita.

Adjusting to Decker's fast lope, I wished I'd asked my mama which happened first: Stuckey on the four-wheeler, or Reese Trenton on the ranch grabbing Charley.

Or, maybe it wasn't Reese Trenton. Did Oscar ride in? Had he been hiding out and now made a move for Charley? Why?

I rode and considered Sabino Arriaga and how I was afraid he'd lay claim to my dog. I thought about Steinhammer asking me who was in the car at Starbucks. She hadn't asked who the waif was who had just popped in on Ivy and me.

She'd known. So, probably Melinda was right about the cops turning Solar into an informant.

Things were not fitting like my favorite old jeans.

The dust cloud from Stuckey's four-wheeler pretty well took the course Decker and I had ridden before—the fast way to the place where someone had snuck onto Reese Trenton's property the day before. Maybe I'd believed too much of what Trenton had alleged.

Decker was not feeling inspired under me. I reckon the multiple hill rides I'd given him had taken a toll. It felt like I was running out of horse.

The sound of the four-wheeler roaring ahead suddenly stopped dead. Stuckey had shut it down. I squeezed Decker harder, eking another trot out of the boy, and we reached the edge of the Beaumont ranch. Between the thud of hoof falls flickered men's voices, full of anger, though I couldn't make out the words.

Rounding some scrubby oak and manzanita, I saw Trenton's upper body first. Behind him, the fence had been cut and peeled back enough to allow a horse. Trenton was ahorseback and didn't have Charley, but his right hand held a pistol, resting on the wide horn of his saddle. I wondered if his horse could possibly be so steady that he was planning to fire. In two more strides, the brush blocked my view of Trenton's horse briefly, but I saw Stuckey, still atop the four-wheeler, drawn down on.

It had been Reese Trenton all along, I realized way too late. The brains, the one who was calling the shots, in on all the goings-on. Everything? Vicente's murder, hurting dogs and doing bad breedings? Dope, too?

Somewhere in this world is a woman who brawls but doesn't want to. In the personality lottery, she somehow got my willingness to fight. I know this to be true because here I am, regularly wanting to fight, but never taking a swing. Doesn't keep me from itching to sock someone now and again and again, though. And that kind of fury either gets me to yelling or shuts me up cold, like now. I eased Decker past more brush and wondered if Duffy was going to show up, and if so, whose side he'd be on.

Stuckey was frozen closer to me, downhill from Trenton, stopped halfway to reaching for the rifle on top of a long shovel, both wedged across the handlebars.

Trenton called out. "And you. You back on out of here."

I was some distance from their standoff, so it took me a breath to realize Trenton knew I was there, and his order was directed at me. I pushed Decker forward one more stride, cleared the bushes, and saw Charley on the ground, panting at the hocks of Trenton's chestnut gelding.

"Charley, come."

Charley scooted to join me.

Trenton took his time swinging off the horse, keeping the pistol on Stuckey.

Stuckey reached forward. I expected he was going for the rifle, but he fired the ignition then twisted the throttle hard as Trenton headed down the slope on bowed, rickety legs.

Turns out Trenton's a whole lot less steady unhorsed. Slick-soled cowboy boots are no good on scree anyways. His feet slid forward, throwing him on his back in front of his horse. The gelding didn't shift a foot.

Stuckey lurched the four-wheeler uphill, past me, a cloud of dust following him like Pigpen.

Decker swerved, unsteady and dropping a shoulder as he mis-stepped on the slope, and damned if I didn't slide right off him, landing hands and feet on the dirt. I reached for the lead rope, but he swung away, out of my grasp.

"Whoa, easy, easy," I whispered, but he took fast steps away. I hollered, "Stuckey, wait. What's going on?"

Thirty feet up the hill, Stuckey eased off the four-wheeler's throttle. The tires locked up, raising another dust cloud. Looking back at me through the murk and the dying roar, Stuckey eyed me, shook his head, and mouthed one word.

Sorry.

"He's the one you want," Trenton croaked from the ground. "I had this handled 'til you showed up. He hurt the dog. And tried to frame a good man. I'm not putting up with this nonsense, and neither should you."

I looked from Trenton to Stuckey and back again. "As I rode up, I thought it was you."

Trenton rolled onto his knees, trying to keep the pistol on Stuckey as he got unsteadily to his feet. "It's him, Missy. He's the one."

Stuckey gunned the four-wheeler straight up the hill, throttle wide open.

Reese leveled the pistol at Stuckey's back, then slowly lowered the sights. He kept his eyes on the ground a second before he turned to look at me. He shook his head and winced an apology of sorts.

"I can't shoot a man in the back."

***

People sometimes accuse others of doing what the accuser has actually done. And others think the wrong person's guilty of something another fellow's done. Guy calls it proxying or transference or something like that. He learned this stuff from his folks and college, and he explains it better than me, but it makes enough sense without more big words.

I'd figured things wrong is all. That whatever hinky business was going on at the Beaumont ranch involved more than one liar, okay. That Oscar was in on everything or anything Gabe and Stuckey and Ivy did, well, maybe not after all. Or Trenton. Stuckey'd looked bad enough often enough.

I raised my chin toward Reese Trenton. "You got proof about him being the one?"

"Not actual proof, no. Never seen him and Elmer Fudd in a room at the same time, but that don't mean they're not one and the same. I can look a man in the eye, know the whole story. The wrong man's not taking the fall for all the mischief on the Beaumont ranch. Not if I can help it."

"I think police proof's a little different," I said.

"I talked to the De La Rosa fella enough to know."

"Who?"

"Oscar."

So that's where Oscar went. To go plead his case with the neighbor. "He's with you?"

Trenton spat tobacco juice and wiped his chin. "He told me everything, so I come to save the dog. Those other yokels don't hold a candle to Oscar."

I'd have like to held a candle under Trenton, and I pointed up the hill. "We've got to catch Stuckey. I think he's the one who hurt my dog."

"Well, hell, young missy, all pardon, but that's what I tried to tell you."

Trenton mounted up and let his good horse fire through the open section of fence. Maybe he knew another way to the summit,

or maybe he was leaving me on my own. With Charley's help, I
caught Decker, positioned him across the slope, then jumped from
the uphill side to get aboard, fingers laced through Decker's mane.

"C'mon, Charley. Let's go, Decker."

That good blood bay gelding labored. It felt like this lope was
using the last of his reserves, but he gave it a good try. We cut west-
ward, away from Trenton's land, toward the true summit, to the
police crime scene, and Charley got left behind, unable to keep up.

Poor Decker was black with sweat, except for where he'd lath-
ered along his shoulders, neck, and chest. His scent filled my nose.
Ordinarily, horse sweat makes me very happy, but now I saw the
man who'd killed a dog in Nevada and another right here on this
ranch. I now realized that I should have paid more attention to the
way Charley avoided Stuckey over the weekend.

Stuckey was bent over at the summit, digging where the stone
boy had stood, the rocks already kicked over in a rubble pile.

I should have asked Ivy how long the stone boy had been there.
Was it Fire's grave marker? I remembered during dinner when
Stuckey admitted to shooting the dog and Gabe said he was buried
in the low land. Why lie?

Then I reconsidered the tip I'd given Steinhammer fifteen or
twenty minutes ago. Things started making sense. I wasn't the only
one who'd noticed that Vicente earned money and didn't use a
bank.

Stuckey stood, looked over his shoulder at the rifle on the
four-wheeler's handlebars, measuring the distance between me
and it and him. A death triangle.

Decker slowed to a trot then a walk, I had to raise my voice to
be heard over the gelding's hard breathing.

"Stuckey, it's over. I know."

I guessed anyways. Stuckey had killed Vicente for Vicente's
buried wages. The guys had seen the rock cairn Vicente made,
guessed he kept his money there. Except they guessed wrong.
Vicente didn't bury his money, certainly not all of it. Eliana had

kept it for him. And after he was gone too long, she sent the extra money home.

Stuckey braced the shovel across his chest and studied me.

I pulled out my cell. Power, yes. Reception, yes. Thank you, summit.

Stuckey whipped the shovel back. I goosed Decker forward, beat Stuckey to the four-wheeler, and tumbled off the horse, letting go of the reins as I grabbed the rifle.

Stuckey gripped the shovel. "This is where Vincent—"

He cut off his whining as I brought the rifle straight up, meaning business.

"His name was Vicente."

Chapter 28

ON MY FAR LEFT, STUCKEY'S RIGHT, someone hollered, "Hold it right there."

From my near right, Stuckey's left, my peripheral vision showed another man edging up hands forward, shouting. I pointed the rifle at the ground between me and Stuckey.

I meant to give everyone a warning shot to back off, but the gun went click instead of bang. So, I guess the thing with those semi-automatic rifles is, is they have to have the slidey-thingy yanked on them the first time.

Well, we all figured out that Rainy wasn't really the cold killer type. We being me and the sweating Sabino Arriaga, who rushed forward, yanked the rifle from my hands, racked it, and pointed it at Stuckey, who'd come to a decision and was fast closing in.

Reese Trenton galloped toward us, hollering, pistol drawn. I wondered about the route he'd used to get from his land onto Ivy's. It had something to do with the north edge of the hill, a route I'd never examined since it was off the Beaumont land.

Decker snorted and danced a widening circle around all of us, ending up at the west edge. He snorted at the treacherously steep descent to the interstate that Sabino Arriaga had just climbed. There was no way a soft conditioned horse like Decker, especially having already been ridden hard, would go down that slope. Only one horse in a few hundred would be capable of the descent. Decker spun, but his dragging rope reins caught on brush and he quieted.

Charley panted up, eyeing all of us. Stuckey, Trenton, and Sabino all looked at each other, one with a shovel, two with guns. This had to stop. Everybody needed to just sit down. Two seconds ago, I'd been the one in the best position to make them do it.

Sabino stared at Stuckey but spoke to me. "Did he kill my uncle?"

It seemed a bad time to say that yeah, I thought so.

Trenton reined up hard. "I told you idiots to hold it right there."

Stuckey checked the distance between himself and the three of us he could put in striking distance, me and Reese Trenton and Sabino Arriaga.

Before today, I'd never gotten *why* Vicente was killed. Maybe the question was not who had the most to gain, but who had something to gain. Or who had something to hide.

"Stuckey," I asked, "are you looking for his money?"

"What money?"

"Vicente's cash." I was running out of patience and clearly not the only one. Trenton shifted on his horse. Sabino looked from Stuckey to me and back again.

Stuckey looked purely puzzled at our confusion. "I ain't doing nothing bad. I'm looking for Fire."

"Fire?"

"I think Gabe prolly buried him up here. It ain't right. Ivy asked us to get him cremated."

I remembered how Gabe didn't come to the summit, even that first time I rode on the Beaumont ranch. It's not true that people go back to the scene of the crime. People avoid it like the pox.

"Why'd you have that livestock collar, Stuckey? Why'd you

have it hidden in your locker?" Both were good questions I was too late in asking,

Stuckey studied his feet. It was clear he'd been getting static from someone about this. "I don't know. It's just, I seen it and I thought, I don't know, but I saved it. Put it away."

"You saw it where? When? Tell us what happened."

Sabino lowered the rifle. Trenton lowered his pistol. Charley lowered his head, eyeing us like we were so many misbehaving calves. Stuckey sniffed and rubbed his head, spreading dirt across his sweaty face. "It was after . . . after I accidentally shot Fire. And, you know, Gabe took care of that. He always took care of me before. He's smart."

"The collar, Stuckey."

Trenton raised his voice, the presiding judge at our hilltop trial. "He's the one who mutilated the dog!"

"Gabe cut him." Stuckey pointed at Charley and turned to face Trenton. "He said it was just in case you checked. But you didn't stay for the breeding."

I snapped. "You held Charley down while Gabe cut his ears?"

Stuckey's chin quivered, along with his voice. "Yes'm. I know it ain't right. Gabe had me hold him good."

Go ahead and shoot him, fellas.

Oh, the thoughts that dance in my mind, loom like forest fires, need to be beat back.

"The collar, Stuckey. Tell me about the livestock collar."

"Gabe threw it away in the forge room one night. I saw him washing his hands. It was after Vin—" He cleared his throat hard, shooting Sabino and me careful looks. "It was after I killed Fire. After we bred Flame in his place. After Vicente took off—"

"Vicente never left," I said.

Stuckey frowned and rubbed his head. "Well, we all thought he did is what I mean. It was after it seemed like he took off."

I looked at Trenton, a man who was a good enough judge of

character to believe everything Oscar told him and come to try to rescue Charley from the ranch.

My mind flashed on Gabe's clothes being covered in dirt not long before Ol' Blue went dead. Ol' Blue wasn't getting any juice. Gabe had crawled underneath and disabled my truck, I figured. Maybe popped the fuel line. He was a cool customer to be heading down for the official police interview and polygraph after all he'd done, counting on not being asked the right questions. I shook my head and reminded Stuckey of where he was supposed to be right that minute, getting a ride from Gabe to go talk to the police. "Then everything gets straightened out."

"No, he ain't," Stuckey said. "He packed up all his stuff."

"He's not going to the police interview?"

Stuckey shook his head and snorted. "He's going to Canada. And he wasn't going to dig Fire up for Ivy, so I had to."

Sabino pointed at Stuckey but kept the rifle pointed at the ground and asked me, "He is not the one?"

Trenton snapped. "Well, it was one of them!" His horse pinned its ears but stood steady.

I asked Stuckey, "Gabe's the one who killed Vicente and—"

"Well, it wasn't anyone else—"

"And he's running? He's getting away?"

Stuckey nodded. "Guess so."

I wondered if Gabe had to fuel up, maybe buy some road food. Maybe take the smaller roads before he crossed town and hit the interstate that would curve around to the bottom of the very hill we stood on. In the worst way, I wanted this to be over. I called my Intended and never felt better than the split second the line opened and I heard his voice.

"Rainy! I'm coming for you. We're all almost there."

Best news ever.

"I'm in a pickle," I said. "There's a man we've got to stop. He's trying to get away and—"

"Stay where you are. Don't move. Where are you?"

"Where are you? He's going to be on the interstate any minute, heading north in a hurry, driving a beater green full-size old Ford Bronco with Nevada plates. He's the problem. His name's—"

Unbelievably, Guy hung up on me.

Chapter 29

THE TRIANGLE OF MEN AROUND ME—SABINO Arriaga, Stuckey, and Trenton, still ahorseback—eyed each other. The three critters—Trenton's horse, Decker, and Charley—shifted in place. The distant hum of interstate traffic over the hill's steep west edge filled out the wind then changed for the worse.

A semitruck gassed its air horn over and over. Car horns blared, tires locked up and laid rubber. Sounded like the makings of a major pileup.

Cell phone still in my hand, I skidded a half-dozen steps down the west edge of the hill. Charley moved to follow me. I didn't need my old fellow sliding down that treacherous slope.

"Charley, stay."

Charley obeys a good thirty commands, which is a whole pile more than Guy.

A semitruck-and-trailer was crosswise on the northbound side of the interstate, blocking all lanes. Easy odds on who'd caused that mess and thank goodness for him.

I scrambled back up to the top, hollering at Trenton. "I've got to get down there pronto. I think my fellow passed the word to my daddy, and he's trying to stop Gabe for us. Please, you watch over my Charley dog another hour." I tried to catch Decker's lead rope.

Reese Trenton managed not to look like I was full of good ideas. "You've seen that *Man from Snowy River* picture too many times." He stepped off his horse and thrust the reins toward me.

"Huh?"

"It's your rodeo," he said. He waved for me to mount up as he released his reins and he edged toward Decker, reaching for the loose lead rope on the halter, murmuring, "Easy there, boy, steady."

I mounted Trenton's gelding and felt a lot of horse under me. Yeah, a whole lot. And I was real glad that Trenton and I used the same length of stirrup, 'cause when I pointed this horse at the edge, it jumped.

We landed in a downhill gallop, every footfall sliding on the steep scree, the horse leaping again and again, front end catching us and lifting, faster and faster. The wind forced tears that blurred my vision. I hung on to the saddle horn like it was the doorknob to heaven.

Halfway down the hill, the view was good enough to glimpse the mess of the stopped northbound lanes. A Shasta County deputy car, apparently responding to a radio call he'd received up north, barreled down the southbound lanes.

Bam! One north-bounder—a beater green Bronco—detoured the mess of stopped traffic by off-roading it, busted through the hard wire fence that ran along the freeway. The dust cloud created by Gabe's off-roading rose to meet us, but I could still see that the Shasta deputy wouldn't be able to cross the median and to the break in the fence. I angled this incredible Quarter Horse under me. He agreed to the new line, hindquarters catching us and thrusting us across and down the slope.

When we hit bottom, the horse was entirely unfazed by the car horns and congestion. He took my cue to sprint after the Bronco which cut inland past the big hill. Shrubbery clotted along the interstate fence on my left. A solid cross fence loomed less than a few hundred yards ahead of the Bronco. Would he stop? Do a brody and charge us? Try to make it through the bushes and break through the interstate fence again, then speed north?

Gabe put the pedal down, flattened a T-post with the center of his Bronco. The cross fence popped, wire strands flinging back like someone had thrown a brick onto a guitar. I reined in hard. Trenton's gelding dropped his haunches and plowed the dirt with his hind end but got us stopped before we hit the wire. It wasn't barbed wire, but I still wasn't going to chance snagging a fetlock in a loop of the ruined fence. I walked the horse over the broken strands holding my breath. Ahead, Gabe was slowing to dart around a hundred head of scattering cattle.

Trenton's cattle. I saw him far to my right, having used his secret route off the north end of the big hill. Made sense he'd have such trails. And I saw he rode like an expert, even riding one-handed, bareback, and clutching my dog to his body. I kicked Trenton's horse back up to a gallop.

Ahead of Gabe, the shrubs thickened to real trees, a forest that wouldn't allow a Bronco through. Whether or not there was another cross fence ahead, the trees would stop both Gabe's northbound run and any try to get back to the interstate. If only the cattle were thicker, they could stop Gabe to the east.

Reese Trenton tried to push cattle toward the Bronco, but they were scattering, having too much real estate to spread out on. He didn't have enough control over the herd to get them to block Gabe in.

I shouted, "Charley! Charley!"

Trenton reined up, doubled over, and let Charley down to the ground. Then he loped Decker on, still doing his bit to try to make the herd trap Gabe, but his effort wouldn't do near enough.

"Charley," I screamed from the saddle, "come bye."

He did, swooping with hidden taps of power from within his tired little old self, gathering the herd, packing them tight. Before they met the Bronco, I reversed him with another command.

"Away to me."

When Charley turned, the cattle pushed away from him, packing in tighter on the oncoming vehicle. When Charley was exactly behind them, his presence would push the herd toward me. I pulled up Trenton's awesome gelding to holler a stop command to my great dog.

"Lie down!"

The Bronco slowed but kept coming at the cattle. I moved the horse to take the flank position Reese was shooting for. He saw my move and angled back, around, ready to support the final push.

"Walk up, Charley. Walk up!"

Charley moved up on the herd, head low, daring the cattle, showing the hundreds *you shall not pass*.

They milled, uncertain.

My Charley stood his ground, finding a depth of courage possessed only by the bravest hearts.

The tough part about playing chicken is not flinching. At all.

It's a mighty tall order.

It's also a lot to ask of a herd of hundreds of startled cattle moving alongside the interstate: turn around and face an oncoming, off-road vehicle.

Find the dog and cowboy and the screaming woman on the great gelding more of a threat than the old Ford Bronco.

They chose well.

***

The police showed up then, which was not bad timing all around. Six batches of them, explaining they'd been planning a raid on the Beaumont ranch after they bagged trying to sting Ivy's drug operation through Solar.

Charley moved all the air in that cow pasture through his good dog lungs. If we stayed, birds would drop out of the sky on account of him sucking up all the oxygen.

The way I wanted Guy, his voice, his warmth, his face, right there, right then was big.

Then Guy showed up in the back of a police car, him and Hollis Nunn—having explained to the responding cops following the dirt tracks from the broken interstate fence—that the cowgirl was instrumental to the events. Guy and Hollis got out of the back seat and got their arms around me, pulling me off Reese Trenton's blowing horse.

My brain tried and tried to engage, but it was slipping its clutch something fierce. "You hung up on me." I couldn't get my arms around Guy soon enough to suit myself. He was here. My Guy had come for me, and his wraparound hug and body press felt more than wonderful.

"Oh, Rainy." Guy nuzzled my hair.

Gabe went into handcuffs then into the patrol car's back seat, right where he belonged. I realized it was him in his navy blue baseball cap that Trenton had spied digging a grave, and I wondered if it had been intended for Oscar—where Gabe planned to lay all the blame—or Stuckey, or even me, The cops called for a four-wheel-drive tow truck to impound the Bronco, and I told the driver I might need him for Ol' Blue back at the ranch.

Yeah, it took a while and plenty of talking to get this mess sorted out.

Sabino and Stuckey trundled down Reese Trenton's north slope path off the hill on the four-wheeler. The police spotted the rifle in the handlebars and screamed at them to dismount with their hands in the air.

Soon as he was clear enough of the cops, I went to Sabino. Without meeting his gaze, I tucked my chin in to try again. "I need to keep this dog. I love him. He belonged to your uncle, like the donkey and maybe the mule. The donkey is out with the sheep where he likes it. The mule needs a job. But this dog, he's got a job with me and I love him." The repetitions necessary to make Sabino Arriaga understand that my dog was rightfully his uncle's property made it real.

When he seemed clear, I said it simple, "Let me keep this dog."

"He carved."

"Huh?"

"My uncle carved on wood, sometimes on trees."

I nodded, knowing, because just about everyone who loves the West has heard tell of how Basque herders long carved things on trees in those vast flocks they've managed in the Great Basin and beyond.

But then Sabino Arriaga told me, "You may keep the dog for my uncle."

"I'll do that. I'll honor them both."

Yeah, it was some time before the police escorted us back to the ranch with a tow truck that it turned out we didn't need, because Hollis Nunn is a sharper tack than most.

At the ranch, where my indignant and glorious mama was making all kinds of friends with all kinds of police, Hollis Nunn crawled under Ol' Blue and spent just a few minutes cussing in the dirt. When he slid out, his back and legs were all dirty from crawling under Ol' Blue without a creeper.

"The connector to the CPS was unplugged," Hollis said. "Hard to find, and hard to get to."

I dusted him off with both hands, happy that my truck was fine. It had been Gabe who poisoned the hot food Eliana made for Vicente. Gabe who made Oscar deliver the meal. Gabe who dug up Vicente's summit cache of money and buried Fire there. Gabe who stranded me by tampering with Ol' Blue, Gabe who dug the grave on Reese Trenton's land. I still wondered if he planned it for me or for Stuckey or Oscar. I was just glad that his half-formed notion of how to pin his crime on someone else had collapsed into the idea of running for the border.

"How'd you know about the Beaumonts and drugs, Mama?"

"Everybody in Hollywood knows. That, and I got a role in the western I was trying to tell you about, based on some work I did on a guest spot and the fact that I'm a cowgirl's mother."

I laughed, hugged her, and congratulated her all to goodness. At some point, Ivy had heard from Milt about Dara Dale. Who knew? The police had tried to sting Ivy through Solar, but still had enough to charge possession and distribution, which Ivy had been doing through her dog supplements ever since the Beaumonts bought a chunk of Reese Trenton's family ranch.

***

Dragoon sold, so I had an empty trailer to haul back up to Cowdry, but I had a couple things to tend before I could leave. First, I talked to Sabino about Eliana then crossed my fingers and hoped for the best. She needed someone in her corner. She needed work with someone who wouldn't just use her like Ivy did. It would take her a good while to re-earn Vicente's wages, but I was sure Sabino could take the long view.

Then I went back to the Beaumont ranch to see about the mule. It was Oscar who stood up and said I should be allowed to take Shoeless Joe away, if Sabino Arriaga was all right with the arrangement. Stuckey was of course fine with the suggestion, and Gabe wasn't there to vote, wearing a jailbird's jumpsuit as a guest of the state.

The flock wasn't too far from the barn at the time, and the donkey jack watched it all when we approached his big son. Guy hung onto the lead rope while Shoeless Joe played kite. Mules don't cotton to being bullied.

"Steady there, Joe. Guy, ease up on that line."

"There's someone I'd like you to meet," I told Joe when I got Guy to lighten up tension to the halter. The mule relaxed, and I led him away from his father's flock.

At the back of Hollis Nunn's stock trailer, hitched to Ol' Blue, the shoeless mule swiveled his tremendous ears, considered my request, then stepped in like a boss.

"She's a good person," I promised Joe as I latched the trailer doors. "We'll have you at your new home by the end of the week. Got fences to build."

The men were all waiting for me, Stuckey, Oscar, and Reese Trenton. They had a chunk of cargo on the back of a four-wheeler.

"What's this?" I asked though I could see what it was. It was a Whisper Momma forge, used but in real nice condition. Stuckey and Duffy had found a relined forge and added a new regulator and propane cylinder. "What's going on?"

Stuckey was all shy smiles. "This is a forge party."

"A what?" I asked.

They were laughing at me, not with me.

"We buy you a forge," Oscar explained.

Trenton said, "Stuckey paid for most of it. Said he owed you an apology. The prosecutor likes it when restitution is made."

Come to find out, Stuckey had used advance wages he would earn from Reese Trenton. Stuckey had done his level best to find my keys, too—he'd thrown them after he drove Ol' Blue onto through the east gate—but ended up promising to pay for new keys to be made.

"A man ought to be able to live down his mistakes if he tries hard enough," Trenton said. He'd hired both Oscar and Stuckey. He was going to keep mentoring Stuckey at shoeing too. Good thing. It's a job for a younger person's back.

***

On Wednesday afternoon, at the edge of our home pasture, under an arbor Hollis and Donna had built and brought, Guy and I said, "I do."

The preacher waved around and pointed at my left hand, in the buff for one more moment. My ring finger's never had so much attention. Months back, when I proposed, which was some time after he proposed, I'd told Guy I didn't need an engagement ring. We'd picked out our titanium wedding bands together, and I'd handed his over to Melinda for safekeeping. Guy had fussed about where to put mine before his folks got to town. He'd long settled on his buddy Biff as his best man, but given that Biff is a poker player, Guy hadn't felt like ring-keeping made a good extra chore for the man.

Never met these new in-laws before today. His father is the one Guy picked to watch over my ring until we were all assembled under the arbor. And then Guy's folks made noise about taking time at a B&B they'd booked in Gris Loup, not too far from Cowdry. We ate clams and scallops and shrimp. There was beef and pulled pork plus side dishes and every kind of noodle and green salad. Bowls of Guy's salsa and guacamole that shames the supposed Tex-Mex offered on the West Coast, especially what's found in the Pacific Northwest. We'd been eating enough to feed an army when my daddy said something about fruit on sticks being served.

Guy grinned. "Dessert kebabs."

My daddy said, "You mean, like, marshmallows? S'mores?"

I've logged some hard time hearing cooking school stories and I'm sure I'll only do more, being married to Guy. Like he'll hear my shoeing stories. We're for keeps. I sort of tried to calm my daddy down. But after all, he hadn't hesitated to block an interstate when Guy asked him to.

Grilled fruit kebobs, drizzled in dark chocolate sauce, turn out to be the bee's knees.

***

Time to get back to work. I'd calls from clients, a new client who wanted shoes tapped for removeable studs, a reschedule, and a thrown shoe to deal with, plus next day, I was to bring Joe the mule john out to Melinda. He'd spent the night with my herd like he was born to it. Melinda's only got a half-acre, but her neighbor has more land. She's going to make a go of becoming a backcountry rider. I let the mule bid goodbye to Guy's little half-Arab colt, Pinto Bean, while I rubbed the Kid's giant draft horse nose and took in the warmth when Red held his chestnut face against my body. I rubbed noggins with both hands for as long as it took for all of us to feel like we were together again.

"He's barefoot," Melinda said when I opened the stock trailer.

Shoeless Joe stepped out of the trailer like a mail-order bride, and I properly introduced him to his future person. "Melinda, Joe. Joe, Melinda." Then I stepped away to give them the personal time such an encounter deserves. I took a lap around her pasture checking the new fencing. We still needed to string some lower strands of electric tape. I took my time before coming back to check on the new couple.

"He doesn't look like a Joe to me," Melinda said. "Maybe a Louie?"

I considered the mule's face, a great mix of future wisdom, goofy, and stern.

"Yeah," I agreed. "Louie fits."

In a few hours, we finished the fencing for Louie's pasture.

TAP AND DIE

THE FOURTH
HORSESHOER MYSTERY

A sample from the next Rainy Dale horseshoer mystery . . .
TAP and DIE

Chapter 1

B ANG! CRACK!
     This part of central Oregon doesn't get too much fire in the sky, but today's was enough to make my good old dog Charley hunker into the footwell on Ol' Blue's passenger side. Near the gravel driveway's entrance, my client had a spanking-new barn under construction, and the framing gun blasting away up there was another reason Charley gave me that fearful, disapproving gaze when we'd parked in the mud down by this converted storage shed that was never meant to house a horse.

The big gray Thoroughbred now wore half of the four special shoes I'd tapped the night before. The cracking rainstorm was the only reason I was shoeing inside Quicksilver's makeshift ten-by-twelve stall. Poor guy.

My mind strayed to Guy, my Guy, my husband—wow, that h-word feels funny still. Made my left thumb touch the wedding ring.

Wish we hadn't had that blowup last night.

Three months married, and we've hit a dealbreaker.

Bang! The construction project up Buddy Holmes's driveway added more disruptive noise to the mix. The horse owner, Shannon, bent and kissed Quicksilver right between the nostrils. "You have many horses that stand like this? Especially off-track Thoroughbreds?"

I shook my head and drove another nail into his left hind. "He's awesome." Red, my horse, wasn't too fond of environmental percussion, but he'd have stood just as well.

Shannon was all goo-goo eyes at her big boy. "And he jumps like a gazelle. We're going to kill it at Bend."

Yeah, the High Desert Classics, always the last two weeks in July, were coming up fast. I'd be thrilled if a client of mine finished high in the ribbons. I don't have many jumper clients here in Cowdry, which is as cattle-oriented as it sounds. Of all my tools, my tap-and-die set is one that gets the least use. I keep the set in Ol' Blue, but generally use it at home, prepping the night before a job since so few clients need the threaded holes drilled and tapped into shoe heels.

I plugged the stud holes in Quicksilver's new shoes with little rubber stoppers. Just before a big competition, Shannon would remove the stoppers and screw-in stud caulks to help her giant jumper get traction.

She's a new client, and new to our little town, another transplant from California, with dreams of flipping the jumper world on its head. Going to have to do some traveling to compete her gentle gray Thoroughbred over the big sticks, as she calls grand prix jumping.

As if we needed more noise, her boyfriend Buddy chose that moment to rumble up in his crew cab truck, jacked up with an overloud tranny and exhaust, plus a sound system bumping a beat that vibrated my chest.

"Darling," he hollered through the half-down driver's window, "I'm headed to town. You be safe, you hear?"

She crooked her index finger at him. He grinned and climbed

out, braving the rain to come stick his face in the shed with us. She leaned toward him for a kiss then stroked a finger along his jaw. "Mmmm. I like it. Don't listen to Darren. That was canned wine talking anyway."

Laughing, Buddy reddened and rubbed his chin. "I kind of miss it."

Bang!

They both looked up the curving driveway where the building project was under way. At least the next time I shod Quicksilver, we'd be in the aisle of that new four-horse barn, dry and roomy, not cramped into an old converted storage shed.

"I'm going to hire on with their construction crew." Buddy beamed as he stepped back into the rain and headed for his truck. "They're going to have a lot of work coming up."

Shannon rolled her eyes and muttered to me or her horse, "He's been saying that for weeks. Like, why wait 'til after the big Phipps deal goes through? Why not hire on with regular hours now?"

I figured Buddy didn't hear her last comment on account of his truck's boom-beat, which was still threatening to make my ears bleed.

More bangs echoed from up the driveway as Buddy escaped the pelting rain by climbing back into his monster truck. "Can't believe they didn't cancel construction today on account of the weather," he hollered. "That little gal is so cool."

He cranked on his steering wheel. The tires dug into the mud, splattering through a U-turn. Quicksilver peaceably ignored it all as the truck motored up the hill.

Shannon exhaled a long, put-upon sigh, and spoke to the shed's low ceiling. "Not cool, Buddy, going on and on to your girlfriend about how cool another woman is. Not cool at all."

Keeping my head down, staying tucked under Quicksilver was a safe place to be. I let finishing that hoof absorb my attention, while my client went on about her fella owning a piece of the planet, single-wide trailer included, for taking care of old man Phipps and his hundred-acre hill. Shannon puffed an annoyed little snort through her teeth as she muttered her final assessment. "Margo Plicatus is *not* oh so cool."

I paused, turning my head to consider her lie, breathing in the horsey scent of Quicksilver's belly. I didn't know the person up there framing the new barn, but I knew for sure and for certain that the builder's name wasn't Margo Plicatus. Time for me to tune out everything but the hoof in my face.

After a spell, Shannon roused herself. "Hey, Rainy, he stands great. Let me just tie him to the stall chain for a minute, all right? I've got to pee. Left my checkbook up at the house anyway, so I'll bring it down." She shimmied out of the too-small stall before I could say a word.

I pulled my hoof stand from underneath Quicksilver's belly and plunked it a yard in front of his right shoulder. "Just drop his lead rope. I'm ready to clinch this hoof."

She ducked her head against the rain as she walked up the hill, disappearing around the driveway's curve.

Bang, bang!

The construction work near their trailer house up there punched on, but Quicksilver stood like a gem while I finished that hoof and the next one. Thunder and downpour and man-made noises weren't worth a yawn from this sensible fellow, even his pasture mate—a grade horse whinnying and pawing for feed or attention in the clearing behind the shed—didn't swivel his ears. I worked in peace for a good spell, glancing once or twice at the soaked, shelterless horse, unhappy behind a single strand of electric webbing propped up on temp posts. The rain was pouring so bad, I wasn't surprised when Shannon drove down in her little red Mustang fifteen minutes later.

As I finished the last shoe and straightened out my back, I told her, "I hope you clean up at the Classics."

"Thanks. I'm going to need him reshod in five weeks flat." She rubbed her hands together complaining about the weak water heater in Buddy's trailer house.

We scheduled the appointment into my book, I gave her a card with the date and time noted, then gave thanks as I took her check, which showed a more impressive number than my regular straight shoeing fee on account of the eight tapped holes for screws I'd carved into the metal.

She checked her cell, gave me a grin and a wave. "I'm late. Going to beat you out of here."

I was still getting rained on, hefting my tools back into Ol' Blue, when the sound of her little Mustang powering away on the paved road beyond Buddy's gravel driveway faded. Dandy, 'cause Shannon beating me out of there let me feel free to get Charley out for a pee.

"Come on. You know you need to."

My good old yellow Aussie checked the sky as if he could determine whether any more thunderclaps were due in the minute he'd need, then hopped out, handled his business, and reloaded himself in Ol' Blue. The rain kicked up like someone cranked the faucet wide open, uncountable big drops drenching all that stood ready to rust. As we rumbled by the half-framed barn near Buddy's old single-wide trailer, I told Charley we'd be in a dry aisle next time. Couldn't help glancing at the half-framed walls, ladder leaning against the north side, open rafters not yet holding any roofing above the future stalls that edged the concrete center aisle.

That's when I saw the person laying on the aisle, Vibram soles facing me, boot toes pointing to the sky through the unsheeted rafters.

I started to roll Ol' Blue's driver's window down for a better look, then just put it in neutral and stomped on the emergency brake, glad this upper part of Buddy's driveway was on the flat.

Opening my driver's door, I hollered, "You okay?" but I was already dismounting my truck, striding toward the sight, then jog-scuttling toward the gal in the aisle.

"Whoa!" The word came out as I saw rain splatter in the blood pooled around her head.

A bare wisp of her breath frosted up as her lips moved in a soundless word or two. I reached, gently touched her chin on my way to her neck with my left fingertips. She was cool, though she wore a thick wool sweater and rain pants over jeans—the cuffs soaked to a dark blue above her boots.

"I'll get you an ambulance."

My cell phone is a pay-as-you-go type, which I've learned means I'm considered a second- or third-tier customer and actually have poorer coverage than those smartphone people with a gajillion hours and data plans and the like. Out here at the base of Fly Hill is a no coverage place for me.

Standing in the rain, I looked where two trucks sat stupid: near the southwest corner of the new barn was a navy crew cab marked PISTORUS CONSTRUCTION above the driver's door, and on the driveway was Ol' Blue with DALE'S HORSESHOEING and our house number on the door. Charley cocked his head at me from the front seat, obviously considering bailing out as I'd left the driver's door open. In the other direction was Buddy's trailer, and I ran for it.

Buddy's front door was locked. I gave less than a second's thought to running around the place trying all the windows and doors. The window on the right side of the door showed the kitchenette with, bless him, a real telephone. So many folks don't have landlines these days. I took one step back and swung my right Blundstone boot forward, kicking the doorknob with all my power.

Hard enough that the interior molding crashed into the living room with the thin aluminum door.

At the kitchen wall phone, I hit the three digits.

"You need an ambulance at Buddy Holmes's place, bottom of Fly Hill. A gal came off a ladder while building the barn here and she's hurt pretty bad."

"What is the address?"

Oh.

My.

I know how to follow one road then another, motoring Ol'

Blue from one client's barn to the next. Reciting addresses? Not so much my strength. "It's off the old Schmitt ranch road, you know, the cutoff from Fly Lake." I turned, came face-to-face with a mounted deer head when all I wanted was to look out a window.

Bambi's dad's dead head—antlers used to hang ball caps with Cat diesel and John Deere logos—was mounted next to the kitchen window over the sink full of dirty dishes. Little curtain there and the phone cord was too short a leash. Above the dinette was a dirty window that let me see the half-framed barn, the ladder in the rain quickening my pulse as a reminder of the bloody-headed woman on the concrete below those open roof rafters.

The sounds of keyboards clattering and radios squelching burst in the background as the dispatcher went on. "Is she breathing?"

Twenty questions is not an enjoyable activity for me. "That's something to check on, all right. You send help. I'm going back out there right now."

I dropped the phone, but heard the dispatcher hollering at me to stay on the line. I ran back out Buddy's busted front door, thrilled to hear the scream of distant sirens. We'd lucked out if first responders were already in the area. Normally, it could have been a quarter hour or twice that to get help.

The injured woman wasn't moving a lick as I ran up. Couldn't tell from there if she was still breathing.

At her shoulder, I dropped to my knees on the concrete slab. The pool of blood making a halo around her head seemed bigger. She was fully unconscious, but when I knelt with my ear over her chest—studying as hard as I would a hoof—the minimal rise and fall of her breathing showed.

All I could think to do was grab a horse blanket out of Ol' Blue to cover her up.

Butte County Deputy Melinda Kellan beat the paramedics to the scene by a good couple of minutes and made me feel better with the way she swept to the injured gal's side, checking her pulse and going over the head wound with a flashlight. She sent me exactly one quick, dark stink eye as she spoke codes into her radio so fast that I couldn't understand the gibberish.

Melinda is my best friend—no, check that, Guy is my best friend, provided he's still talking to me—but Mel is my best girlfriend.

"I wasn't sure what to do for her," I said.

Melinda swore a quick one, as she is wont to do and she missed the young ladies' oath about not talking like a trucker, then added, "Lucky fire and rescue is close, too. We were all at a false alarm at the lake."

Sure enough, an ambulance and fire engine pulled in together, lumbering like they'd started a race with Melinda, but she drove a racehorse of a sedan compared to the dually diesel draft horses of vehicles that paramedics and firefighters ride.

The fire captain pointed at Ol' Blue, and one firefighter hopped in my truck, helping himself to backing it up a good fifty feet down the hill. I had a quick thought that Charley may bail out of the truck when a stranger jumped in—he and I had a little experience with that sort of thing not too long ago, and it was more than a little tricky to resolve when he took off.

I can't stand losing someone I love.

One paramedic said something to the fire captain, who then pointed at a firefighter who didn't look old enough to go in a bar, apparently assigning him to impersonate an IV pole. The kid was pretty good at the job, holding a plastic bag of intravenous fluid above his head, squeezing it as directed by the medic, who was shaking her braids, saying, "I don't like it, head injury with significant hemorrhage. C-spine precautions and let's roll."

The captain and other firefighters hustled, fetching a backboard and neck collar from the ambulance. The IV-pole firefighter groaned as he watched them put the collar on the woman.

"Oh, man, it's Ms. Pistorus. I had her for English, senior year."

The other medic spoke between squeezes on a blood pressure cuff. "She the one who had the thing with that kid—"

"Let's *roll!*" snapped the first paramedic.

While the medics sped through their paces—vitals and an injection in the IV, oxygen mask and a heart monitor that exposed the woman down to her bra as she lay there under the rain—Melinda reached into the gal's pockets, pulled out a cell phone with a thin wallet attached from the gal's right rear, and helped herself to a driver's license, which she stuck in her gun belt. Then Melinda stomped over to a pile of lumber under a blue tarp, yanked the tarp free with one hand.

"Rainy, be tentpoles." She spread her arms wide and snapped one long edge of the tarp like it was a sheet and she was making a bed. I grabbed the flapping edge and we formed a canopy over the medics and victim.

The paramedic at the unconscious woman's head turned on his knees and grabbed Melinda's leg with one latex-gloved hand, smearing blood on her uniform pants, making her drop one corner of the tarp as she leaned down to listen to him speak urgently into her ear.

She eyed him hard, then the victim, then spoke into her radio. The firefighters all stepped up with a gurney and helped load the patient. One got promoted to ambulance driver and the rig pulled away, lights and siren.

"We have to talk," Melinda told me.

"Later. I have another client scheduled. I'm going to be late."

"I'll write you a note."

"I don't need your fu—flipping note. I need to get gone. Horses to shoe."

"Statement to give," she countered. "I have our detective en route."

"Huh? Why?"

"Margo Pictorus didn't crack her skull falling off the ladder, Rainy. She was shot."

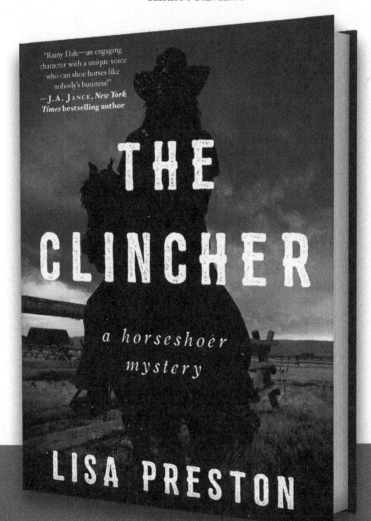

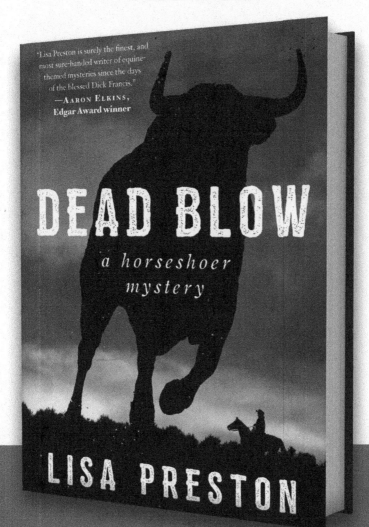